Sipping
Sangria

Jan Romes

WINE AND SWEAT PANTS SERIES BOOK 2

Big love to my husband, kids, grandkids, daughter-in-law, son-in-law, and siblings. Thank you for your constant love and support. You're the best!

<u>Special dedication</u>

In loving memory of my mom and her sisters, whose quirks and sense of humors provided great inspiration for my characters and the situations I put them in.

Dear Readers,

I was tickled to receive such incredible feedback from *No Sweat Pants Allowed - Wine Club* (book #1 in the Wine and Sweat Pants series). Many readers said they laughed out loud at some of the scenes while others could picture Elaina, Tawny, Stephanie, and Grace as people they knew in real life. (Just between you and me, those four amazing women are fashioned after people I know in real life) Stony, the adorable Husky, is the spitting image of my granddog, Jax. Lula, the independent feline has all the traits of Katt, the hunter cat, who used to place scary treasures on my Welcome mat.

One particular reader touched my heart by saying she was starting over as a single woman and when she read No Sweat Pants Allowed - Wine Club she could relate to the characters journeys to regain their footing because that's what she was going through.

It brought me so much joy to write *No Sweat Pants Allowed - Wine Club* that I had to continue Elaina's story with *Sipping Sangria* (book #2 in the series). As in the first book, you can look forward to plenty of humor, warmth, sarcasm, and mischief.

And yes, book #3 is on the horizon.

Will there be a book #4 and #5? Stay tuned to find out. Until then...

Wishing you happiness, laughter, and true friends who love you at your best and your worst!

Love,
Jan

'A friend is someone with whom
you dare to be yourself.'

~ *Frank Crane*

Sipping Sangria

Chapter One

~ Monkey with a meat cleaver ~

Elaina Samuels smiled, remembering the day she met Tawny Westerfield, Stephanie Mathews, and Grace Cordray at the cash-for-gold event and how she'd adopted the mantra 'Not my circus; not my monkeys' in hopes of warding off their chaos when she had plenty of her own. Had she kept on walking when she'd spotted Grace in distress, she would've missed out on three of the funniest, quirkiest, most loving women on the planet. It still amazed her how easily they'd clicked. They each had something huge and traumatic going on in their lives. While seeking emotional support from complete strangers was bizarre on every level, that's exactly what happened. They'd gone to the jewelry store to remove the sparkly, platinum shackles that kept them from moving on with their lives. What happened instead was more freeing and healing than anything they could've imagined. Essentially four like-minded misfits had found one another. Elaina raised her glass of blackberry wine.

"To living together for six months without killing each other."

They clinked glasses.

Tawny looked around the winery. "This is where we came after we got even with my ex." Her cheeks rose high with a grin. "Best. Time. Ever."

Steph made a face. "What's this *we* stuff? The only thing you did was drive the getaway car and you didn't do such a hot job of it. Your fleeing-the-scene skills stunk up the place. We came to the car barely able to breathe from running and you kept moving it ahead so we couldn't get in."

"I know, right?" Tawny's expressive brown eyes were filled with mischief.

Elaina sputtered the sip of wine she'd just taken and Grace almost fell off her bar stool laughing. It took Steph a good thirty seconds to catch up to the funny side of things.

"Priceless." Elaina blotted her mouth with a drink napkin and reflected on the night they'd given Tawny's ex – Grady Westerfield – a bit of comeuppance. Grady had an aversion to certain textures so they'd smeared shortening on his mailbox, welcome mat, trash can, and car door handles. He deserved a lot worse but it was the only thing they could think of at the time that wouldn't land them in jail.

"We should become payback specialists with a revenge-for-hire service." Steph tipped her wine glass and missed her mouth. Droplets of red wine found the front of her shirt.

Shortly after the Grady-caper, Steph had introduced the idea for the revenge business and had been given the thumbs down. As far as Elaina was concerned it was still a no. "Girl, when you get something in your head it's stuck there for life."

Steph pleaded her case. "We'd have people lined up outside our door. You'd be surprised how many folks would pay for us to perform harmless pranks on people who've given them fits."

"Not happening."

Steph fanned out her hands. "I can see the sign above your garage doors – *Sweat Revenge*."

Grace's forehead crinkled. "Don't you mean Sweet Revenge?"

"How does that even make sense? We weren't the No *Sweet* Pants Wine Club."

Elaina held out her glass to Rachel. "I'm going to need more wine to deal with these jokers."

Rachel, the winery employee they'd met after the Grady-caper, snapped her fingers. "I thought y'all looked familiar. You're the sweat club ladies."

Steph cleared up the error. "Not the sweat club. We *were* the No Sweat Pants Allowed – Wine Club."

"What do y'all go by now?"

Elaina couldn't resist. "Elaina, Tawny, Steph, and Grace."

Steph steered the conversation in a different direction with an off-the-wall question. "Why do they call these oyster crackers? They taste like regular crackers." She took a handful from the crystal dish on the counter and began tossing them one by one into her mouth.

"They *are* regular crackers. They're used to distract your taste buds should you switch to a different wine." Grace teased by moving the dish out of Steph's reach.

Rachel still had a confused expression. "Y'all are allowed to wear sweat pants now?"

Grace slurped from her glass and smacked her lips. "Yep. Sweat pants. Sweet pants. Yoga pants. No pants. It's all good."

"We *always* wear pants," Elaina stated emphatically and inclined her head toward Grace. "Too much wine brings out her hidden hussy."

"It's not the wine, which by the way is delicious. It's these guys. I'm totally me when I'm around them – whether they like it or not." Grace put her teeth together in a toothy grin.

Elaina revisited Steph's suggestion. "I'm giving a no-vote to Sweat Revenge." A tiny part of her wanted to embrace the idea for one more job, but she couldn't, even though Arden Wellby Samuels needed to get his just desserts. He'd been a thorn in her side long before their divorce. Lately, he was pushing the thorn in deeper, trying to hit an artery. But the small satisfaction she'd get from a harmless prank would embarrass her to the core if she got caught. As a member of Cherry Ridge's Chamber of Commerce she had to be good. Elaina tapped her glass, picturing devious things she could do to her perfectionist ex; like impaling his lawn with spike heels or sprinkling it with bird seed. People and birds weren't allowed on his grass. Another thought, more devious than the first, made her chuckle inwardly. She could deliver a gaggle of geese to his property. Their massive droppings would infuriate Arden to no end. Her subconscious cut into the wicked scheme with brain cramping assurance that he'd get her misdeed on tape and play it back a zillion times when he took her to court. Since Arden was a financial wiz the damage tally would be per blade of grass. By the time he was done, she'd owe him so much money she'd have to return the house and fitness center she got in the divorce settlement. Elaina winced at having to toe the line where he was concerned. He could be bad; she couldn't. It was the same when they were married. Arden had been forceful and demanding with regard to how she looked when she went out in public and even harsher about how she behaved. If she as much as frowned at something and he noticed, she'd hear about it when they got home. Yet behind her back, he was as imperfect as they came. He was a groping womanizer. Resurrecting his misdeeds angered her all over again and she was about to tell Steph that Sweat Revenge was on but Rachel swayed her thoughts.

Rachel pointed to Grace. "You're the one who wore the catwoman mask."

Grace feigned innocence. "I have no idea what you're talking about." With her eyes forward, she fumbled for something in her purse. "I'd like to buy a cheese plate so Steph will stop eating all your crackers."

"She can eat as many as she wants. We have tons of those things."

"Seriously, Rach', we'd like a cheese plate."

"Okey dokey. Be right back." Rachel disappeared into the back room. In a flash she returned with a ready-made plate of assorted cheeses with a cluster of red grapes in the center. She startled at Grace who'd slipped into the mask. "Oh my gosh!" Her laugh started out as a small cackle but grew into full-blown laughter.

Elaina fist-bumped Grace.

After Rachel composed herself she put a hand on her chest. "You've made my day but I may need a defibrillator to restart my heart."

"Tawn' can fix you right up. She's a nurse."

An older couple entered the winery at that precise moment. Their eyes opened wide when they caught sight of Grace in the mask. They walked backward until they were out the door.

Tawny was off the bar stool in a flash. "They think you're being robbed."

Rachel waved away the concern. "I'm sure they don't." She shoved the cork back in the wine bottle.

"My gut says they're calling 9-1-1."

"Awesome," Elaina said. "With my luck it'll be those same two officers who showed up at our place when you locked me out of the house. They thought I was breaking in."

Steph cocked an eyebrow. "Maybe they'll frisk you this time."

"Ha. Ha. You're a riot, Mathews."

Steph's shoulders rose and fell with a sigh. "I could use a good frisking."

Elaina slanted a look at Grace and then at Tawny

whose head snapped around at Steph's comment. Steph had been seeing Jack Kirby for almost five months. He was an easy going guy who seemed to adore Steph. "Something we should know?"

Steph negated the possibility by firing off a hasty, "No."

Tawny excused herself and headed to the Ladies room.

Elaina gently elbowed Steph. "No doesn't always mean no. Sometimes it means yes."

"Sometimes it means leave well enough alone."

"Oh-kay. When you're ready to talk, I'll listen."

Steph offered a weak smile.

Red and blue flashing lights appeared in the window.

"Let the frisking begin," Elaina quipped.

* * *

Tawny exited the restroom and rushed out of the winery with her arms raised in surrender.

Grace arched an eyebrow. "You don't think..." She trailed off the thought.

Elaina shrugged. "I wouldn't put it past her."

Steph looked lost where the conversation was concerned. Suddenly her green eyes lit with understanding. "Tawny dialed 9-1-1?"

Grace raised her eyebrows up and down. "We'll soon find out."

Rachel's eyes rounded with surprise. "Is there anything you ladies won't do?"

"A ton of things." Elaina swirled the wine in her glass,

hedging on going outside.

Grace flicked Elaina on the wrist. "Such as?"

"We'd be here all day once I got started."

Grace slid from the bar stool. "Come on, sweat club. It's time to save Tawny...from herself."

"Uh, you might want to remove the mask."

"Good plan." Grace stuffed the mask back in her purse. She strutted out the door like she was walking the red carpet at a Hollywood premiere.

Elaina muttered, "Not my circus; not my monkeys."

"You'd be lost without us," Steph quipped.

There had been a huge learning curve when it came to four women cohabitating. Idiosyncrasies had pooled with hormones. Hormones had pooled with the grunge of their pasts. The past wreaked havoc with the present. Basically, they'd gotten under each other's skin to the point Tawny, Grace, and Steph had temporarily moved out. It had taken Tawny's adorable Husky – affectionately known as Stony – to go missing to put them back together. Sort of. Elaina thought everything would be peachy from that point on but she soon realized Stony wasn't enough to fix their issues. It had taken Steph's breast cancer scare to put everything into perspective. They put aside their differences and rallied around Steph. Since then, life had been mostly awesome. "You're right. I'd be a raving lunatic without you. Wait. I'm a raving lunatic *with* you." Elaina smiled and walked outside into the brilliant October sunshine with Steph and Rachel fast on her heels. They were so close if she'd made an abrupt stop they would've knocked her over.

Tawny stood spread eagle against the police cruiser. Elaina burst out laughing because no one was paying any attention to Tawn'. One officer was in conversation with Grace, while the other was a few yards away with the couple who'd supposedly placed the call.

Elaina sidled beside Grace. "Everything okay?"

"This kind officer understands the mask was just one of those crazy things people do." Her smile thinned. "I was about to explain why I carry it around."

Elaina was mildly stunned that Grace would consider sharing how the mask was the last fun thing she'd shared with Brince before he passed away. It took a moment to realize something subtle yet remarkable could be taking place. She decided to back away to give Grace some space. Before Elaina could actually move though, Rachel crowded in.

"I'm the employee on duty, officer. There was no ill intent on Grace's part by wearing the mask; although it scared the bejesus out of me for a second." Rachel chuckled. "It was just bad timing those folks walked in when they did. From their vantage point, things had to look suspicious."

"I'm truly sorry for causing mayhem," Grace said in an unusually soft voice.

The officer's blue eyes danced with what appeared to be amusement. He coughed, possibly to get his professional bearings. "Not a problem." He shifted in place and Elaina wondered if it was from wanting to hear Grace's explanation but knowing it wouldn't happen now with so many people gathered around; or maybe being surrounded by hot babes made him nervous. Sheesh. She was starting to think like Tawny and Grace.

The couple who thought there had been a robbery in progress wandered up with the other officer and apologized for jumping to conclusions.

Grace patted the woman's arm. "You did what you thought was necessary. Could I buy you and your husband a glass of wine?" She leaned into the officer's personal space. "I'd buy you a drink too, Officer T. Marley, but you're on duty. Rain check?"

The officer politely declined.

Tawny and Steph wandered up.

Elaina noticed that Steph stepped back right away.

Tawny shouldered Grace. "You vixen. Offering to buy Officer Marley a drink."

"Me vixen? You stretched out over the cruiser hoping to be patted down."

Tawny rapidly batted her long eyelashes. "I was prepared to moan as well."

The second officer snickered and he got 'the look' from Officer Marley. They both tipped their hats. "Have a good day."

Elaina waited for them to get in the cruiser and to pull from the parking lot before she said, "My heart was thudding against my ribs."

"Mine too, probably not for the same reason." Grace traipsed away.

* * *

Steph perched on a stool again. The huge mirror behind the wine bar reflected a change in her expression. Instead of a carefree smile, her mouth was a thin, straight line. She was also clenching her hands so hard her knuckles were white.

Elaina took the adjacent stool. "Earlier you were clowning around and wolfing down crackers. Now you look as if you want to duke it out with whoever looks at you wrong. What's up?"

"Nothing a meat cleaver won't fix."

"Okay then." Elaina gave Steph a few moments to use or not use the imaginary cleaver in her mind. "I'll keep bugging you until you explain."

Steph uncurled her hands and inclined her head to the right. "The 9-1-1 callers are Corbett's aunt and uncle. I didn't recognize them at first since I only met them once. Outside in the true light, I figured out who they were at the same time they figured out who I am. They looked away so fast their heads should've snapped off." She puffed out a sigh. "Corbett must've painted himself as the victim of our breakup."

The snake Steph had been engaged to, broke their engagement via text message. She'd found out later he'd been playing around behind her back. Corbett clearly was not the victim. Not by a long shot. Elaina rubbed Steph's back. "They're related to the slithering beast. It's natural for them to take his side. You should go over and offer sympathy."

Steph's frown deepened. "Why?"

"You were fortunate to escape Corbett. They're stuck

with him forever."

The stiff corners of Steph's mouth eased into a lopsided smile. "You always put a unique spin on things." She motioned for Rachel. "I'd like to buy those innocent kinsmen a bottle of whatever they're drinking."

Rachel looked confused. "Huh?"

Elaina watched with interest as Steph explained in a hushed tone that the 9-1-1 callers were sadly linked to the no-good, egg-sucking reptilian poacher who wouldn't know a good thing if it pranced naked into his snake pit.

"Umm, okay. What do you want me to say when I deliver the wine?"

"Tell them they're going to need it to cope with their lot in life."

"Stephhhh," Elaina warned.

Steph put on a fake smile. "Nix that, Rach'. Tell them to have a sweet day."

"Better."

Grace slid off her stool. "We've caused enough mayhem for one day. Let's head home and have a soak in the hot tub."

"You have a hot tub? I'd do anything to have one."

Tawny came to stand beside Grace. "Best watch what you say, Rachel. It makes you sound like a villainess." She cracked a smile. "Our type of gal."

Elaina finished the last of her wine. "You're welcome to join us when you get off work."

Rachel slanted a look at the clock. "Sweet offer, but I have a few hours before I can clock out."

Elaina scribbled her address on a napkin. "If you can't

make it tonight, come some other time. We'd love to hang out with you."

"Seriously?"

"Sure. Why not?"

"You wouldn't feel weird having me there? I'm only twenty-two."

"We're only twenty...seven," Tawny fibbed.

"Tawny's *forty*-seven. She's the geezer of the bunch." Elaina wrinkled her nose at Tawny.

"Don't listen to them. They're mid-lifers, just like me. To answer your question, no, it wouldn't be weird. You'd fit in with this motley crew just fine. You're welcome to bring a friend. Right, Elaina?"

"Right. I have just one rule – no smoking."

Tawny was known to occasionally burn one on the back porch. "No smoking in the house anyway. The warden lets me smoke outside. Except for weed. She draws the line when it comes to weed."

Elaina rolled her eyes. "This conversation is going nowhere fast." She paid their tab and added another twenty dollar bill for a tip. "Stony is probably cussing us in dog-speak because he has to pee. And Lula, well, who knows what that sneaky cat is up to. Stop by anytime, Rachel. We always have wine or margaritas on hand."

"Pssst. Just remember to leave your weed at home," Tawny reiterated humorously and winked.

Elaina tugged Tawny outside and to her SUV. "What it is with you and weed? Like I really need to ask."

"What's that supposed to mean?"

"We both know every time you mention marijuana

it's because you're wound tight. Translation: guy trouble."

"I wasn't wound tight tonight."

"No you were not." Elaina climbed into the Escalade. "I used my phone to take a picture of you getting jiggy with the police cruiser."

"Let me see."

Elaina handed over the phone. "Nice sidestepping about guy trouble, by the way."

"Thank you."

When Grace and Steph belted in, Elaina looked around the seat. "Want to fill us in as to why you wanted to be frisked, Steph."

Steph sifted air through her teeth. "It was an off-the-cuff remark."

"Nuh uh. It meant something."

Steph dropped her head. "Jack and I, well..."

"Your love life is going through a drought?" Grace asked.

"You might say that." Steph groaned. "Jack and I share a love for cooking, but the only place he gets cookin' these days is in the kitchen."

"Of course he cooks in the kitchen. Why would he want to make a soufflé in the garage?" Tawny stuck out her tongue.

"Funny. Not."

"Sorry. I shouldn't be teasing *you* when things are about as parched as they can get with me and Carter," Tawny admitted.

Ah ha! Now they were getting somewhere.

Tawny went on to say Carter blamed his lack of libido

on lack of car sales this month. "He gets pissy if he isn't the top salesman at the dealership."

Grace peeked around Tawny's seat. "If he doesn't sell a Porsche his sex drive plummets?"

"Weird, right?"

Elaina tried to smooth things over. "Life can sometimes get in the way of lust."

"Hence the need for weed."

Chapter Two

~ Hair dye and nipple rings ~

Stony barreled into the kitchen with a happy yowl.

Tawny patted her chest and the sweet hairy dog leaped up to drag his tongue across her cheek. Just as quickly he dropped down and pressed his nose against the patio door. Tawny hooked the leash to his collar and spoke in a gooey voice. "It's not my fault we were gone so long. I couldn't get these lushes to leave the winery."

"Your master embellishes, Stone-man." Elaina opened the patio door and stepped out of the way to keep from getting mowed over.

Stony bolted into the fresh air at breakneck speed dragging Tawny behind him. On the way to his designated sprinkling area, he knocked over a terra cotta planter filled with potting soil and brown, curled-up leaves that had once been a vibrant plant.

Elaina heard the planter crack as it hit the concrete patio. "That's what I get for procrastinating on putting things away before cold weather moved in."

"He would've knocked it over regardless of the

season." Steph began checking the selection of wine in the wine rack.

Stony was a much-loved, spoiled Husky who could do no wrong in any of their eyes – even if he broke things. Lula was the same; only a much-loved, spoiled cat. Elaina smiled at how the household had changed. Instead of a quiet, sterile, organized environment there was laughter, barking, meowing, clutter, and hair on just about everything despite attempts to keep it at a minimum. "Tomorrow is supposed to be warmer, which means it'll be a good opportunity to work outside. I plan to clean and close the pool."

"Noooo. Don't do it. Once you put the cover on snow is just around the corner," Steph whined.

Grace took a glass from the cabinet. "We live in Ohio. Snow happens."

"Apparently flirting with the men in blue also happens," Elaina mumbled under her breath.

Grace clicked her tongue. "Not only does snow happen but also steaming piles of assumption."

"I didn't assume anything. I saw it with my eyes and heard it with my ears. You were attracted to Officer T. Marley."

Grace peered over the edge of her glass. "His name is Ted."

Steph took a bottle of Merlot from the rack. "What about Dalton James?"

"What about him?"

"You and Dalton are still an item, right?"

"About that..." Grace sat at the kitchen table.

Steph rubbed her hands together. "Go on."

Elaina opened a package of deli turkey and voila! Lula magically appeared. "There you are." Tearing off a corner from a slice of turkey, she crouched to treat the black stray they'd taken in. "Did you behave while we were gone?"

Lula meowed.

"I'll take that as a yes, but I doubt it's accurate. Further inspection of the house will give way to the truth."

"The meow was for you to hand over the turkey, not a fib that she was good. We all know she wasn't. Lula seems to have a thing for the accent pillows on my bed and for my laptop. I always find the pillows on the floor. When I'm working on the laptop, she plops down across the keyboard. I thought she was jealous because I pay more attention to the computer than her. According to a Google search the reason cats love computers and TV's has to do with visual stimuli. Of course there's the possibility she just wants to annoy me."

Steph crossed her arms. "Ever notice when Grace doesn't want to answer something specific she goes off in an entirely different direction with the conversation?"

Elaina raised her eyebrows. "It hasn't escaped me." She sat down next to Grace. "You were about to tell us about Dalton."

"There's really nothing to tell. We go out once in a while."

Elaina hopped up to get the garlic dill pickles from the fridge. She wrapped a turkey slice around a pickle spear. "I'm starting to see a pattern."

Steph joined them at the table. "See? Told ya, Elaina."

"Yeah, I got Grace's pattern. I'm talking about a different one." Before taking a bite of the turkey-pickle wrap, she explained, "We're no longer hot for the guys in our lives and they're no longer hot for us. I'm not saying we don't care about them and vice versa, but things have cooled off."

"Michael Rexx still smooches you the second he sees you, whether we're standing right there or not."

Elaina rubbed her forehead. "I think it's become a habit more than anything."

"Sounds like a great habit to have."

Tawny and Stony returned. "What's a great habit to have?"

"Michael swaps spit with Elaina before he even says hello."

Elaina shrugged. "The Kisser doesn't come around much these days though."

Tawny snagged a pickle from the jar. "I never gave it much thought until now. He isn't here every weekend like he used to be."

"Elaina said she sees a pattern."

Elaina winced and brought Tawny up-to-date. "Grace hasn't explained how things are with Dalton but tonight she hit on Officer Ted. Steph, you were dying to be frisked. Tawny admitted earlier things are dry with Carter. And Michael is pulling away from me. Our relationships with the guys appear to have grown stagnant."

Tawny ignored Stony's calculated stare at her pickle. "What do you think we should do?"

Grace's light blue eyes glistened. "I'm for spicing things up and see where we land."

"Uh oh," Elaina snorted, "this can't be good."

"I propose getting tattoos and nipple rings."

Steph choked on a bite of pickle. "My nipples are going to remain just as they are, thank you very much." She splayed her hand so it partially protected her chest. "If a tattoo artist came at me with a needle I'd pass out."

"They don't come at you." Tawny pressed a pretend needle into Steph's arm. "You lay there and let them create something unique. I'd love to get a tat." She flicked Elaina on the wrist. "Let's do it."

"Ixnay the nipple ring and the tattoo. I'm not getting either of those to keep Michael interested. My gut says he's moved on even though he hasn't formally cut me loose."

"It's because you're an old fogey. Get a tattoo and show him you're still hip." Tawny took a second pickle and crunched it with a grin.

"I've gone almost forty-four years without a tattoo. I plan on going another forty-four without one. Same goes for a nipple ring."

"How about a tongue ring?" Grace laughed.

"You used to be so quiet and reserved. What happened?"

"I moved in here."

"Whatever. You can talk about piercing tongues or ears or eyes, butts, whatever. I'm taking my boring body upstairs to get in my swimsuit." Elaina messed up Grace's hair as she walked away. Get a tattoo? Pfft. No way. Not happening. While she admired some of the exquisite body art on some of the members at her fitness center, she'd also heard a few say they regretted getting it done.

In her bedroom, Elaina removed her blouse and bra and stared in the mirror. She shivered at the thought of her breasts being perforated for the sake of jewelry. With her luck, she'd get an infection. She could hear the doctor now, 'What possessed you to get a nipple ring?' She turned sideways and tried to picture a little silver hoop sticking out. *If* she got one, which she wouldn't, she'd make sure Arden got a glimpse. The shock value might be worth the pain and risk of infection.

* * *

"Did you see that?" Tawny stretched her neck to look around Elaina.

Grace blotted sweat from her face with a towel. "See what?"

"I could've sworn I saw someone poke their head around the man-cave." Tawny pulled up out of the hot tub, grabbed her t-shirt and yanked it on. Barefoot, she ran toward the climate-controlled building that once housed Arden's vintage automobile collection.

Elaina also climbed from the hot tub and speed-walked to catch up with Tawny. She tugged at the bottom of Tawny's shirt to make her stop. In a quiet voice she said it was probably a squirrel.

Tawny raised both eyebrows and held them in the up

position. "Unless this particular rodent got a blonde dye job and took growth hormones, it isn't a squirrel."

"Your eyes could be playing tricks on you." Elaina pondered the possibility someone was spying on them and was instantly ticked. "If someone is there they would've had to walk past us or scale the fence." Arden had a huge wooden fence built to block out the scraggly vacant lot behind their property. He'd cussed out the owner more than once for not taking care of the ground and threatened to get the city involved, which would mean a hefty fine. The guy had laughed in Arden's face. A week later the property became an even bigger eyesore. A load of old bricks had been dumped in the center of the lot. These days the bricks were gone and in their place, a realtor sign.

"My eyes are fine." Tawny signaled for Elaina to go to the left and she'd go to the right.

Adrenaline spiked Elaina's pulse as she peeked around the corner of the building. Brown eyes blinked from the opposite corner. "There's no one here except us." She stepped into the open and inspected the fence; looking for a sign someone had trespassed. All the boards appeared to be intact.

Tawny scratched her head. "I saw someone. I did."

"I believe you." Elaina's gut indicted Arden right away. While there wasn't any physical evidence to back up the accusation, she wouldn't put anything past him. "The who, how, and why have me baffled."

Grace traipsed onto the scene with a rake raised high.

"What were you going to do with that? Rake leaves

off the guy?" Tawny teased.

"Well yeahhhh."

Steph brought Stony. "Stone-man will sniff him out."

Grace poked Steph with the handle of the rake. "He's a Husky not a bloodhound."

"Dogs have a keen sense when it comes to scent."

"The scent of bacon. When it comes to tracking humans they have to be trained." Tawny shook her head. "It wasn't my imagination. I saw someone."

"Are you trying to convince us? Or yourself?" Grace offered a suggestion. "It could've been a wine induced hallucination."

"Very funny. While it seems like we always have wine we really don't drink as much as it seems and we certainly don't drink enough to bring on mirages."

Steph was still hung up on Stony finding the perpetrator. "Look, he's sniffing." A few seconds later he hiked his leg and peed on an oak tree.

A cold shiver tracked up Elaina's spine. She squinted up at the tree, wondering if a large blonde *squirrel* was ready to pounce.

Grace offered her two-cents. "It might've been a peeping Tom trying to get a look at torpedo boobs."

"Duhhhh. Who wouldn't want a look at these? They're spectacular!" Tawny cupped the underside of her boobs and lifted them high. She laughed her way back to the hot tub.

Elaina silently marveled at how far Tawny had come. Steph had made progress regarding her chest as well. When they first met, Tawny grumbled about the burden of having a huge chest. She'd wanted to get a breast reduction procedure. On the flip side, Steph had bellyached about not having a chest and thought implants were the way to go. These days they seemed content with the bodies God have given them. Carter and Jack's influence might be part of the reason but Elaina hoped it was also the comfort of good friends. Personally, Elaina felt better about herself too because of Tawny, Steph, and Grace. They were positive energy.

Halfway back to the hot tub Elaina experienced a strong feeling of being watched. She glanced over her shoulder. In the fast-growing tech world, it was possible for their every move to be captured via a secret camera or drone. It still didn't explain what Tawny had seen, but that was a mystery to be solved later. Elaina put a hand behind her back with the intention of extending her middle finger, but dropped her hand to her side. She didn't flip people off. There had been numerous occasions where it would've been a fitting response yet she didn't allow herself to engage in that special kind of sign language. It wasn't because she was goodie two-shoes. It was the fear of not being able to stop once she started. Elaina turned around, crossed her arms, and sneered as hard as her face would allow. If someone *was* lurking, they'd get the message. The finger that wanted in on the action seemed to have a mind and life of its own. Up it went. "Capture that!"

* * *

Tawny propped against the kitchen counter and stirred her strawberry Greek yogurt. "Carter texted me last night."

Elaina poured a cup of coffee and took a much needed sip. "Let me guess, he has visions of being top dog this month."

"He begged me again to trade Ferdinand in on a Lexus. While I'd love a Lexus, the balance in my checking and saving accounts wouldn't buy a bicycle let alone a car. The loan officer at the bank would have a good laugh if I applied for a loan."

"Have you mentioned your financial situation with Carter?"

"I have. He listens about as well as Lula."

Elaina blew the steam from her hot coffee and indulged in another careful sip. "His senses are marred by that new car smell."

Tawny spooned yogurt into her mouth and licked her lips. "Or by the color green."

Steph entered the kitchen; her face glistening with the sheen of perspiration from having done her workout. "What about green?"

"Green has a sound all its own. Cha-ching!"

Not yet in tune with the conversation, Steph asked what the color brown sounded like.

"Brown is one of my favorite colors. To me it hums 'ahhhh'. This discussion, however, really isn't about colors or sounds. It has to do with Carter. He's bullying Tawny to relinquish Ferdinand, her beloved Malibu."

"Carter is hot and all, but he's a bit of a nag." Steph

took a Tupperware container of baby carrots from the refrigerator.

"He's definitely hot. And definitely a nag. The night we met was the first time he bugged me about buying a new car from him. We've been dating for five months and he's still at it. He's hell bent on me having something shiny and expensive to park in the driveway. If he wasn't so good looking I'd kick him to the curb for calling Ferdinand a junker." Tawny groaned. "In some ways he reminds me of Grady. He wants what he wants and not what I want."

Steph munched a carrot. "You should pay attention to that, Tawn'. It's a warning sign."

Tawny put an arm around Steph. "You're a wise little owl, Stephanie Mathews, but you eat carrots like a beaver gnawing a log."

Steph put her teeth together in a toothy grin. "I love you, too."

Grace strolled into the kitchen and did a three-sixty turn. "What do you think?"

Elaina sat her cup aside. "Me likey."

"It says 'wild child', but I'm with Elaina – me likey." Tawny gingerly touched the purple streaks in Grace's hair.

Steph cocked her head and studied Grace's new look. "Yesterday you wanted a nipple ring and tattoo. Today it's purple hair. What's bringing about these changes?"

Grace shrugged. "It's normal to do something drastic post-breakup." She winced. "It's not actually post-breakup yet, but soon."

Elaina's mouth unhinged at the jaw. "No kidding?"

"I like Dalton. I do. I just can't see me with him long term."

"You used to write Mrs. Dalton James on your notebooks."

"In high school. A lot of years have come and gone since then." Grace smirked. "I've discovered the fantasy is better than reality. Besides, I haven't given myself enough time to enjoy all life has to offer a single woman."

"Did you have a fight?" Steph inquired.

"No. That's just it. We never fight."

Steph looked baffled. "You're breaking up with Dalton because you didn't fight? What kind of sense does that make?"

"It makes perfect sense. You get to know a lot about a person during a fight; what they firmly believe, what they're willing to negotiate, how they resolve issues. Dalton doesn't stand his ground or express his true feelings on anything. He does a dance I call the two-step side-step. In some ways it's charming; mostly it's annoying." Grace put her hands on her head in frustration. "It's niceness insanity. I want to scream 'Just fight with me all ready'."

"Because Dalton refuses to fight you'll never have incredible, make-up sex," Tawny teased.

Grace made a zero with her fingers. "No chance whatsoever."

Elaina wouldn't weigh in because she hated fighting in all its forms.

"Did you explain that to Dalton?" Steph asked.

"I did. He wouldn't even fight about fighting. He

merely lifted his shoulders in a shrug. Don't get me wrong, he's a super guy. We're just not on the same page and I don't feel as though our hearts are in synch."

Tawny's brows knitted together. "You're okay with breaking up?"

"Yep."

Steph placed a hand on Grace's shoulder. "Do you really mean that? Or are you trying to camouflage your disappointment?"

"I'm not disappointed. It is what it is."

"If you're on board with the breakup then why the hair streaks?"

"Psychologically, it's like 'now what?' I'm 99.9% sure I'm doing the right thing. The .1% prompted the streaks."

Elaina nodded in agreement. "It takes a lot of strength to set your world right."

"I couldn't do it without you. You gals aren't just my best friends, you're my safety net. If I make a mistake, you'll catch me." Grace smiled. "And you'll fight with me once in a while too."

Chapter Three

~ *Dent me, wreck me, any way you want me* ~

Elaina put the car door handle in a death grip. "That light was redder than red, Steph!"

"What light?"

At Steph's glassy-eyed stare, Elaina poked her in the ribs. "Snap out of whatever daydream you're in and concentrate on your driving."

"Did I really run the light?"

Elaina tilted her head with a critical look. "Uh, yeahhhh. We were lucky there wasn't a car coming from the opposite direction. And *you* were darn lucky there wasn't a cop there to catch you." She turned the volume down on the radio. "We've had our fair share of interaction with the law." She watched Steph drum her thumbs on the steering wheel and slip back into the same oblivion. "We're not crash dummies, Steph. If you hit something it won't be a collision simulation. It'll be the real thing."

"I'm not going to hit anything." At the corner of Main and Seventh Streets, Steph stomped the brakes, lurching them forward.

Elaina sent off a quick text message to Tawny – *Call the Bureau of Motor Vehicles and have them revoke Steph's driver's license.*

Is she burning rubber with her tires again?

Again?

I have no idea. Thought I'd throw that in to heighten whatever fun you're having.

Not having!!!

Steph proceeded to Main and Eighth.

A black cat just ran out in front of us. That can't be good.

WE have a black cat. Tawny continued to heckle. *Speak soothingly to the driver.*

I'll speak soothingly all right – with a flick to her temple. Elaina tucked her phone in the side pocket of her purse. "Want to tell me why you can't seem to concentrate on getting from point A to point B without scaring me?"

Steph flinched like she'd just zoned back in. "A little preoccupied I guess."

"Did you even see the cat?"

"What cat?"

Elaina would've dropped her face into her hands and shook her head but someone had to keep an eye on the road. "Put. The. Car. In. Park." She held out her palm for the keys.

"I can't park the car at a stop sign. Besides, we're a block from home."

"Twenty-three percent of reported crashes occur within a mile of home."

Steph pointed to Elaina. "You're staying there. I'm

staying here. I'll get us home without injury."

Elaina muttered "doubtful" under her breath and straight-armed the dashboard until they were safely parked in their driveway. She shouted a theatrical, "Halleluiah!"

"Drama queen."

"Bad driver."

They broke into a laugh.

Steph started to get out of the car and Elaina tugged her back. "Tell me why you're preoccupied?"

"What do you think Jack meant when he said he has something important to ask me?"

Elaina frowned. "This is the first I'm hearing about it."

"Didn't I tell you?"

"No. You said very little from home to the grocery and back. You were too busy trying to dent your car."

Steph wrinkled her nose with that familiar faraway look in her eyes. Good thing the keys were out of the ignition. "He suggested we do dinner tonight, which isn't unusual, but he was acting kind of weird and nervous when he said we needed to talk. You don't suppose... Surely he isn't going to..." She stopped to chew her thumbnail.

"You're having an entire conversation, with yourself, in your head. Try saying things out loud so I can hear."

"What if he asks me to marry him?"

Elaina wasn't aware Steph and Jack's relationship had advanced to the point of a marriage proposal; especially in light of Steph wanting to be frisked at the winery. "Were you getting engagement vibes?"

"See that's just it – I wasn't feeling anything other than comfortable companionship. I wouldn't mind a little more pizzazz but nothing that includes wedding rings." Steph put a hand on her forehead. "Unless it's the opposite of wedding rings."

"Don't stress yourself out. It could be something simple. You haven't met Jack's folks yet. Maybe he's planning a weekend getaway so you can meet them."

"That's what I like about you, Elaina. You ooze positivity."

Elaina made a face. "Oozing anything sounds gross, even if it is positivity."

Steph finally smiled. "You always lighten my mood."

"I do what I can. Now let's get these groceries put away so you can get all gussied up for whatever awaits you tonight."

"Did I mention we're eating dinner here?"

"Another tidbit you left out. It doesn't matter though. The house is yours. Grace, Tawny, and I will make ourselves scarce."

"Just don't leave."

Elaina grabbed a bag of groceries from the back seat. "You want us close by?"

Steph nodded. "Not too close. You know in case..."

"Stop right there." Elaina put up a hand. "I want to be able to eat at the kitchen table without picturing what may have taken place on it."

* * *

Grace did calf stretches while Tawny used a stretch band for her arms. Elaina slowed her movements on the stationary bike to lower her heart rate after a half hour of hard pedaling.

"We shouldn't be working out at eight o'clock in the evening." Grace sat down, extended her legs, and reached for her toes. "It's going to rev us up so we can't sleep. Instead of snoring, we'll be prowling the hallways."

"Prowl quietly. I'll be dreaming about the new doctor who's doing a six-month stint in ER." Tawny put a hand across her heart and blinked rapidly. "His name is Parker Addison. When he speaks I get warm all over."

Grace lifted an eyebrow. "You little vixen."

"Uh huh." Tawny fanned herself and joined Grace on the mat.

"You've not mentioned him before. Tell us about him."

"When we talk we're eye to eye."

"So not tall," Grace stated.

"Height isn't everything. His eyes are sky blue."

Grace winked at Elaina. "His eyes are *sky* blue."

Tawny pushed Grace to make her fall sideways. "He smells amazing. I can't seem to pin down the fragrance."

"It could be eucalyptus." Grace righted herself and grabbed a kettle bell weight from the rack.

"It's not eucalyptus." Tawny sighed dreamily. "All the nurses want him."

Elaina chuckled at the constant banter between Tawny and Grace. They were brilliant women who had mischievous, humorous sides few people got to see. At the hospital, Tawny was all business, as she should be. It was the same with Grace. Her boss was a stiff professional who expected similar behavior from his bank employees. When they got home, their true personalities emerged. "If he asked you out, would you go?"

Tawny expelled a soft whimper. "A thousand times yes. He won't ask."

"Because?"

"Because I'm ancient and he recently turned forty."

Elaina understood where Tawny was coming from. When men dated younger women they got an 'Atta boy' and a pat on the back. When women dated younger men they got raised eyebrows and were called cougars. "You're not a wimp, Westerfield."

"True, but I am forty-seven." She cocked her head with a reflective look in her eyes. "When I'm old enough to retire, Parker will be fifty-eight."

"Think of all the money you'll save him by getting the senior citizen discount when you go out to eat."

"Ha. You're hilarious." Tawny stood and did a bicep wall stretch. "His age really isn't the issue. Parker doesn't know I exist until he needs my assistance in suturing a wound or when he has to set a broken arm or leg." She jiggled with a laugh. "Would it kill him to look at my boobs once in a while?"

Elaina tried not to smile. "Maybe he sneaks glances."

"Yeah. No. He doesn't. Realistically, the only way he and I will hook up is in my dreams. Even that won't happen now that we've exercised. The three of us will be wide awake and traipsing up and down the hall."

Elaina climbed off the bike and grabbed a towel to blot a trail of perspiration before it dripped into her eyes. "Exercise, regardless of the time of day, reduces stress and stimulates endorphins which should allow you to doze off...so you can kiss a hunky doctor or help him shove a needle and surgical thread through someone's skin."

Grace wrinkled her nose. "You could've stopped at hunky doctor."

Tawny's mouth dimpled with a grin. "Elaina, you're a walking-talking blog post about the benefits of exercise and eating right." She laced her fingers and stretched her arms high above her head. "You made us go meatless tonight. Blah. Blah. Blah. 'Cutting meat out of one meal per week could lessen the gunk in your arteries.' If exercise doesn't keep me awake, the lack of real food will."

"Grilled asparagus and salad with fat-free dressing *is* real food."

"Wanna bet? My body's in shock. It wants steak medallions with hot, buttery mushrooms on top."

Elaina's stomach did a flip at the thought of biting into a succulent piece of steak. She sighed. Some days it was hard to walk the talk. "Your body's fine. It's your emotions trying to trick you into eating comfort food."

"Forget the steak. I could go for a cheeseburger right now." Grace gave Tawny a high-five and checked her watch. "How long do we have to hang back while Steph and Jack make googley eyes at each other?"

Elaina snickered, knowing the second they were in the house they'd raid the refrigerator. "Until Steph gives us the all clear."

"I hope it's soon." Tawny lifted her arm and sniffed. "I need a shower."

Grace pinched her nostrils closed and walked backward. "You smell like Swiss cheese."

Steph opened the door at the exact moment Grace stepped in front of it.

Grace flinched. "You almost bonked me with the door."

"Then watch where you're going." Steph looked down at the floor.

"Stay away from, Tawn'. She smells like cheese."

"Thanks for the warning." Steph still avoided making eye contact. "You can come out of hiding, Jack has gone home."

Grace followed Steph out of the exercise room.

Tawny tugged Elaina's shirt to keep her from leaving. "Is it my imagination or was there a quiver in Steph's voice?"

"Not your imagination."

"What do you suppose happened?"

"Or rather what didn't happen?"

"Huh?"

No sex on the kitchen table. Hopefully. Elaina gestured to the door. "Let's go help Steph over whatever hill or hump Jack tossed in her way."

They found Steph standing at the kitchen counter adding club soda to the punchbowl of sangria she'd made earlier. "Care to sample my concoction? The club soda is to make it fizzy."

Earlier Steph had thrown together brandy, lemonade

concentrate, a smidgen of lemon and orange juice, red wine, triple sec, and a small amount of sugar. She'd floated slices of fruit in it to make it fancy. It didn't look as if she and Jack had touched a drop.

Elaina took stemware glasses from the hutch and passed them around. "We'll give it a whirl." She sampled the sangria. "Mmm. Tasty." She took another sip. "This just might become my beverage of choice."

"I'm glad you like it." Steph chugged the sangria like it was water.

"For the record, are we helping you drown your sorrows? Or is this a celebration?"

Steph huffed out a breath.

"You're putting off distress signals." Elaina guided her to a chair.

The quiver in Steph's voice returned. "Jack's moving to Portland and asked me to go along."

Elaina shot a look at Tawny, whose eyebrows were arched high. "Portland, Indiana?"

"Maine."

"Maine?" Elaina was beyond shocked. She'd gotten used to having Steph around. Loved her naivety and caring soul.

Grace ladled more sangria into Steph's glass. "You're leaving us?"

"I don't know. Maybe." Steph cleared her throat. "A small part of me wants to ditch the potholes I dug in Ohio with all my bad decisions and start fresh on new pavement somewhere else. The rest of me can't imagine leaving you guys."

Elaina took the chair next to Steph. "I don't even want to think about going a day without you, Steph, but that's me being selfish. If you need a new beginning, go for it. Besides, we'll only be apart distance-wise. Thanks to technology we can bug you with endless text messages." It was difficult to be upbeat when the thought of not having Steph around was squeezing her heart. "There's also Skype and Facetime so you can see our ugly mugs on a regular basis." Elaina swallowed hard to push down an unexpected burst of sadness. She didn't want Steph or Tawny or Grace to leave. They were her strength. They drove her crazy at times but mostly they kept her sane. If love took them to Timbuktu or Portland, Maine, she had to let them go. Elaina knew that Steph still wrestled with how things had gone with Corbett the snake and also the month-long marriage mistake she'd made directly after graduating from high school. Plus being an executive assistant to a hyper boss was a huge stress ball for her too. There were days when Steph came home so knotted up she could barely move. "Whatever you decide, I'll support you a hundred percent."

Tawny crossed her arms at her chest. "Jack wants to whisk you away." She shook her head. "That's a lot to process."

"His parents and sister are making the move ahead of him." Steph dropped her face in her hands and muffled through her fingers, "Something or other about an uncle who bought a bed and breakfast a few years back and now he wants out from under the responsibility. He's selling the business to Jack's dad but it's going to be a family venture."

"What does it specifically mean for you?"

Steph lowered her hands. "Mountains. Snow. Finding a place to live. Looking for a new job. The list is endless."

Tawny frowned straight away. "I get the bit about having to find a job because a bed and breakfast can only support so many people, but aren't you and Jack going to live together?"

Steph tugged at her bottom lip with her teeth. "Not right away. He doesn't want to upset his parents."

Jack deserved big points for considering his parents feelings. At the same time, it seemed odd for him to ask Steph to pull up stakes and then treat her as if she was just a girl he was dating. Jack Kirby either had 'nads the size of boulders or he was a complete and utter doofus. Elaina kept those thoughts to herself since Steph appeared to be on the verge of panic.

The tremble in Steph's tone increased. "Before I make a decision, I'm going to scout out Portland."

"We could go with you," Grace offered.

"I have to do this on my own."

Tawny sat in the chair opposite Steph and swiveled to face her. "You mentioned ditching the potholes for smoother pavement. You didn't say a word about being in love with Jack and how you'd follow him to the end of the earth."

Steph rubbed her forehead. "I'm in love with him."

"I'm not buying it. That should've been the first thing out of your mouth."

Steph puckered her face. "Well it wasn't."

Elaina fished an orange slice from her glass and chewed on the rind now spongy from having soaked up alcohol. "When is all this going down?"

"Jack gave the grocery his two-week notice today. He'll leave Ohio as soon as he packs and finds someone to sublease his apartment. His parents and sister are leaving on Monday. I'll wait until November to fly out. If I like what I see..." She didn't finish.

Ohhhh, Steph! Elaina had to bite back that this new circumstance for Jack and his family didn't happen overnight. They had to have known about it for a while. Yet Jack waited to spring it on her. An uneasy feeling settled in the pit of Elaina's stomach. She wrapped her arms around Steph and kissed her temple. "It'll be good."

Grace held up her glass for them to clink. "To being brave and following your heart."

Steph took a significant swallow of sangria first and then joined in the toast. She guzzled another swallow and presented her own toast. "To not wrecking my life by digging another pothole."

Chapter Four

- *Patch it!* -

Elaina led Stony into the park on North Street, trying to dig herself out of the funk that settled in after Steph announced she might be relocating to Maine. It was weird being distraught about her leaving, especially since there was a strong possibility Tawny and Grace would find love and eventually leave too. "The world isn't ending, Steph is chasing her happiness," she said aloud, hoping if her ears heard it her heart would accept it.

Stony glanced back like he understood the conversation and her angst. She'd been mumbling about Steph leaving for seven city blocks. The poor dog had to wonder what she was going on and on about.

Elaina crouched and planted a kiss on his head. "Why am I so weepy, Stone-man?" She knew the answer. The last few years had been emotionally rough. She'd lost both parents in a car wreck and shortly afterward her marriage fell to pieces. Her heart had taken direct hits both times. Meeting the girls at that cash-for-gold event had come at the right time. Without them, she'd still be a mess. Tawny, Grace, and Steph made her laugh and talked her into doing bizarre things. They were good for her on so many levels. On the flip side, living together was supposed to help them get their bearings as well. Maybe Steph had gotten hers.

"Stonyyyyy." A little red-haired girl with pigtails squealed with delight. She looked to be four or five and was barely able to get her arms around his neck to give him a hug. "You're the cutest dog in the world." She rubbed her face against his soft ears.

A few more kids wandered over.

Stony stood still while they made over him. They petted him, looked in his ears, touched his wet nose, and lifted his gums to inspect his teeth.

"Careful. He doesn't bite but his mouth is sensitive." Elaina shared a random fact. "He loves to get his teeth brushed."

The red-haired girl giggled. "He can't hold a toothbrush."

"You're right, he can't." Elaina was set to explain that Stony waits for her to finish brushing her teeth so he can have a turn. It was too much information for the kids so she simply said. "We help him."

"My mom says she hates brushing Roscoe's teeth because he tries to bite her," one boy offered. Another said his dog Cartwright runs when he sees a toothbrush.

The little red-haired girl looked up at Elaina. "I just love Stony."

"Me too."

The girl touched Stony's nose with hers, giggled

again, and took off for the swing set. She must've been the leader of the pack because the other kids followed.

"Gorgeous dog."

Elaina half-turned to acknowledge a tall, thin brunette. "Thanks."

The woman bent down to check out Stony. "I've begged my husband for a Husky. So far I've gotten a maybe." She smoothed her hand over his back. "He's well-behaved."

"I can't take the credit. He actually belongs to my roommate. She's put in the time to make him a lovable ball of fur."

The woman straightened to a stand. "You look familiar."

Elaina assumed it was because she owned the fitness center. "I get that a lot."

"I'm Lita Brandywine."

"Nice to meet you."

Lita cocked her head with a look of contemplation and then snapped her fingers. "You're involved with Michael Rexx."

Elaina smiled in spite of being jarred by the comment. She and Michael had kept their relationship low-key for his daughter's sake. Zoe was eight years old and not in a good place emotionally regarding her parents' divorce. According to Michael, she'd been acting out in school lately and would burst into tears over the least little thing. Zoe was aware of Elaina and vice versa, but they were never in each other's space. Elaina hadn't been in Michael's space either for the last few weeks. It was odd that he'd been absent from the fitness center too. As a truck driver, his job was mostly sedentary so he craved exercise to stay fit. Lately, he hadn't craved her or his workout. Elaina scrambled for an appropriate response. "We occasionally go out."

Lita nodded. "So I've been told."

Elaina squinted with suspicion. "Are you related to Michael?" That seemed to be the safest question out of the six racing through her head.

Lita offered little. "No."

"Lawyer? Neighbor? Close friend?"

A strange sparkle lit Lita's eyes.

The question all but answered itself. "You're a friend of his ex."

Lita looked away. "We're best friends."

Elaina inhaled a breath and released it with a difficult inquiry. "Are you here to tell me to back off?"

Lita returned her gaze to Elaina's. "Liz would have my head on a platter if I said anything of the sort. I saw you walking the dog on Canal Street and my curiosity got the better of me. I didn't mean to follow you and I certainly had no intention of speaking with you." She lifted her shoulders and let them fall. "But here I am."

"Best friends are awesome. I have three I'd I do anything for." *Even chase down whoever was seeing their exes if I thought it would help them in any way.* Elaina put some slack in Stony's leash so he could hike his leg on a tree. "Now that we've *bumped* into each other, what comes next?"

Lita blurted out that Michael and Liz were taking

steps to get back together.

Elaina was rendered speechless for just a moment. She wasn't sure if her mouth fell open or not. "Oh" was all she was capable of saying. She was stunned yet her mind rushed back to the last conversation she'd had with Michael. He'd bared his soul about the guilt he felt for interrupting Zoe's happiness. He'd also said Liz was going to counseling. Perhaps in one of those counseling sessions Liz identified what caused their marital rift and wanted a chance to make things right. Elaina's eyes burned with tears that wanted to surface but she wouldn't allow. She hurt, yet how could she fault anyone for giving or getting a second chance?

Stony picked that precise moment to shove his nose where it didn't belong.

Lita jerked.

Stony's invasive way of getting to know someone broke the tension. Elaina uncoiled the tightness in her body with a nervous laugh and yanked on the leash. "I'm so sorry. Sometimes with no warning Stone-man goes for the goods. Typical male."

"I hear that." Lita splayed a hand in front of her lady bits but she didn't keep an eye on Stony. She seemed more concerned with Elaina. "I could tell by your expression you weren't aware Michael and Liz were trying to patch things up."

The tears Elaina managed to override with laughter came on. "I didn't know."

"I should've kept my mouth shut." Lita sounded genuinely troubled. "It's just that Liz cries all the time because she ruined something great."

"I understand." Elaina puffed out a sigh. "I won't nark you out to Michael."

"Thank you. Liz has been there for me over the years and I'm trying to be there for her."

It took all her strength, but Elaina ended things on a positive note. "Good friends are hard to come by. Liz is lucky to have you. Thank you for telling me about Michael and Liz." Elaina tugged on Stony's leash. "We really should be going."

"Will you be okay?"

Elaina lifted her chin. She'd make herself be okay. "Yes."

* * *

"Where's the new bottle of ketchup you bought when you went shopping with Steph?" Tawny clattered items in the pantry and closed the door with a slam.

Grace and Elaina glanced at each other with a questioning look. Tawny wasn't all daisies and rainbows in the morning but she seldom got everyone's attention by knocking things around. Once she was out of bed and showered the sharp edges of her crack-of-dawn crankiness smoothed out. Not this morning, however.

Elaina walked to the pantry, found the bottle of ketchup setting on the second shelf in plain view, and handed it to Tawny.

Tawny clutched the bottle to her chest for a few seconds before trying...and failing...to flip open the cap.

Grace snorted.

Elaina was careful not to do the same. She took the bottle from Tawny's mitts and unscrewed the cap to peel back the protective seal. Returning the cap, she opened the lid. "Here you go." She eyed the hot dog Tawny was having at six o'clock in the morning. Elaina wouldn't judge. She'd been known to eat strange things for breakfast; never a hot dog. In her case, the weird breakfast choices were usually spawned from a rough night with Arden. After the encounter with Lita yesterday that she still hadn't shared with the others, she could've easily gotten up this morning and popped a whole package of hotdogs in the microwave. "Someone or something has ticked you off. Grady?"

"No." Tawny parted the sandwich bun and squirted so much ketchup it leaked over the sides. She winced and jammed the plastic bottle down on the bottle. "My day just keeps getting better."

Elaina leaned against the counter with a Granny Smith apple.

Tawny groaned like she was in pain. "I was trying to keep this quiet so I could surprise you. Like everything else my emotions trip me up."

"You're making a lot of racket for trying to keep quiet." Grace's eyes widened. "Don't tell me you leaving us too."

A small, somewhat-wicked smile curved Tawny's mouth. "The thought of not seeing me every morning, even though I'm a grouch, is hard to imagine. Am I right?"

Grace didn't mince words. "You're about to wear that hotdog."

"Good to know." Tawny shoved a significant bite of sandwich into her mouth.

Grace held up two fingers to measure a half-inch. "She puts this much information out there to make us crazy."

Tawny laid the hotdog on a napkin and blotted the corners of her mouth before she responded. "I'm not leaving you. Although, by the time I'm done with my plan you might help me pack my bags." She reached for the hot dog and Grace blocked her.

"No more weenie," Grace said animatedly, "until you give us good info instead of sketchy malarkey."

Elaina almost choked on a bite of apple.

Another groan, gritty and threatening from Tawny, made Grace surrender the hotdog.

"So here's the deal." Tawny tapped the table with her index finger. "On multiple occasions I've expressed a desire to quit smoking. Every time I take a stab at it, something worse than smoking happens and I end up puffing more instead of less." She thwarted any questions by throwing a hand in the air. "Relax. Nothing happened. Yet." Shifting in her chair, Tawny said she'd laid awake last night thinking about her sons, Bo and Quentin, and it hit her that one of these days she'd get a phone call from one of them saying they decided to settle down.

Grace turned to Elaina. "I'm not getting a clear picture, are you?"

"Patience," Elaina urged.

Tawny looked longingly at the coffee pot.

"I'm on it." Elaina took three cups from the cupboard and filled them with piping hot coffee.

Tawny hopped from her chair and retrieved the bottle of Kahlua they kept in the refrigerator. She splashed some into her cup.

Grace curled her lip. "Hotdogs and Kahlua. Yum." She shuddered for effect. "What are you thinking, woman?"

"I'm thinking you should mind your own beeswax." Tawny blew the steam from the coffee and indulged in a sip. "I tossed and turned and couldn't get my thoughts in line. It was as though my subconscious staged a coup and held me a knifepoint until I addressed my bad habit."

"You have more than one bad habit."

Tawny wrinkled her nose. "You're on a roll, heckler."

An impish expression flashed across Grace's face. "Sorry. Continue."

"My boys will someday be dads. I'll be a grandma. I want to stop smoking so I have the lung capacity to chase grandkids."

Grace raised her eyebrows. "I did not see that coming."

Elaina smoothed a hand across Tawny's shoulders. "Awesome, Tawn'."

Tawny shrugged. "Part awesome. Part mid-life crisis. The more I thought about being a nana, the more I wanted a cigarette. I almost sneaked out of the house to burn one at two-thirty in the morning. The craving was so strong I would've ripped someone apart limb by limb if they got in my way."

Grace strayed into dangerous territory. "The craving is still strong. You're assaulting ketchup bottles."

Tawny tightened her eyelids to a squint. "And I'm still capable of limb carnage."

"I'm not poking fun. I'm tickled for you. I just happen to have a mouth on me."

"Truer words have never been spoken." Tawny finally smiled.

"Good thing you're friends." Elaina thought of two other good friends. She tasted her coffee to distract thoughts of Lita and Liz. "How can we help?"

Tawny took another bite of hotdog and licked ketchup from the corners of her mouth. "By not over-reacting when I over-react. Nicotine withdrawal is going to turn me upside down and sideways."

"We won't overreact. Will we, Grace?"

"You won't." Grace put her teeth together in a toothy grin.

"We'll do whatever you need, Tawn'. The good news is it only takes three days to get rid of all the nicotine in your body. The bad news is the side effects that accompany withdrawal will hit you the hardest right about then."

"You know that as a fitness trainer?"

"Nope. It comes from having dealt with it firsthand." At Tawny's wide-eyed look of surprise, Elaina explained, "Not me. My parents. One summer they both decided to quit smoking. Let me just say things got so tense I wanted to go live with my aunt in Seattle for a while. Thank goodness they made it to day four without killing each other or biting the head off a bat. It wasn't easy, but they kicked the habit."

"I won't make any promises but I'll try not to bite your heads off and I do believe bats are safe at this time."

"We're here for you, no matter what."

Grace followed Tawny's lead and poured a little Kahlua in her coffee. "We definitely are."

Tawny smirked. "You say that now."

Stony stuck his head around the doorway and looked at them with his big blue eyes.

"Stone-man, would you like a hotdog?" Elaina didn't have to ask twice. Stony was by her side before she blinked. She tore the end off Tawny's breakfast.

"Heyyyy."

"Your owner's a bit stingy this morning." There was a routine they went through before Stony got a treat. Elaina fisted her hand. "Sit." Stony obeyed. She opened her palm. "Shake." The adorable pooch placed his paw in her hand. Elaina held up two fingers and then lowered them for Stony to go down on his belly. She was sure he was thinking 'just give it to me all ready' but he followed her instructions to a tee.

"You're going to need a nicotine patch and I'm going to need the rest of that hotdog." Grace grabbed the bun, took a dramatic chomp, and fled upstairs with the rest of the sandwich.

"Game on." Tawny took off after Grace.

Elaina shook her head when Stony raced after them. This early morning commotion was just a taste of what was to come. Perhaps this time she really would catch a flight to Seattle to live with her aunt for three days. Not only was Tawny going to upset the rhythm of the house, but also Steph. And Michael. Crap. Before all was said and done, she'd nix cereal for hot dogs.

* * *

"Grace, noooo," Elaina advised in a quiet shout when she reached the top of the stairs.

Grace slanted an evil grin and darted into Steph's room instead of her own.

Steph wouldn't be happy to be bothered so early on a scheduled day off from work. Plus, she'd told them last night she was staying up to watch the cooking shows she'd recorded on the downstairs DVR. Knowing Steph's love for cooking, she possibly didn't hit the sack until around three.

Elaina flicked on the hallway light but Steph's room remained dark with the exception of a tiny sliver of light beaming in from the street lamp in front of the house.

Grace's laugh was loud and depraved as she skirted around Steph's bed.

Tawny was no match for Grace's agility. She rounded the doorway and couldn't put on the brakes quick enough. She bumped into the bed with her thigh.

Caught up in the excitement, Stony took a leap and landed smack dab on top of Steph.

Steph screamed herself awake.

Between broken breaths from having run up the stairs, Tawny apologized. "Sorry, Steph." She put a hand on her chest, possibly to get her heart to stop thudding. "This is Grace's fault." She pointed a finger at Stony. "Get down."

"I'm guilty as sin," Grace admitted.

Elaina advised Steph that Tawny was abandoning nicotine and it might be wise to either sleep with a light on or lock her bedroom door from now on.

A deep yawn rolled slowly from Steph's chest. "Huh?"

"Tobacco."

Steph rubbed sleep from her eyes. "What about it?"

Elaina felt like a half-wit for explaining Tawny's situation to a semi-conscious person. "Tawny's trying to quit smoking."

"What does that have to do with everyone being in my room? Seriously."

"Grace stole Tawny's hotdog."

Steph's forehead creased into a mess of lines. "A hotdog?"

Tawny lifted an eyebrow. "At least I'm not wearing lizard pajamas."

"They're geckos."

"Geckos *are* lizards," Grace clarified.

"Get out of my room."

Chapter Five

~ *Lies, ties, and catnip!* ~

Elaina wouldn't chase Michael down for him to confirm or deny Lita's revelation. She stood firm on that pledge, for at least a good hour. Somehow she found herself standing in front of his condominium complex with two chocolate milkshakes. She walked up the sidewalk. Halfway to his condo she turned on her heel and went back to the parking lot.

Taking a pull of chocolaty goodness from the straw, it was delicious yet bittersweet in the memories it rousted. Michael loved milkshakes. Their date-nights always included a shake, usually after a movie or a walk in the park.

Her inner voice urged her to either speak with him or go home.

Elaina breathed in a lungful of air and exhaled as she proceeded up the sidewalk that would take her to the door marked 104 in black metallic numerals. She noticed his curtains were open and there were no sheers – so much for the element of surprise. Elaina made a snap decision to circle around the building instead of walking past the window.

Finally, at his door she fisted her hand to knock but held off. Michael didn't owe her an explanation or closure. Not really. Still, getting the low-down about him reuniting with his ex-wife from a second-hand source didn't set well. Her knuckles were almost on the wood when she lost her nerve. She retraced her steps back to the Escalade and slumped against the bumper, trying to understand how Michael had gone from an eager wooer and straight-forward vocal guy to being absent and silent. Elaina remembered something he'd said shortly after they met – 'I'd rather be open and honest about my life and my feelings so you know who I am and why I do the things I do'. That's the Michael she'd grown fond of; not this elusive creature of the past three weeks who reportedly moved on or moved back without a word.

Staring at the brick building as though it was an ominous creature, Elaina contemplated her next move. There was no reason she couldn't drop by for a visit and she did have milkshakes going to waste. "Whoever said ignorance is bliss must've had a screw loose." The not-knowing bit was making her nuts. She growled low and feral. "Avoiding me isn't an exit strategy, Michael." She had a powerful urge to throw the milkshakes at his pickup truck. Instead, she winced at how easy it was to give into anger. These out-of-control thoughts had to stop. Wanting to deliver geese to Arden's property and contemplating giving Michael's truck a bath in chocolate was so unlike her. She was no angel but she wasn't vindictive, normally. Why now? The question made her dig deep. It didn't take long to come up with a motive – she didn't want to be made a fool, again. Elaina frowned when another potent thought surfaced – the fear of being messed with emotionally had made her hold back with Michael. To be honest, she hadn't been 'all in'. She'd given him a lot of herself, but not everything. She hadn't given him the level of affection he sought. She also hadn't told her closest friends about this surprising development with Michael. Apparently she wasn't 'all in' with them either.

Moisture formed on the outside of the milkshake cups and she almost dropped one.

"Get it together, Samuels. Either do this or go home." Blowing out a breath, Elaina squared her shoulders and raised her head high. She marched up the L-shaped sidewalk. Instead of circumventing the window this time, she strode past and took a look.

Her pulse stopped beating.

Sitting on the couch was Michael, his daughter Zoe, and a long-haired blonde that had to be Liz. They were scrunched together, laughing. It was a joyful scene – for them. Elaina tried to rein in on a mixed bag of emotions. She was glad for Michael, yet she wanted to thrust her knee into his delicate manly parts for leaving her hanging. Her subconscious steadied her with the reminder that Zoe was a sweet girl caught up in the pain of divorce. Zoe deserved to get her family unit back intact. Elaina leaned into that logic, but it didn't remedy her hurt feelings. While she and Michael hadn't declared love for one another, they'd been intimate. It had taken a while for it to happen, but once it did, Elaina felt more content than she had in a long time. They'd grown comfortable with one another and would occasionally curl up on her sofa and talk about their previous entanglements. Michael had once said he wanted to stay as far away from his ex as he could get. It would be easier to think he'd lied; she knew he hadn't.

Elaina blinked back tears. Maybe if she'd been 'all in'...

* * *

Steph furrowed her brows at the brown and pumpkin-colored diamond-patterned tie twisted around the doorknob of Tawny's bedroom door. "What do you think it means?"

Elaina masked her distress from the visit to Michael's place with a fake smile. "I know what it meant in college. I'm not sure it applies in this case."

Grace tiptoed down the short hallway and rested an ear against the door.

Elaina jerked her thumb for the tauntress to back away. Yeah, like that would happen. Grace was as self-governing and noncompliant as Lula.

The door was suddenly yanked open. Tawny stepped into the hallway and jammed her hands on her hips. "Helloooo! Tie on the door!"

Grace flinched but leaned right and left, trying to look around Tawny. "Who's in there?"

Sarcasm rolled off Tawny in waves. "The milkman. The UPS guy. Some random stranger who happened to drive by. The mayor. City Council. You name it. They're in there."

Steph didn't leave well enough alone. "We don't have a milkman."

"Exactly!" Tawny's scathing loudness boomed off the walls.

"Okay then." Steph cast off a bit of loudness too. "That leaves the UPS guy, a random stranger, the mayor, City Council, and most of the men in Cherry Ridge!"

An eye roll accompanied Tawny's groan. "I. Need. A. Cigarette." She ducked back into the bedroom and vibrated the door with a hard slam.

Grace braved the wrath of a woman on the edge and hollered through the wood. "Where'd ya get the tie, hussy?" She received a muffled, "I rummaged through your stuff." Grace's light blue eyes darkened. "If you touched Brince's ties I'll strangle you."

"Pfft. You'd have to break down the door to make it happen."

"Don't think a thick piece of oak will stop me."

Elaina coughed to get Grace's attention. "If you dish it out, you have to be able to take it."

"Meaning?"

"She's toying with you," Elaina snickered, but she softened right away. "She'd never touch Brince's things. Take a good look at the tie. The Brince you've described would've never worn something so gaudy."

"You're right. Brince had taste." Grace flipped back

into heckling mode. "Where'd ya get the tie, clown?"

"I'll have you know I bought it for Grady for his birthday, or Easter, or Ground Hog Day." Tawny finally gave into a laugh. "I might've bought it to get back at him for forgetting our anniversary."

"You're a first-class nut job."

"Takes one to know one."

"True that."

Trying to cope with the not-so-funny things going on in her head while putting up with her roomies whacked-out behavior was wearing on Elaina. "This is only day two."

Steph moved Grace out of the way to speak to Tawny. "You don't have to stay in your room."

"Oh yes I do."

"We'll be close by if you need us." Elaina relocated to the kitchen, deep in thought. She startled when Grace tapped her on the shoulder.

"Sooooooooo," Grace drew out the word until she could no longer add o's. "We know what's ailing Tawny. What's ailing *you*?"

Was she that transparent? Elaina looked down at the floor instead of meeting Grace and Steph's inquiring gazes. "The only thing ailing me is a lack of wine." From the corner hutch where she kept fancy glassware, she took a goblet and filled it to the rim with blackberry Merlot.

Grace bumped Steph with her forearm. "Here we go again. When something's bugging her she has a full glass of wine, not to mention RBF. When we call her on it, she plays dumb."

Elaina gulped down a third of the wine. "What's RBF?"

Grace clicked her tongue. "Something I learned from the new girl at work. She's a hoot! You'd love her."

"Not enough info...about RBF...not the new girl at work." Elaina gulped another healthy swallow of Merlot at the same time Grace said, "RBF. Resting bitch face." She spit wine across the counter and some came out her nose.

Steph laughed so hard she had to hold her stomach. All of the sudden she stopped. Her mirthful expression sobered. "The RBF is because of me, isn't it? You're upset because I may become a Mainiac."

Grace was quick to point out that she was already a maniac.

"You'd starve as a comedienne." Steph raised her shoulder in haughty rebuttal but amusement returned to her green eyes. "M-a-i-n-i-a-c; someone from Maine."

"You'll be a Mainiac maniac."

"Clever. Not."

"Is Steph right?" Grace asked.

"That you're not clever? Yes, she's absolutely correct." Elaina hollered for Stony. He barreled into the kitchen at full speed. "Want to go for a walk?"

Stony's tail did double-time.

Elaina hooked the leash to his collar.

"No walks until you answer the question."

Stony was raring to go. Elaina wrapped the leash around her hand several times to keep him in place until she was ready. "No she isn't right. I'm not upset that you might leave, Steph. If Jack Kirby is your joy and Portland is your destiny, then so be it."

"If the RBF isn't about me, then who's it about?"

Elaina rubbed the tense muscles at the back of her neck. It was time to be 'all in' with them. "Michael."

Grace crouched to pet Stony and looked up at Elaina. "I assume you found out why he's been missing in action."

Elaina swallowed hard. "He's getting back with his ex."

Steph was all over the situation with sympathy. She patted Elaina's arm. "Aww! I'm sorry."

"It's fine. Really." Elaina exhaled noisily. "Where's the nearest tattoo parlor?"

Grace softly said, "Atta girl. When life gives us lemons, we don't make freaking lemonade. We drink wine and get tattoos."

"How'd he tell you?" Steph asked.

"He didn't. Lita Brandywine tracked me down to deliver the news."

Steph's brows twitched together. "I know her. She was a grade below me in school. Tall, thin chick with dark hair?"

"Yep. She happens to be Liz's best friend."

Grace scoffed. "I wouldn't put much stock in what a friend of his ex had to say. Besties lie for each other."

Elaina stretched her neck from side to side. "She didn't lie."

Lula had sneaked into the kitchen and jumped onto Stony's back.

Stony howled and almost separated Elaina's hand from her wrist when he tried to break loose to chase the wicked feline.

"What the heck is up with Lula?"

Grace drew her shoulders up in contrived innocence. "She needed catnip. We could all use a little catnip. Apparently."

Chapter Six

- It's complicated! -

"Tell me it's not snowing on October fifteenth," Steph moaned.

Elaina parted the curtains to look out the living room window. Huge beautiful flakes floated effortlessly from the sky and melted as soon as they hit the ground. The month of October usually gave way to warm days and cool nights, not frozen precipitation. The snow was a surprise given that three days ago the temperature hovered near eighty degrees. That was Ohio though. There were times they experienced all four seasons in one week. "Umm, it's snow."

Steph moaned again, louder this time. "Mother Nature must be off her rocker. Or the witch can't read a calendar."

Elaina had a hunch Steph's mood stemmed from something other than snow. She wouldn't pry just yet because sometimes a girl needed to work things out in her head. "A perfect day for sitting in the hot tub."

"Swimsuits in the snow? I don't think so."

"We could make mulled wine and sip it while snowflakes fall in our hair."

Steph closed her eyes halfway. "Why are you so cheery?"

Elaina gave Steph big points for not adding, 'when Michael is being a butthead'. "I want it to be a good day, that's all. And I could really go for a hot tub party."

"I'll wave at you from the kitchen."

With her phone, Elaina did a Google search. "You'd better prepare yourself for snow. It says Portland, Maine averages seventy-two inches of the white stuff a year." She smiled devilishly. "You and Jack could go snow tubing."

"Bite me."

Tawny looked over the banister at the top of the stairs. "What are we biting?"

"Elaina has a dark side."

To anyone other than those living in the house, Steph's comment would've been met with furrowed eyebrows or at least a "huh?" Tawny seemed to understand the sideways remark. "We all do."

Elaina's grin widened. "Did I mention the east coast also gets the occasional nor'easter?"

Steph was trying to fend off a smile but the corners of her mouth dimpled. "Keep it up, Samuels, and you'll find ground glass in your scrambled eggs tomorrow morning."

"I prefer dill, but hey, you're an awesome cook that made me a fan of succotash. You could probably work wonders with glass." The mere thought of succotash used to make Elaina queasy. Shortly after they decided to live together,

Steph became the unofficial cook. One night she made succotash and pressured Elaina into trying a spoonful. Expecting her taste buds to stage a coup, Elaina had been pleasantly surprised at the burst of flavors that met her tongue. Instead of just corn and lima beans, there was bacon. Everything was better with bacon. There was also onion, garlic, tiny bits of carrot, diced jalapeno pepper, and cherry tomatoes. A secret ingredient or spice made Elaina wolf it down. When she asked what the mystery component had been Steph replied, 'love'. It turned out to be sesame oil. Elaina smiled. Steph's imagination and fearlessness to experiment with food was remarkable. She threw stuff together most people wouldn't begin to consider. Essentially, Stephanie Mathews could be a top chef in a five-star restaurant. She loved food. Food loved her. It was a romance made in heaven but continued in the kitchen.

Steph raised her eyebrows up and down mischievously. "I'll skip the glass...for now."

Tawny plodded down the stairs still dressed in her terry cloth bathrobe even though it was just after two in the afternoon, on a Saturday yet to boot. Dusky circles under her eyes indicated a lack of sleep. "One more day," she grumbled. "One more grueling day. Nicotine can kiss my arse."

"You've got this, Tawny," Elaina said.

"Tell that to the monster inside who wants to inhale a cigarette so badly." She whimpered. "The struggle is real."

Steph was out of the recliner in a nano-second. She

slung an arm around Tawny's shoulders. "The monster wants to hang out in the hot tub and drink mulled wine."

Elaina covered her mouth with her hand; astonished and tickled at the same time that whatever was bugging Steph was put on the back burner so she could comfort Tawny.

What a unique blend of characters she had as roomies. The longer they lived together the more alike they became. Grace had been full of grief at the loss of Brince. These days she was full of piss and vinegar. Tawny had been an over-worked stressed-out nurse. She was still over-worked but she seemed to take a more relaxed attitude toward life. And, she was trying to quit smoking. When Steph moved in, her self-esteem was in the toilet. She fought weight issues and her knack for picking the wrong guy. These days she was still concerned about stepping on the scale but she didn't obsess about it. The jury was still out about her selection of men. Jack Kirby seemed like a decent guy. He didn't say much but he made Steph smile a lot. That alone was awesome. Elaina thought about how she'd changed since having the support of three crazy but incredible women in her life. Like Tawny, she was more relaxed. She could be herself – sometimes hyper, cranky, or gushing with sweetness. The best thing – she didn't have to walk on eggshells every moment of the day like she had to when she was married to Arden.

Grace came inside from getting the mail and drew back theatrically when she saw Tawny. "What's with the zombie eyes?"

"The apocalypse has begun. Didn't you get the memo?" Tawny didn't wait for Grace to slide in a snappy comeback. "Hop to it, ladies. The mulled wine isn't going to make itself."

Steph chuckled. "That's right. Chop. Chop. Elaina, zest an orange and then juice it. Grace, find a bottle of Cabernet Sauvignon. Tawny, rummage through the cabinets for cinnamon sticks, cloves, honey, and anise."

Tawny cocked an eyebrow. "What are *you* going to do?"

"Make sure the minions don't slack."

Elaina grinned at Steph. "The kitchen is your happy place."

"I've never thought of it like that, but yeah, it is."

"I still think you should write a cookbook and/or have your own cooking show."

Steph's face brightened. "I would love to do both. I can picture it now. *Steph's Kitchen. 8PM Eastern Time, 7PM Central.*"

"More like *Hell's Kitchen*," Tawny mumbled.

"Don't diss Gordon Ramsay. He's my role model. Not only does he expect culinary perfection, he's an incredible humanitarian who gives back." Steph took a gallon of apple cider from the refrigerator and poured four cups into a large saucepan.

"You're *our* role model." Elaina handed Steph the cutting board which held a small pile of orange zest. "You've nailed the art of bossing people around. Your cooking, in my humble opinion, is perfect. And you're more of a giver than a taker. All you need now is an opportunity to showcase your talent and who you are as a person."

Grace uncorked the bottle and added the wine to the apple cider. "Damn skippy you're our role model."

"Thanks, you guys. You're good for my ego." Steph took the other items from Tawny to finish the recipe. "Realistically, I don't see any kind of showcase happening. I may be moving to Maine and will live out my days working in an office again instead of a kitchen."

"This is supposed to simmer for at least ten minutes." Tawny dipped a spoon into the pan for a sample. "Mmm. Have a taste." She took three other spoons from the drawer and passed them around.

Steph's eyes rolled back in her head after she sampled the concoction. "Delish'."

Grace spooned a taste into her mouth and smacked her lips. "My mouth is aquiver."

"Aquiver?" Tawny mocked.

Elaina helped herself to a spoonful. "Mmm. Mmm. My mouth is also aquiver." She elbowed Grace. "By the time we get our swimsuits on it should be done." She advanced to the stairs but stopped when someone thundered the front door with a knock.

Their long-haired furry protector barked repeatedly.

Tawny traipsed to the door and smashed an eye against the peek hole. "Brace yourself, Elaina. Tall, dark and arrogant has paid you a visit."

Elaina puckered her face in revulsion. "I must've pissed off the gods." She grumbled her way to Tawny. "There's no other explanation. First Michael. Now Arden. Yay me."

"Do you want me to tell him to bug off?"

"No. I'll talk to him. I'd rather toss him a cobra but with my luck, the two venomous vipers would become fast friends."

Tawny opened the door just enough to hold a conversation. She pretended not to recognize Arden. "Whatever you're selling we don't need any."

Stony continued to bark and tried to push his way outside.

Arden stood his ground. "Cute." His infamous grating tone didn't seem to affect Tawny even a little.

"I thought so too, dude," Tawny quipped in a valley girl voice.

Elaina stepped into view. "What brings you to the commune?" She suppressed a laugh at the dig. Arden had verbally bashed her about running a commune the day he found out the girls had moved in.

Awareness flashed across his face. "Good one, Elaina." His follow-up snicker was mirthless. "Call off the hairy beast...and your dog."

Tawny glared. "You're a real piece of work, Wellby."

Arden volleyed back the glare at her use of his middle name.

Elaina smiled at Tawny with her eyes. "I'll take it from here."

Tawny used two fingers to tell Arden she'd be watching him.

When it was the two of them at the door Elaina expressed her surprise. "I'm shocked to see you. Not blown-away shocked, just slightly stunned." Although 'slightly' was underselling it.

"No doubt." Arden shifted from foot to foot, which gave the impression he was nervous.

Elaina was sure his unease was an act to get her to let down her guard. She crossed her arms. "Care to clue me in?"

He moved in close and dropped his voice to a whisper. "I came to ask you something."

Every muscle in Elaina's body tightened. "Oh?"

Arden cleared his throat. "Would you have dinner with me tomorrow night?"

Elaina uttered a silent expletive. "I...uh..." She blinked up at him. "Why?"

"I'd really like to have dinner with you."

That was not an explanation. Elaina smacked the left side of her head hoping to get the part of her brain responsible for logic, to provide the real reason. The hit wasn't enough to jar the cogs into making clear his motivation. Although she had a hunch it might be his endless quest to the get house and fitness center he'd given up in the divorce. A few months ago he'd made it known he wanted both properties back. His tone had been demanding and a bit threatening. Elaina had stood her ground and told him to take a flying leap. *Perhaps* he thought time had softened her stance. *Perhaps* he also thought wining and dining her would get her to sign over the deeds. *Perhaps* he was still a clueless jackal. "Sure. Why not."

Arden reached for her hand but Stony wedged between them to prevent the contact. Stony followed up with a growl.

"Good dog," Tawny said over Elaina's shoulder.

Arden stepped back as if he thought Tawny would command Stony to take a bite out of him. "Six o'clock?"

"Six is fine."

Tawny moved Elaina out of the way and shut the door with her foot. "What are you doing?"

"It's complicated," Elaina muttered, half-dazed.

"It's not complicated. It's a bizarre case of rebounding. You rebounded from Arden with Michael. Now you're rebounding from Michael with Arden. Complicated? Pfft!"

* * *

Grace appeared on the patio wearing a two-piece swimsuit, boots, and ear muffs.

"Just when I thought the day couldn't get weirder, there's Grace dressed in her finest." Tawny shook her head. "No wonder I smoke."

Grace did a three-sixty turn to show off her fashion sense; or lack thereof. "Chic. Don't you think?" She removed the boots but kept the ear muffs on when she climbed into the hot tub next to Steph. "We have to loosen these two up." Nodding toward Tawny and Elaina she stated the obvious, "They're a mess. One is trying to cope with strong physical urges. The other is Tawny."

Elaina snorted. "I don't have strong physical urges. Wait. I do. I have the *urge* to wrap my hands around your spindly little neck."

"Your mouth says 'no, no, no', but your body language

said 'yes, yes, yes,' when Arden was here. I saw it. Did you see it, Steph?"

"Ohhh yeah." Mischief bubbled out of Steph. "She was saying yes. Big time. You need an intervention. Let's begin by talking smack about Arden."

"We're not going to trash him."

"Because?"

Elaina looked away.

"We were right," Tawny said. "She still has the hots for him."

Elaina gave Tawny the evil eye. "Discussing me, were you?"

A guilty grin cornered all three of their mouths. "You might say that," Tawny admitted."

"I *did* say that." Elaina's shoulders rose and fell with a sigh. "I don't have the hots for Wellby. I have...I don't know...something that needs rectified. I'm not sure what it is. When I saw him at the door, I was both intrigued and repulsed. Mostly repulsed."

"We'll help you sort it out. By talking," Steph drew out the word, "smaaaack. Start by telling us something about the pointy-headed fish that only you know."

Elaina tapped her mugged. Arden Samuels was the ultimate cliché when it came to looks. He was *all that and a bag of chips.* He turned the heads of both women and men. His cocky, overconfident, do-as-I-say personality, however, lessened his appeal. He could go from a perfect ten to a measly two just by opening his mouth. "Umm, he gets irked when his morning newspaper isn't on the porch by 6AM sharp."

Steph's wink to Grace had evil plot written all over it.

Elaina inhaled. "He has the most amazing scent."

Tawny flicked at a bubble. "That explains why you broke out in a sweat."

Elaina adamantly denied the claim.

"You were glistening. There were beads of moisture on your forehead, above your lip, and who knows where else."

"Stop. Just stop," Elaina smirked, "biatch!"

"What?" Tawny laughed so hard she snorted. "You did not just call me a biatch."

Grace snickered. "We've ruined Elaina. Before she met us she was the epitome of class. Now look at her. She's slurping mulled wine from an insulated mug that says 'Diva' and calling Tawn' a biatch. Our work here is done."

Steph moved so one of the hot tub jets hit her lower back. "Hey! I bought that mug. It's classy."

"Whatever. Keep going."

"This is in no way helpful."

"It is to us."

Elaina gave Grace a pointed look but couldn't resist one more crack about Arden. "He'd blow a blood vessel if he watched you cook, Steph. You dance around the kitchen while being elbow-deep in spices and ingredients. Arden is a one-thing-at-a-time kind of guy. If he used the cinnamon, he'd have to put it away. If he used the nutmeg, yep, you guessed it; he'd have to return it to the cabinet. God forbid a few grains of salt would land on the counter. He'd have to clean them up before he could continue."

"So he wouldn't shake his groove thing while cooking?" Tawny surmised.

"Honestly, I don't think he has a groove thing."

Steph shook her head with amazement. "It would take all day to cook a meal."

"Exactly. We dined out a lot. To save time."

Grace mimicked a pulling motion.

"I know. I know. Keep sifting the dirt." Elaina lifted out of the hot water to give her body a break from the heat. "He attended a City Council meeting and asked them to ban clotheslines."

"That's preposterous." Steph looked over the edge of her mug. "Why do clotheslines bother him?"

Tawny put up a hand. "I got this one. Wellby has a problem when people hang their delicates out to dry. Am I right?"

The cool air made Elaina shiver. She dunked down to her chin. "I'd like to say you're wrong, but you're not. He'd mumble under his breath every time he drove by a house with clothes on the line. Should any of the garments happen to be underwear or bras, he'd go into a rant about dense people."

"What did you ever see in the loon?" Steph asked.

"He was fairly normal until he made his first million. After that he went crackers."

Grace caught a snowflake with her tongue. "He's supposed to be engaged yet he asked you to dinner."

"I almost asked about his betrothed. Instead, I accepted the dinner invitation."

"You're curious. I would be too." Tawny removed

the lid to her mug and poured more hot wine from the insulated carafe setting on the corner of the tub.

Steph held out her mug. "Fill 'er up." She tried to put the lid back on the mug and spilled wine in the bubbly water. "My bad." She righted the lid and offered her thoughts. "Maybe Arden's changed."

Grace said they should put that theory to a test. Before she could say how, they were distracted by the sun.

Steph raised her face to the sky. "The snow madness is over." Those words were barely out of her mouth when the clouds slammed shut and dime-size hail fell with a vengeance.

"You jinxed us." Tawny tried to hurry from the hot tub only to skid out of control.

Steph sprang into action and grabbed a handful of Tawny's swimsuit top to keep her from going over the side of the tub headfirst. The material ripped at the hook letting Tawny's extraordinary chest free of its bondage.

When Tawny got her footing she was inches from Grace.

Grace shielded her face with her hand. "Watch it. You could put an eye out with those things."

They'd had just enough wine to find that hysterically funny.

Chapter Seven

- *Picnics and G-spots!* -

Elaina tilted her head with amazement as Grace spread butter on her biscuit.

Tawny toed Elaina with her shoe. She picked up a wrapped rectangle of butter from the crystal dish in the center of the table and pretended to study it. "Real butter. Only thirty-six calories." She turned it over several times. "Not many restaurants serve real butter these days." She handed it to Grace who absently took it and started to remove the foil wrap. "Grace, you either love butter or you're in some kind of trance."

"Huh?"

Elaina, Steph, and Tawny said "trance" at the same time.

"You've buttered the same biscuit three times. You were quiet during Mass – a first for you. When we drove around looking for a place to eat that didn't have a one-hour wait, you didn't nag Elaina to forget breakfast so we could go to Juan's for Mexican food and margaritas. "Did you step on a rusty nail and get lock-jaw?"

Grace didn't sass back – another first. She merely shook her head.

The waitress arrived with a large oval tray heaping with food. She handed a plate of whole wheat pancakes to Tawny. Elaina took the bowl of grapefruit sections and low-fat cottage cheese. Crepes filled with custard and drizzled with strawberry sauce went to Steph. Lastly, a platter with three over-easy eggs, a short stack of blueberry pancakes, two strips of bacon, two sausage links, and home fries was handed to Grace.

Tawny and Elaina exchanged glances. "When you ordered the lumberjack plate did you know it was enough food to feed a small country?"

Grace pressed her lips together.

"Grace?" Steph prompted.

Grace moved a sausage link around on the plate with her fork. "This was Brince's favorite place to eat. He always ordered breakfast combo number five – the lumberjack plate."

Pieces of the puzzle started to fall into place when Elaina noted the wedding rings on Grace's left hand. The day they'd met at the cash-for-gold event Grace had moved them to her right hand.

The waitress skirted away but she returned in a flash with a fresh pot of coffee. "Can I top off your cups?"

"Actually, we're not staying. We'd like to-go containers for our food."

Steph almost had a bite of crepe to her mouth. She gave Elaina a perplexed look and lowered her fork. "We would?"

"Yes, we would."

The waitress's eyebrows furrowed into a frown. "Is anything wrong?"

"The food and service are perfect. It's just that we've decided to take our food to the east side of town for a picnic. Could we get to-go cups for our coffee also?"

"Sure, hon. Not a problem."

Steph shoved the forkful of crepe into her mouth and said between chews, "It's not picnic weather."

Elaina was well aware it was fifty-eight degrees with enough wind to make the tree tops sway. "The sun's shining."

It took a good fifteen minutes to convince them the picnic needed to happen.

After leaving a hefty tip for the waitress's trouble, they piled into Elaina's Cadillac Escalade.

"Oh goody. A picnic. I can hardly wait." Tawny's sarcasm was playful.

Grace was still abnormally quiet.

Steph enjoyed her coffee via the sip-tab of her Styrofoam cup and said "ahh" after each slurp.

Ten minutes later Elaina pulled off the paved roadway and onto the stone drive of Shady Oaks Cemetery.

Grace broke her silence and leaned forward to peer around Elaina's seat. "What are you doing?"

"I thought Brince might like some company."

Grace drooped against the backseat and covered her face. Her sobs were instant and loud.

Steph unlatched her seatbelt and drew Grace into her arms. "We don't have to stay."

Grace untangled herself from Steph and used the heels of her palms to wipe her eyes. "Yes we do. I miss Brince so much today it hurts. It's been almost three years since I kissed him goodbye."

Awareness registered in Steph's expression. "Well then, let's get this picnic underway while our food is still warm."

On a blanket spread under a giant oak tree near Brince's headstone they sat in the cool, crisp, autumn air and dined without speaking. Leaves fell from the trees and rustled in the breeze.

Grace rolled one of the sausage links in a pancake and wandered over to Brince to have a private conversation. Even from a distance it was easy to see streams of tears trailing unrestrained down her cheeks. She knelt on the ground and ran a hand over the smooth marble stone etched with his name. Nibbling the corner of the pancake, she held it out as though offering the next bite to Brince.

Elaina blotted tears with a napkin. Tawny and Steph did the same to their eyes.

"Should we go to her?" Tawny asked quietly.

Elaina could barely speak. "No. This is between them."

When Grace came back there were traces of mascara under each eye, but a tender smile at her lips. "Thank you. I needed that."

Elaina nodded. "You're welcome."

"Now," Tawny said, "let's drive around town and count how many clotheslines we can find."

Grace sniffed and then chuckled. "Let's do it."

"Four single women with nothing better to do on a Sunday afternoon than count clotheslines." Elaina finished her coffee. "We could really rev things up by stopping at the gas station for pumpkin spice lattes."

Tawny grinned at Steph and Grace over the headrest. "Look out Cherry Ridge, the Sweat Pants ladies are on the move."

"We could go bowling." Steph's suggestion was met with resistance. "Or we could head home and help Elaina find something sexy for her date with Arden."

"Yeah that's not happening."

"The bowling? Or the search for something sexy?"

"I already know what I'm going to wear – layers that include: a turtleneck sweater, three blouses, a pair of long underwear, two pairs of granny panties, wool slacks, and a matching jacket. Knee-high socks are a must. And boots."

"If you had a chastity belt, would you wear that too?" Grace teased.

Elaina smiled to herself. Grace was feeling better. "Arden is after something. I doubt it's sex but I can't take the chance. I don't want to put off the slightest sexual vibe because he'll use it to his advantage."

"You know what you have to do then – fight fire with fire. Let him *think* he has the upper-hand. You know that little black dress he wouldn't allow you to wear because he thought it made you look slutty?"

* * *

80

"Fifteen clotheslines on Maple Street alone." Grace rubbed her hands together. "Oh the fun we could have."

Elaina looked in the rearview mirror. "Don't even think about it."

Grace stretched up to meet Elaina's gaze in the mirror. "You're not the boss of me."

"Nor do I want to be. I'd be tearing my hair out by the handfuls." She couldn't keep a straight face. "Seriously. No. You can mess with anyone else, not Arden."

"Fear of retaliation?"

"Big time. He has connections far and wide. He'll sit back and laugh while they do his dirty work."

"He's not a mob boss. He's a financial investor."

Again in the mirror, Elaina gave Grace a pointed look.

"He'd never suspect us. Anyone from City Council could be the..."

"N-O."

"Killjoy."

Elaina smirked. "I prefer to think of it as self-preservation."

"You need to grow a pair."

"I'd need testosterone for that to happen."

Tawny poked Elaina on the arm. "FYI – you have testosterone swimming around in your veins." At Elaina's narrowed eyelids, she coated her words with laughter. "Ovaries produce both testosterone and estrogen. Small amounts of testosterone are released into your bloodstream. You might not be able to *grow a pair*, but you have some hidden manliness."

Elaina deepened her voice to imitate masculinity.

"Whatever."

"Enough about ovaries. Show us where Arden lives." Grace put up her palms. "It's a clothesline expedition nothing more. I want to see how many I'll find on his street."

"You won't find anything resembling a clothesline. He lives in a swanky neighborhood and is a member of a homeowner's association. Knowing Arden, he schmoozed his way into the organization and was voted president. That way he could dictate what people were allowed to do on their properties. You won't find any gardens or sheds either. He hates plants and he thinks sheds are tacky."

"He had a shed."

Tawny corrected Steph. "Oh honey, he didn't have a shed, he had a car museum."

Elaina felt a sudden rush of guilt for man-bashing Arden the past few days. Not that she owed him allegiance but he'd been her first love. She'd given the barracuda her heart and virginity. He hadn't thought much of either one, but still, whether she liked it or not, a part of her would always belong to him. Elaina made a right turn instead of left.

"Nice try." Tawny jerked her thumb to the east. "He lives that way."

When these women got something in their heads...

Elaina put on chunky sunglasses and turned down the sun visor as she drove onto Hemingway Lane. "The brick castle at the end of the cul-de-sac belongs to Arden."

Tawny's mouth gaped open. "Holy mackerel. That *is*

a castle. I'm surprised it doesn't have a moat to keep out the riff raff." She slapped her thigh. "Us."

"He doesn't need a moat. He has a high-tech security system."

"Complete with infrared lasers?"

"Of course," Elaina joked. "If you're conspiring to mess with him, you'd better think twice. Those lasers will cut you in half."

"We could go all Tom Cruise on him and repel from a helicopter."

Elaina wrinkled her nose with amusement. "I don't see that happening."

"Me either." Tawny motioned for her to move the Escalade closer.

Elaina drove forward another hundred feet. "Is that what I think it is?"

"If you're referring to the For-Sale sign in his front yard, then yes."

People had referred to her home as a mansion. It was nice but in no way did it fall into that category. Arden's home, however, qualified as one; at least from the outside. The day she dropped off a package that had mistakenly been delivered to her house, he'd answered the door but body-blocked her from seeing anything inside. At the time, she'd been too intimidated to care and wanted to get out of there as fast as possible. Staring at the place now, she noted three floors and more square footage than a small factory. The large picture windows in the front displayed an ornate winding staircase with crystal chandeliers hanging from the ceiling on each level.

Steph asked the big question tumbling around in all their thoughts. "Why would he sell such an amazing home?"

Elaina's gut instinct prompted her answer. "My guess is it's too much for him to maintain."

"He could hire a maid and a gardener."

In all likelihood Arden had hired a maid but he was so finicky the woman may have lasted a month, tops. Elaina kept that criticism as a thought only. "He definitely wouldn't have a gardener on his payroll. Even though he hates plants, Arden loves his lawn. No one is allowed to walk on it let alone mow it."

"He's a class-A weirdo."

"We all have our quirks." Elaina was surprised by her defense of him.

Grace yawned. "I'm falling asleep back here. Let's go bowling."

A half hour later they were sporting red, white, and blue bowling shoes, and drinking soda because the bowling alley didn't have a Sunday liquor license.

Tawny crowed that she'd gotten a turkey – three strikes in a row. She puffed out her chest and acted like bowling was her life. She showed Steph the proper form and told her to visualize the ball hitting the headpin.

Steph wasn't receptive to the advice. "My ball prefers the gutter."

Tawny drummed the score sheet with the little stub of a pencil the bowling alley provided. Most bowling alleys used electronic scoring these days. Cherry Ridge Lanes was a bit behind the times and still used paper score sheets. "This is the third frame and you have a grand total of twelve points. Keep your arm straight and aim for the G-spot." She gave Steph a toothy grin. "I mean the headpin."

Steph mocked Tawny by repeating and amplifying the advice. "Keep your arm straight and aim for the G-spot." She rolled the ball. It stayed out of the gutter and putted down the lane like it had all day. "They must've polished the lane with Turtle Wax. Bwahaha!"

"Mathews, you're one strange puppy."

"Not breaking news."

Grace retrieved her bowling ball from the ball return and patiently waited.

Steph's ball hit the headpin with little to no force whatsoever. To everyone's surprise, all the pins toppled, one by one. "Whoop! A strike! Take that, Westerfield."

The women bowling next to them cracked up laughing. One woman shook her head. "Looks like she found the G-spot."

Tawny's face colored in an instant. "I probably should've kept my voice down."

"Nah. It's all good. You've been nonstop entertainment since you arrived." The woman raised her penciled-in eyebrows. "I can't wait to tell my husband to...keep his arm straight."

* * *

At five minutes till six Elaina tried to wear out the carpet between the kitchen and the front door.

Grace smoothed a hand across Elaina's back. "Why so nervous?"

"I feel like I'm about to be ambushed."

"Stay alert but don't rule out the possibility he realized he lost a good thing and wants you back."

Elaina blew on her newly polished fingernails to finish drying them. "He definitely lost a good thing." She released some pent-up tension with a chuckle. "That goes without saying." She walked to the coat closet and searched for a light jacket that wouldn't look too hideous with the sleeveless dress. The plan to wear layers still had merit, but Tawny pointed out that after a while she'd be so hot she'd start taking things off, giving Arden hope. "There's nothing he could say or do to win me back."

Tawny sneaked up behind Elaina and sprayed her with heavy musk perfume.

"Sheesh." Elaina fanned away the lingering mist. "That's come-and-get-me perfume."

Steph glanced up from her phone. Ever since they'd gotten home she'd been texting back and forth with Jack. "I'd go after you." She jiggled with a laugh.

"When things end badly with Arden – and they will – it's you and me, babe."

Tawny opened the curtains just enough to eyeball the street. "Ready yourself, wench. He's here."

"Wench," Elaina repeated and rolled her eyes.

Tawny shuffled to Elaina and tucked a wayward wisp of blonde hair behind her ear. "Whatever he wants, say no. Unless he wants to give you a million dollars, then say yes."

Elaina scanned the living room. "He might offer a million for the house."

"Wow. A million. I can't imagine that much cash." Tawny called for Stony. She messed with his ears until he laid his head in her hand. "Bite Arden," she said in a ghostly voice. "Bite Arden," she repeated.

"No biting, Stone-man."

Stony cocked his head. The lovable pooch wouldn't take a bite out of anyone unless he sensed real danger. He left Tawny to brush against Elaina. Hundreds of dog hairs stuck to her dress.

"Marking your territory, boy?" Elaina traipsed to the utility room where she kept the sticky roller.

Grace was two steps ahead of her. "Here you go. Don't take them all off in case you need to put a few in his food."

With the help of her wicked funny friends the bulk of Elaina's tension was gone. "Thanks. I needed that."

Grace smiled. "I said those exact words to you earlier."

Elaina squeezed Grace's hand.

Tawny swung open the door before Arden had a chance to knock.

Arden flinched at the abrupt reception then sneered.

Tawny sneered back and held up two fingers. "Two things: no hanky panky and she'd better be home by eleven."

"Smart ass." Arden gaze swung past Tawny to find Elaina. "Are you ready?"

About as ready as a rabbit about to be eaten by a fox. Elaina took a mental breath, nodded, and grabbed her red satin clutch from the lamp table.

Tawny still blocked the doorway. "Don't try anything funny, Wellby. She's got pepper spray and a taser that can immobilize you from fifteen feet away."

The lines at the corners of Arden's eyes deepened into a harsh squint.

"I don't have either of those things." Elaina stepped out on the porch.

Arden looped his arm.

Elaina hesitated, not wanting to make physical contact this soon. He gave her the smile that used to make her melt. She had no choice but to take his arm. Looking back at the trio of spectators huddled in the doorway she stretched her mouth in a noiseless wince.

When they got to Arden's BMW, he opened the door and helped her get in.

Tawny yelled something but the wind carried most of it away. Elaina pieced together the few words that came through - 'Don't...him...spot.' *Don't let him near the G-spot.*

Arden slid into the driver's seat. "What did she say?"

"Don't let him take you bowling."

"That isn't what she said." A dark, commanding brow shot up. "Your friends think I'm scum."

Elaina shrugged. "They're protective."

"Well, they don't need to get their panties in a bunch. It's just dinner."

So you say.

Chapter Eight

~ *Argyle socks and lacy thongs!* ~

Elaina shifted in her chair. Not only was she uncomfortable sitting across from her ex-husband, a feeling of being watched made things even more awkward. She did a subtle scan of the posh restaurant. No one seemed to be paying them any attention, which meant her over-active imagination was trying to rescue her with distraction. Tawny may have planted the seed of suspicion yesterday. After Steph and Grace had gone to bed, she and Tawny stayed up and finished the last of the mulled wine. Tawny remarked how great the wine tasted and had gone on to say that giving up smoking had put her into a heightened state of sensory sensitivity. Elaina had bolstered the statement saying it was normal for taste buds to actually enjoy flavor again when most of the nicotine is gone from a body. Tawny went from joking to serious in a pulse beat. 'I'm not talking about the sense of taste. I'm referring to seeing someone when we were in the hot tub. It wasn't an illusion or shadow. There wasn't any evidence left behind to back up my claim but I know what I saw.' Elaina said she trusted Tawny's gut. On their way upstairs, Tawny thanked her but, 'Don't trust just my instinct, also trust yours.' At the moment, her gut was telling her someone had an eye glued to them. It may have more to do with Arden than her, but they were being monitored.

Arden broke into her suspicions by leaning so far forward he was halfway across the table. "You look amazing in that dress." His eyes lowered to the plunging neckline.

"Thank you." It took all her willpower not to mention he'd complained about that very dress the day she bought it. She'd let the girls talk her into sexing things up to drive Arden crazy. The dress was making him crazy all right. His eyes constantly strayed to the swell of her breasts.

"I mean it, sweetheart. You're more than just enticing. You're beautiful."

Elaina's throat convulsed with a gag. She covered it with a cough and reached for her water glass.

Arden thwarted the move by grabbing her hand and putting it to his lips. He stared at her over the rim of her knuckles and swept his long lashes slowly, seductively over his eyes.

Her gag reflex settled in an instant and Elaina spiraled into a warm haze of confusion. Arden's amazing scent floated across the table and his masculine voice appealed to those sneaky hormones that messed with her libido.

"I've missed you so much, Elaina. I look in the mirror every day and call myself an idiot for screwing things up between us."

The clank of silverware at the next table was as good as a flick. Elaina shook her head to clear whatever madness was trying to make her forget who she was with. "Aren't you engaged?"

A muscle ticked in Arden's jaw. "No."

Elaina withdrew her hand. "Shouldn't there be more to your answer?"

"She wanted to take a break." The tightness in his tenor warned her to let it go.

Elaina wouldn't let it go. She'd kowtowed to that tone for more years than she should have. "You told her you were through. Finished."

"I don't do breaks." Arden finished his scotch on the rocks and held up the glass for the waiter to bring him another one. If they'd been the only ones in the place, that move would've brought their waiter to them in a snap. Since every table in the restaurant was occupied, so were the waiters. "What does it take to get good service these days?"

Arden's impatience prompted Elaina to say the first sarcastic thing that came to mind. "A megaphone."

"Don't be ridiculous."

"Then don't expect people to jump when you think they should."

The firm set of his chin indicated he wasn't thrilled with her backtalk but he threw her for a loop with his response. "I forget myself sometimes."

Wow. Did Arden Samuels actually admit to having a flaw? Her brain couldn't process it. "Then lower the glass. Our waiter will be here when he gets a chance."

The napkin on her lap fell to the floor. Elaina bent sideways to retrieve it. As she straightened she caught Arden ogling her cleavage. "So your fiancée...

"...either wants to be with me or she doesn't. End of story."

Elaina couldn't resist. "Being dumped sucks the life right out of you, doesn't it?"

Arden looked like he wanted to spit nails at the brutal truth of what he'd done to her and was now being done to him.

Elaina no longer feared the barracuda and poked him with a verbal stick. "Why did she need a break?"

"We're not going to discuss my broken engagement," he barked.

The waiter came to the table at that exact moment. He hadn't heard the content of the conversation just the increase in volume. "Is everything okay here?"

"It will be as soon as you get me another scotch."

The waiter spared a wary glance at Elaina.

She confirmed they were fine with a fake smile.

"More iced tea?"

Elaina had deliberately stayed away from alcohol as a way to keep her wits about her. *What the heck was I thinking?* "I'll have a wine spritzer. Thank you." She waited until the waiter was gone and then turned up the heat. "I get that you don't want to discuss a failed alliance."

Arden flashed a scowl.

"Surely you can understand my curiosity. Your dinner invitation came at a time when you should have been soul-deep in love with your fiancée. You had to have anticipated questions."

"I anticipated them. I'm just not going to answer them. Let's talk about you and me."

Arden hadn't changed one iota. He was still an arrogant asshat. "There is no 'you and me'."

"It may seem that way to you but..."

Elaina jabbed him with her fork; not hard, just enough to make him stop talking for a second. "You tossed me aside for the gal who now wants to take a break from you."

His forehead creased into an accordion of lines. "There's no need to make a scene."

"It's the only way to penetrate that thick noggin of yours."

"I don't want to fight."

"What *do* you want?"

"For us to be a couple again."

"Don't BS me, Arden. I'm not a complete moron and neither are you. What you broke is beyond repair. What is it you're really after?" Elaina trembled from the force of not just talking back to him but for also standing up for what she knew to be true – that this dinner had nothing to do with them getting back together.

Arden's eyes opened so wide they could've easily fallen out of their sockets. A hiss slid between his clenched teeth.

Elaina felt empowered. She pulled back her shoulders and met his gaze without blinking; no longer intimidated by the man who used to rake her with condemnation.

"I want..." He looked away. "I thought we could come to a suitable agreement with regards to..."

Again, Elaina didn't let him finish. It was rude to cut him off but she decided to follow Tawny's advice to 'fight fire with fire'. "The house?"

Arden gave her his full consideration with flecks of cold steel in his eyes. "What's happened to you?"

"I'm the same woman. When we were married I held my tongue because I didn't want things to get ugly. I was a fool then. I'm not now." She displayed her left hand that was minus her wedding rings.

Arden went into a rant that she had a twisted view of their marriage and how she'd only heard what she'd wanted to hear.

Elaina didn't hang on to his every word when she was Mrs. Arden Samuels. That much was accurate. No one tunes into every second of what someone says. It's human nature to get distracted and miss a word or two. "I heard plenty."

Again, he went off half-cocked something or other about men getting short-changed these days.

The feeling of being hawked from afar, intensified.

Elaina searched the perimeter of the restaurant, half-expecting to see his fiancée duck behind the hostess podium or the fountain located in the middle of the dining room. Instead she caught sight of a familiar head of red hair. A smile started to tweak the corners of her mouth until she spied someone else, also familiar. *Son of a...*

Arden snapped his fingers to draw her back. "You're not even listening."

Elaina put her hands on the table to push up and out of her chair.

"Don't go. We should let go of the past and start over. Tonight. By being civil with each other and then see where it leads."

"I doubt you'll remain civil once I tell you I'm not giving up the house." Elaina didn't wait for his reaction. She scanned the room again and discovered the two familiar people were gone.

"Elaina, please." Arden used his hands to turn her face to him. "I'm willing to pay twice what it's worth."

There it was – the offer Elaina knew would come sooner or later. "Not. For. Sale. At. Any. Price."

* * *

When their food arrived, Arden's lawyer, Cornell Reeceton, made an unexpected and untimely appearance. He pretended surprise at seeing them. Elaina knew without a doubt there was no surprise involved.

Arden invited Cornell to join them.

Cornell politely declined. "I don't want to be a bother."

"It's no imposition. We'd love to have you. Wouldn't we, Elaina?"

Put on the spot, Elaina had no choice but to agree. "It would be a pleasure."

"If you're sure..."

The only thing Elaina was sure of was that this was a setup.

Cornell gave her shoulder a soft squeeze as if they were old and dear friends. "It's good to see you, Elaina." Without a second prompting from Arden, he took a seat and stowed his briefcase under the table. "It's doubly good to see the two of you together."

A briefcase? On a Sunday evening? Cornell could've pulled a weekender at the office but chances were he didn't. He came to the restaurant at Arden's request. It didn't take an Einstein to deduce there were papers in the briefcase for her to sign should they wrestle the house out from under her.

The waiter zipped to the table with a place setting, menu, and glass of water for Cornell.

Cornell paid no attention to the waiter and keyed on Elaina. "What are you up to these days?"

Elaina was tempted to say, "I haven't grown an inch. I'm still five five-foot-four." Instead, she said, "Sipping sangria in sweat pants." She jiggled with a laugh when Cornell shot Arden an is-she-kidding look.

Arden didn't look pleased. He lifted a warning brow at Elaina.

It was difficult being wedged between the guy who divorced her and the one who represented him in the divorce proceedings. Elaina made an excuse to leave the table. "I need to powder my nose." It was probably unwise to leave Arden and Cornell alone but she needed a few minutes to collect herself before they tag-teamed her. Plus she had to prove she hadn't lost her mind and that seeing Steph hadn't been a hallucination. Seeing Michael hadn't been one either. In fact, for the tiniest of moments, Elaina could've she could've sworn she and Michael had made eye contact. He might've been looking in her direction without having homed in on her. Things like that happened to Elaina all the time. She'd wave to someone only to discover they weren't looking at her at all but rather someone beside or behind her.

Rounding the corner to the Ladies room, she almost slammed into Steph.

Steph's mouth curved into a sheepish grin. Tucked behind her was Grace and Tawny.

Elaina gave them a make believe look of annoyance. "I'm not sure if I should throttle you or hug you."

Grace wrinkled her nose humorously. "I'd go with the hug."

"And how are things going with the barracuda?" Tawny asked.

"Not great."

Tawny latched onto Elaina's wrist. "We're here to kidnap you."

Elaina tugged loose. "You can't kidnap me."

Her wrist was gripped by Grace this time. "I wanted to bring a pillowcase to slip over your head. Steph voted it down." She mocked Steph, 'We'll mess up her hair.' Why did I listen? You're one of those women who look great with messed up hair. In the morning when you shuffle downstairs before you've used a hairbrush, you look amazingly mussed. The rest of us look like Christopher Lloyd from *Back to the Future*. How do you do it?"

"I sleep like a mummy; hair smoothed just so on my pillow, hands at my side." It was a silly answer but Elaina needed silly right now.

Steph was brilliant in so many ways, but sometimes a tad naïve. "Really?"

"No. Not really. Grace and I are just being colorful. By the way, I love you ladies. Thanks for the attempted abduction." Elaina wrenched Grace's hand off with ease. "I'd rather go with you than back to the table, especially after Arden confessed that this," she made air-quotes, "date...isn't a date after all. Duh. Hello. I was born at night, just not last night. He finally stopped skirting the issue and asked about buying the house – for twice the value. Then what do you know? Cornell Reeceton makes an appearance." She fine-tuned her sarcasm. "I don't want to *dine* with them but I'm not leaving until I know everything they're up to."

Steph's phone plinked with an incoming text message. She took a quick look and stuffed the phone in the back pocket of her jeans. "We could get a table close to you. For moral support."

"Not necessary. I can handle those two." She smirked. "I was going to add 'with my hands tied behind my back' but you guys probably have rope with you. Thanks for saving me from a pillowcase, Steph."

Steph's smile was tinged with mischief.

"Did you happen to see Michael a few minutes ago?" Elaina inquired.

All three shook their heads.

"How could you not have seen him? He was maybe twenty feet from you."

"We were too busy watching you squirm."

"Gee thanks," she mocked with a smile.

"You know we love you."

"Actually I do. Thanks for always having my back."

"That's what friends are for." Grace checked her watch. "Do you know if the dollar store is still open?"

Tawny put a finger to her lips to shush Grace.

"What?" Elaina asked.

"Nothing."

"Riiiight." Elaina smoothed the front of her dress. "Anyway, back to the shark tank I go. Wish me luck."

"You don't need luck. You need a harpoon."

* * *

Elaina came home to a quiet house. Tawny, Grace, and Steph's cars were in the driveway but it was lights-out upstairs. Odd. It was only ten o'clock. Tawny had a good excuse for going to bed early because she had to be out of the house by six-forty-five tomorrow morning to start her twelve-hour rotation at the hospital. Steph and Grace didn't have to be to work until nine so they seldom headed upstairs before eleven.

Stony scuttled into the kitchen. Lula peeked out from under the table. Elaina petted them both at the same time. "Arden made me a bizarre offer tonight," she quietly said to her furry friends. "He wants the house *and* the gym. Let me tell you, I did not see the bit about the gym coming at all. Arden practically foams at the mouth when he talks about the house but he put me in a state of shock about the gym. When I asked why he wanted it he didn't give me a straight answer, which is nothing new. My guess is he has a potential buyer willing to pay him an arm and a leg for it."

Stony touched her with his wet nose and Lula meowed. They might not understand her words but they definitely understood her tone and offered a unique type of unity. She kissed Stony on the head and did the same to Lula.

Elaina refilled their water dishes.

Stony blinked up at her and then pushed against the glass of the patio doors.

"Yes. We can go for a walk." Elaina stepped out of her high-heeled shoes and into a pair of comfortable slip-on sneakers. From the coat closet, she grabbed a lime green runner's parka. "I'm styling now, aren't I?" She dropped her phone and keys into the pocket, hooked the leash to Stony, and headed outside.

Stony dragged her to his designated spot in the backyard where he hiked his leg for what seemed like ten minutes.

It started to spit rain.

Elaina put up the hood of the parka and walked him around the block twice. When she tried to lead him back inside the house, Stony had other ideas. "Stone-man, it's raining." The moisture falling from the sky was no longer in spit form. It was flat out pouring. "I know I won't melt, but still." She shook her head, remembering who she was talking to. Shortly after Stony came to live with her, he'd scared the bejesus out of her when he joined her in the shower. "I'm trying to reason with a dog who loves to get wet." Her phone rang. "Whoever it is can wait. Come on, boy. One more time around the block. That's it." Her phone rang a second time. "Leave a message all ready." When it rang a third time, she gave in. "Hello."

"It's me."

Elaina scowled. "I haven't changed my mind."

"I'm not calling about the offer. I'm calling about *my* house."

"It's not *your* house. It's *my* house." Sheesh. The guy had bricks for brains.

"Not that house. My house. On Hemingway Lane."

"Oh," she said dryly, even though the hood blew off her head and she was getting soaked to the gills. "What about it?"

"Someone – probably those hooligans you live with – strung a clothesline from my back door to one of my trees. Do you know what they hung on it?" Not leaving her space to answer, he said, "Cloth diapers, a dozen pair of off-brand men's underwear, Argyle socks, some cheap looking bras, and," he groaned, "lace thongs."

Now it made sense. The dollar store. Everyone upstairs pretending to be asleep. "Why would you suspect my friends?"

"Who else would do something so ludicrous?"

"City Council, perhaps. You bellyached to them about clotheslines."

"A year ago," he growled. "They wouldn't wait until now to pull a fast one."

"Have you looked at your security footage? That'll pinpoint the culprit." She said culprit instead of culprits to throw Arden off. *I hope they hid their faces.*

"I'm warning you, Elaina, if it was your friends they'd better watch their step."

"I'm warning *you,* Arden. Don't threaten Steph, Tawny, and Grace."

"Or what?"

Elaina disconnected the call. "Woohoo! Way to go, Sweat Revenge!"

Chapter Nine

~ *Words of wisdom and a little cinnamon!* ~

The smell of homemade cinnamon rolls floated upstairs. Elaina opened her bedroom door at the same time Grace opened hers.

"We can't let her move to Maine. Who will make us cinnamon rolls?" Grace rushed to the stairs.

Elaina wisecracked, "Pillsbury."

Grace sniffed and moaned with pleasure all the way down the stairs and into the kitchen.

"I'll take that as a compliment." Steph pointed to a platter on the counter. "I've also made egg and sausage burritos."

"You're a kitchen goddess." Grace waved her arms up and down in front of her. "I'm not worthy."

Steph beamed with pride. "I'm something. Ain't I?" She handed Elaina and Grace a cup of coffee. "It's the least I can do for my besties."

"What's the catch?" Grace slurped a sip of coffee.

"You have to drive me to the airport after I get off work."

"We do?"

Steph nodded. "Jack got a good deal on a flight and left yesterday even though he still has a week to go on his two-week notice at work. His boss told him to go ahead and go. Jack text-begged. He doesn't want me to wait until November to check out Portland. I couldn't sleep last night so I browsed air fares and booked a flight for tonight."

"It sounds like everything is falling into place, Steph." Elaina poured more coffee into her cup.

"I know. I'm excited. Well, kind of excited."

"You don't have to downplay your excitement on our account. Embrace it."

Grace took a bite of cinnamon roll and licked the frosting from her lips. "This is sudden. What's *your* boss going to say when you tell him you're taking vacation the rest of the week, or however long you're taking off work?"

"I can guarantee he won't make it easy on me like Jack's boss did on him."

"Don't let him bully you." Elaina sat at the table.

"He won't bully me but he'll whine the entire day."

"You could butter him up with cinnamon rolls."

Steph closed her eyes and shuddered. "Let's talk about the weather or the stock market, not my boss. I don't even want to think about him until I have to."

Elaina cocked an eyebrow. "We could talk about clotheslines and lace thongs."

Steph and Grace burst out laughing.

Between bites of burrito, Elaina uttered, "Hooligans."

She almost fell off the chair laughing when Steph called her a hussy.

* * *

Elaina had gone to the gym early to adjust the tension on the leg press machine and to replace the cushioned pads on the hip adductor. She turned on just enough lighting to illuminate those particular pieces of equipment. If she turned on all the lights, the members who arrived a half-hour to forty-five minutes early in hopes of working out before the place actually opened for business, would pile in and try to hurry her progress.

With the leg press taken care of she moved to the hip adductor which was located in front of a row of windows. Thankfully, these windows overlooked the dumpsters instead of the parking lot.

Elaina tried to loosen the bolt on the first cushion. The darn thing wouldn't budge. She squirted it with liquid grease and tried again. No luck. She uttered an expletive and tossed the wrench.

A knock on the glass made her jump.

Staring at her with a goofy grin was Michael. She blew out a breath and motioned for him to come to the rear entrance.

"Elaina," he said when she unlocked the door.

"Michael," she simply replied and braced for… An explanation? The truth? To feel like a fool? None of the above?

He moved toward her and she retreated a few steps.

"I saw you with Arden last night." He advanced on her, and again she backed up. His blondish-brown eyebrows furrowed to the center.

"I saw you too."

There was a long moment of quiet.

"Arden wined and dined me in an attempt to get the house."

"He's still playing that game, huh?"

"Yeah. It didn't work." She cleared her throat. "I hear you're back with Liz."

Michael's blue eyes rounded when he spoke, he stammered. "I, um…where'd you get your information?"

Elaina wouldn't throw Lita under the bus. "Is it true?"

His sigh was labored. "Yes and no."

That wasn't an answer but it's all she needed to hear. "You haven't called or sent me a text for over three weeks."

"I should've called. Work has been nuts and Zoe's been a mess. Liz and I feel it's in Zoe's best interest if we…" He dropped his gaze to the floor.

"It's okay, Michael. Really," she said resignedly. "Your daughter has to come first in your life."

Michael ran his hands through his hair. "This is so hard, Elaina. You're an amazing woman and I don't want to lose you."

"When we first met I told you I was taking a year off from men. I should've stuck to my guns."

Michael's smile was weak. "I pressured you into going out with me. You were so sweet and hard to resist. You still are."

Her heart didn't crack in two but it suffered a few splinters.

He tucked a wisp of hair behind her ear. "When two people stop seeing each other, normally they don't remain friends." His voice trembled. "I don't want us to see each other in a store or restaurant and not say hello. I'm sorry, Elaina. I never thought this would happen."

Tears leaked from the corners of Elaina's eyes. She brushed at them. "You know how I feel about Zoe. About kids in general. They deserve only good things. You're Zoe's good thing. Go be with your daughter and her mama. You and I will remain friends but I'll have to keep my distance – for Liz's sake. If you're going to get remarried, be 'all in'."

Elaina caught sight of the time. "I have to open up or my members will break down the door."

Michael leaned forward and swept his lips across her forehead. "You'll always be special."

"You will be too." She tried to smile but the corners of her mouth wouldn't cooperate. "Out the back door you go, Mr. Rexx. I assume you'll want to cancel the remaining months of your membership."

Michael blew out a breath of air, nodded in affirmation, and said goodbye.

Elaina hurried to the desk for a tissue to blot her eyes. She chugged a much needed drink of water and squared her shoulders in an effort to keep what was left of her composure. On the way to unlock the front door, she lifted her chin, thankful that life had a fresh-start button.

* * *

"How many pair of underwear did you pack?" Tawny loaded Steph's suitcase into the trunk of her Malibu.

"Getting kind of personal, don't you think?"

"Not at all. It'll tell me how long you'll be gone."

"Don't nag, Tawn'. I'll get back when I get back."

Tawny seemed determined to get a time frame. "What are we looking at? A week? A month?"

"Seriously," Steph said firmly, "I'm in no mood to be hassled. The boss copped an attitude right away this morning like I thought he would. He'd go into his office and pout for an hour, come out and yell some more about me being inconsiderate, and then he'd hole up in his office to pout for another hour. Eight hours of that nonsense. When I was cleaning my desk off to go home he told me I should get my priorities straight. I looked him in the eye and told him they were stick-straight."

"I hope your tone had an undercurrent of 'yell at me one more time and see what happens.'"

Steph laughed for the first time since she'd gotten home. "You always fix what ails me. You should move to Portland with me. I'm going to need you."

"I'd love to." Tawny slammed the trunk. "I don't see it happening though. I have too much time invested in my current job. Starting over at a new hospital would be rough. I'd go from working days to pulling the night shift. I'd get a week's vacation instead of three. And I'd drop like a rock on the pay scale."

"I'd be in the same boat. Bank tellers don't make much money to begin with but the pay cut would be brutal." Grace winced.

"Elaina? You care to weigh in?"

"Huh?"

"Haven't you followed the conversation?"

"Sure I have."

"Would you have a problem moving to Portland?"

Elaina rubbed the tense muscles in her neck. "I can't move to Portland. I have a gym to run."

Steph lifted her shoulders and let them fall. "I guess it's just me then."

"And Jack," Tawny added.

"And Jack," Steph repeated.

Tawny bumped Elaina on her way to the driver's side of the car and muttered under her breath that Steph was making a huge mistake.

"It's hers to make."

"I wish just once you'd say something negative or controversial."

"Fine. I will. Men suck." At Tawny's shocked look, Elaina refined the broad statement. "Some men suck." She tweaked it again. "A few men suck."

Tawny smirked.

Elaina made a face. "Actually, only two."

"Arden and Cornell, I assume."

Elaina tapped the roof of the car thoughtfully. "Arden and Michael."

Tawny said point blank, "We *will* discuss this on the way to the airport."

"I don't want to hash out that Arden's a nut case and Michael wants us to remain friends even though he's officially back with Liz. "

"He finally called?"

"He paid me a visit this morning."

"I'm just now hearing about it? What's wrong with you, woman? When the four of us got together we told each other everything. Lately you've been holding out on us. You better cut that shit out."

Steph put her window down. "Less of this," she mimicked talking with her hands. "More of this." She imitated moving the steering wheel. "I'm supposed to be at the airport in an hour."

"Elaina just started to open up. Did you know men suck?"

Grace leaned over Steph to say, "Not all men suck. Dalton doesn't. He stopped in the bank today. Gloria's window was open but he waited until I was finished with a customer so I could take care of him. He asked me to go to a Halloween party."

"Are you going?" Steph asked.

"Absolutely. Despite the fact he won't fight with me, he's a good guy."

Tawny's expression filled with humor. "That's whacked, Grace. Most women would consider Dalton a great guy because he *doesn't* fight."

"I'm not most women."

"No kidding." Tawny twirled her finger by her ear to signify Grace was loco.

"Dalton didn't invite just me. He invited all of us."

Steph frowned. "I won't be able to go."

"We could Facetime you from the party," Elaina suggested.

"Whatever, clowns." Steph tapped her watch. "Step on it, Westerfield."

* * *

True to her word, Tawny wouldn't let the subject of Michael drop. She shushed everyone else so Elaina could talk. By the time they delivered Steph to the TSA security checkpoint line, Elaina had admitted she cared for Michael more than she'd let on. And that it had been difficult urging him to do the right thing. When Grace reminded her that she and Michael's sex life had been just so-so, Elaina shouldered the blame. "My sex drive must be on a retreat because I'm not as interested in intimacy as I should be." She scrunched her face into a tight frown. "I'm forty-three and it's gone."

Tawny should've whispered but she didn't. "You should speak with your gynecologist. He could prescribe something."

The guy behind them in line snorted a laugh, prompting Tawny to add, "For that feminine itch."

Elaina had been tied in knots. Tawny's comment untied each and every knot, and sent her into a hearty belly laugh.

"You haven't lost your libido." Grace tapped Elaina's temple. "You're brain, which happens to be an amazing sex organ, is waiting for that one guy who makes you say 'hubba, hubba'." Grace swiveled around to the nosy guy behind them. "Not you."

When Steph was almost to the TSA agent, they took turns enveloping her in a hug.

"Call us every day," Elaina suggested.

"We want to see Maine through your eyes," Grace said. "Take videos and send them to us."

"Get your keister back here before you run out of underwear." Tawny also turned around to the guy who was chuckling at everything they said. She mischievously raised and lowered her eyebrows.

"Best friends, I take it," he said.

Steph choked back tears. "We're the No Sweat Pants Allowed – Wine Club."

Elaina clarified, "We're sweat pants and sangria these days." She hugged Steph again. "We love you, Steph. Hurry back."

* * *

Tawny held out her wine glass for Rachel to fill. "We thought we'd celebrate Steph's new life with sangria."

"Your foursome is now a threesome?"

Grace said yes.

Tawny and Elaina said no.

Rachel looked confused.

Elaina altered her response to maybe. "Steph doesn't know what she wants but she's on a mission to find out. She asked us to move to Maine. That can't happen."

"Why not?"

"Because…" Elaina paused. The reasons they'd given Steph made them sound like they were already set in their ways. Not so long ago when their happy little foursome wasn't so happy and the other three moved out, Elaina considered selling everything and starting over in Texas. Now that they were back together she couldn't imagine relocating. "I've got nothing."

Tawny and Grace offered the same lame reasons they'd given Steph.

Rachel wasn't buying it. "The average person switches jobs five or six times in their lifetime. As far as the money thing goes, y'all would take a hit. That goes without saying. Look at it this way – y'all can be happy while being poor and eating ramen noodles, or glum with money in your pocket while eating steak without Steph."

"I like steak," Tawny teased.

Rachel tilted her head with a pointed look. "Let me put it another way. Y'all can be happy anywhere as long as you're together. It doesn't have to be in Cherry Ridge."

Elaina looked from Rachel to Tawny to Grace. "She's right."

"My boys live in California and Oregon. I want to move closer not farther away."

"I can't leave Ohio. Brince is buried here."

Rachel topped off their wine glasses without being asked. "There are thousands of flights a day. Some go from Maine to Ohio, if you get my drift."

Chapter Ten

- Tubes of lube! -

Elaina dove to answer the phone. Tawny did the same. They collided with a laugh. Steph had promised to call the home phone every night. Not recognizing the number as Steph's, she assumed it was a sales call. "Hello." The connection was scratchy. "Hello," she said again to prompt the salesman to start his pitch.

"Elaina?"

"Yes."

"Ciao! This is Cody. Is my mom home?"

"Cody, how are you?"

"Doing great, Elaina."

"Awesome. Yes, your mom's here. She's upstairs. It'll just take a second to get her." Elaina covered the phone. "Tawn', get Grace." The downstairs phone and those upstairs didn't work together. You could talk on one or the other, whichever phone had been answered was the one that worked. She'd been meaning to call the phone company to sort out the problem.

Tawny hollered, "Grace, get your butt down here

ASAP. A hottie is calling from Italy."

Elaina did a mental calculation of the time. Italy was six hours ahead which meant it was three in the morning there.

Grace rushed to the banister. "My boy?" The question was redundant. She flew down the stairs. She missed the last step and fell onto the hardwood floor with a loud thud. Her face contorted in pain.

Elaina and Tawny rushed to help.

Tears didn't fill Grace's eyes but you could hear them in her voice. "I might've broken my ankle," she said in a strained whisper.

Tawny knelt to inspect the damage.

Grace put a finger to her lips. "Not a word about it to Cody."

Elaina handed the phone to Grace and took off for the kitchen to get an ice pack. Filling a quart-size Ziploc bag with cubes, she wrapped it in a towel.

Despite the pain, Grace spoke in a cheery, motherly voice. "I've missed you so much, son."

"There's very little swelling. No deformity. It's probably a sprain. When she's done talking to Cody we're taking her to the emergency room to make sure."

Grace overhead the hushed exchange and negated the idea with a head shake. She continued the conversation with Cody. "What kind of news? Are you headed home?" Her light blue eyes jerked open to twice their size. "You're getting married?" Grace put a hand to her forehead. "That's wonderful. I'm a bit surprised though. I had no idea you were dating anyone let alone ready to take such a big step."

Elaina pointed to the kitchen. "Let's give them privacy."

"I want to hear."

Elaina grabbed Tawny by the back of the shirt. "Grace has just been dealt two blows – an injured ankle and the news her only child is getting hitched to someone she doesn't know. She needs breathing room to come to grips with both."

In the kitchen, Tawny scowled. "I disagree. This is when she needs us the most."

"We're not in New York City. We're a hundred feet away. When she's ready for us she'll let us know." Elaina paced, taking an occasional peek at Grace as she passed by the archway separating the living room from the kitchen.

"You know what this means, don't you?" Tawny broke off a banana from the bunch setting by the toaster.

"You'll have to be more specific."

Peeling the banana, she leaned against the counter and crossed her feet for support. "We'll be going to Italy. I have Italian blood flowing through my veins thanks to my great-great-great-grandmother. I'm named after her."

"Tawny doesn't sound Italian."

Tawny shrugged.

"I've never been to Italy. Come to think of it, other than the continental U.S. I've only been in the Caribbean. It's about time my passport got some real use." Elaina made a mental note to check on its whereabouts. It should be in the safe in her room but with all the legal documentation she'd had to provide the lawyer for the division of property during the divorce, the passport might've gotten mixed in.

Alarm flashed through Tawny's brown eyes. "Mine's expired. I've been meaning to renew it but I hadn't planned on going anywhere and it didn't seem like a good use of my money at the time. Since I moved in with you I've been able to save a little. Thank you for that."

"You're welcome." Elaina also took a banana. "Getting a passport renewed isn't too expensive and it's relatively easy. You'll need a new photo ID. The drugstore or post office can take the picture. You mail it along with the renewal application. In a few weeks you'll have it. The only thing that would hold it up is if they find out something shady about you."

"There's nothing shady about me. Not even a parking ticket."

"Your night-driving skills are a bit shady."

"That's why you get to drive me around after dark." Tawny's cocky smile slipped away. "Could the change in our marital statuses hold up our passports?"

"Only if we tie up our exes with duct tape and stuff them in a closet for six months."

"I'm serious."

"So am I. If we stuff them..." At Tawny's concerned look, Elaina cut short the baloney. "As long as your last name remains the same, you should be good to go. To ease your worry, let's find out." She fired up Grace's laptop that sat charging on the far end of the counter.

"Elaina. Tawny," Grace shouted.

In a heartbeat they were by her side.

Grace had tears spilling from the corners of her eyes. "He's getting married to Isabella. She's three years older than him and has a one-year old daughter named Karina."

Elaina cautiously said, "Awesome."

"It is awesome. It's also unsettling." Grace's tears came harder.

Elaina gathered her in a hug and kissed the top of her head, not knowing what to say to offer comfort. If she had kids of her own she'd have a better grasp of what Grace's heart was going through.

"I'm not sure how I'll react when Bo or Quentin drop the marriage bomb. I'm sure it'll be a jolt; a happy one, but a jolt nonetheless." Tawny stooped to take another look at Grace's ankle. "I thought I'd be the first one of us to become a granny."

Grace moved Elaina's arms away so she could put her hands on her head. Her tear-clouded eyes widened as though that tiny bit of reality hadn't sank in until now.

* * *

"I'm gone for twenty-four hours and you're in the ER? Did you get food poisoning from Elaina's cooking?" Steph chortled. "Or did Stony break free and sink his teeth into Arden's thigh?"

"You're a laugh a minute." Elaina was tickled to hear Steph joke around. It was sign things were going well in Portland.

Tawny had her phone on speaker but forgot and put it to her mouth to talk. "Grace twisted her ankle coming down the stairs. Essentially, Grace has no grace."

"Was it a bad sprain?"

"It didn't look bad but with those things you never know. I asked if her ankle made a cracking sound or a pop when she hit the floor. She couldn't remember."

"She might've broken a bone. That would not be good. If she's klutzy on the stairs imagine how she'll be on crutches." As an after-thought Steph asked why Grace's memory was fuzzy. "Did she bump her head when she fell? She could have a concussion."

"Luckily she didn't smack her head. She was in a hurry to get downstairs to talk to Cody on the home phone and missed the last step." Tawny looked at Elaina. "Should I tell her the news?"

"I'd wait for Grace."

"What news? Did she and Dalton have their first fight?"

"We're going to Italy," Tawny blurted.

"Way to wait for Grace," Elaina muttered.

"Who's going to Italy?"

"We all are."

Steph spoke in a rush. "I can't go to Italy. Not with moving to Maine. I don't have the time or the money. Besides, I'm not sure I could be on an airplane for that long. I'm too antsy." She paused to take a breath. "Wait. Why are we going to Italy?"

"Cody's getting married, which is why Grace couldn't remember anything about her foot. He pulled the rug out from under her with the announcement."

"Aww, Cody's getting hitched."

Tawny added that Grace was also going to become a grandma.

"Whaaaat? No wonder she couldn't think straight. I'd be over-the-moon and on overload too if I found out in the same conversation that my son was getting married and that he and his fiancée are having a baby."

"Let me tweak the information for you." Tawny explained about Isabella and Karina.

"Grace will be delighted once the shock wears off. I can't wait to congratulate her." Steph's joy became a whimper. "I don't want to miss out on going to his wedding."

"Don't worry about money," Elaina said. "And just so you know it won't be a direct flight. You'll be able to walk off all that excess energy during layovers."

"I won't let you fund my part of the trip."

Elaina could almost hear Steph's cogs turning.

"I still have my engagement ring from Corbett. He might've been a first class knothead but he wasn't chintzy when it came to the bling."

"Steph, you're a genius," Tawny crowed. "I have money tucked away but not enough to cover a trip abroad. Muahhh! You just made my day. I'm going to turn my platinum into cash." Tawny did a happy dance in her chair. "I won't have to max out my credit cards after all."

"Better not let Carter know you have money at your disposal or you'll be driving to work in a brand new

Lexus while we're in Tuscany drinking wine and eating bruschetta at a sidewalk café."

"Carter better watch it or Ferdinand is going to be the only man in my life."

Elaina noted that Steph had yet to say anything about Jack or Portland. "Is Portland everything you thought it would be?"

It was probably a good ten seconds before Steph answered. "Yeah. It's a cool city."

The hesitation made Elaina dig deeper. "I'll bet Jack swung you in his arms when he picked you up at the Portland International Jetport."

Steph cleared her throat, twice. "He would have if he'd actually been there. As soon as my plane landed I received a text from him saying his rental car was making weird noises and the rental agency was sending someone to work on it. I had to take a taxi to the bed and breakfast. It's awesome, by the way. I expected an older place that had been restored. Not the case. It's a new three-story, ten bedroom brick home. Each room is tastefully furnished with a four poster bed, an electric fireplace, and private bath. Attached to the back is a huge veranda. In the backyard is a stone fire pit circled by benches made of the same stone. At the far end of the property is a white gazebo with rose bushes on each side. It would be the perfect setting for a small wedding. One of the best things, there's a grape arbor. It needs pruning and a little tender loving care, but it has potential. The land takes up a full city block. The Kirby's walked into a gold mine."

"So you've met the Kirby's?"

"Uh huh."

Hmm. No further enlightenment as to whether they were sweet as sugar or mean as hell?

"Will you be staying in one of the rooms at the bed and breakfast until you decide if Portland is for you?"

Another long moment of nothingness.

"Steph?"

"Uh. No. A hotel room was cheaper than a room at the bed and breakfast."

The Kirby's were going to make Steph pay for a room? Elaina frowned and silently called Jack a buffoon. There were some additional questions skirting across her brain but they might stress Steph out if she asked them. "Can you see Casco Bay from your hotel? I hear it's beautiful."

"My room faces the bay. I've been watching the ferry boats return with tourists who went out to the islands. You should see the foliage. The leaves are deep red, bright yellow, and vivid orange. I'm glad I came when I did. In another week all the color will be gone. The farther north you go the leaves are already off the trees."

"Prime time for tourism," Tawny said redundantly. "Is the bed and breakfast filled to capacity?"

"You'd think it would be, but no, it isn't. That might explain why Jack's parents are ouchy."

"The cranky Kirbys. Sounds like a sitcom." Tawny shot Elaina a questioning look.

Elaina slowly moved her head back and forth, urging Tawny to leave well enough alone.

Tawny asked the burning question anyway. "Were

they rude to you?"

"Not exactly. Maybe it's just their personalities or they were having a bad day. Jack's sister, Georgia, was nice though. She's so not like her brother. Where Jack is laidback and mostly quiet, Georgia is hyper and loud. The woman cusses up a storm. If she said the f-bomb once, she said it ten times. I kid you not. And she made it known that she's deliberately single and has no intention of having children. I get that not everyone wants to be a wife or mother, but why she felt the need to share that kind of personal information after knowing me for a grand total of fifteen minutes is baffling." Steph's anxiety carried through the phone. "I'm on Kirby overload, but I'm determined to win them over."

"The cranky Kirbys have a foul-mouthed daughter and a son who..."

Elaina made big eyes to advise Tawny against saying anything bad about Jack. Steph cared about him. They shouldn't give their opinions about him or his gnarly family unless she asked.

Tawny's eyes glistened with defiance. "...has the hots for Stephanie Mathews."

Elaina grinned like a Cheshire cat in appreciation for Tawny doing the right thing.

Despite a rough start with Jack's family, Steph was still on her game. "The cranky Kirbys would make a better reality show than a sitcom."

"Your future sister-in-law should be kept away from the guests," Elaina said without a trace of sarcasm.

"I doubt she'll be my sister-in-law anytime soon. I

think Georgia and Jack have a secret pact to drive their parents batty by staying single."

Georgia sounded like a strong, independent woman who wasn't afraid to put her life choices out there for the world to accept or reject. Her use of colorful language was either to deter or encourage people into her fold. Elaina had gone to school with a genetic copy of Georgia Kirby, only she'd gone by the name of Persimmon. In grade school, much to the shock of their teachers, Persimmon spelled and effectively used four-letter words which earned her plenty of timeouts. In high school health class when they discussed marriage, she'd spouted off that it equaled putting a chain link fence around you for the rest of your life. Elaina smiled at the memory of Persimmon and wondered if she'd softened her stance over the years or if she'd stuck to her convictions. Shortly after graduation she and her family moved to the east coast.

Tawny broke into Elaina's reverie by stating that Jack had long-term plans for him and Steph or he wouldn't have asked her to relocate.

Steph was slow to concur. "I wouldn't jump to that conclusion."

Jack didn't seem to be in any hurry to do much of anything, including making sure his parents recognized his relationship with Steph. Elaina couldn't shake the feeling that something was wrong with the overall picture as it pertained to their friend. Steph had gone to Maine to keep Jack happy, only to be stood up at the airport. Jack could've easily taken a taxi to meet Steph.

His parents could've been more hospitable; if not for Steph's sake, for Jack's. It's what parents do for their sons and daughters. They suck it up. Elaina also had a hard time imagining the bed and breakfast doing well if the Kirbys were crabby. Nothing she heard from Steph was atrocious, but when you combined everything it was cause for concern. Still, she wouldn't offer her two-cents. Steph wasn't just there to see Portland. The trip was to figure out if she fit into Jack's world. Unless all of the Kirby's got their heads out of their keisters, they wouldn't have a successful B & B and they definitely wouldn't have Steph. "We're here if you need us, Steph. Just say the word and *Sweat Revenge* will be there."

Steph laughed. "I knew if I pestered you long enough, you'd come around to the idea a revenge-for-hire service would be a great side business."

"I wouldn't be able to keep a straight face when I applied for a vendor's license at the auditor's office. The clerk would ask what kind of business and I'd lose it."

The double doors opened and a nurse pushed Grace in a wheelchair.

"Hold on a second, Steph. Grace is on her way over to us with her foot in a compression wrap. She has a pair of crutches across her lap."

"Halleluiah! It's not broken!" Grace shouted.

"Woohoo!" Steph said into the phone for all to hear.

"Stephy! I'm glad you're here. Well, not here-here, but here."

Elaina smirked. "I think Grace is under the influence of painkillers."

"We miss you, Steph." Grace's words weren't exactly slurred but they weren't sharp either.

"I can feel the love. Hey, I have to go. Someone's knocking at my door. It better be Jack or he's going to be in a world of hurt when I see him. Words of wisdom, Grace: stay away from sneaky stairs."

The nurse waited for them to finish their gooey goodbyes before she explained Grace's sprain was mild and the attending physician thought her ankle would be fine as soon as the swelling went down. Handing Elaina a prescription for pain meds, she urged them to get it filled on the way home because what they gave Grace would wear off in a couple of hours. "She's not to put any weight on her foot until tomorrow. The doc suggests she follow up with her family physician."

Grace blinked up at the nurse. "I'm flying to another country to become a mother-in-law and grandma."

The nurse's gaze slid to Elaina. "The meds?"

"Not the meds. Her son is getting married in Italy."

"I see. Congratulations!"

Grace held up a finger. "First, we have to high-tail it to Maine to rescue Steph."

Even medicated Grace sensed something wasn't quite right.

Again, the nurse looked to Elaina. "The meds?"

"I wish."

* * *

"We prefer you not smile." The drugstore clerk aimed the

camera. Just as she snapped the photo laughter barreled out of Tawny.

"Sorry. It's hard to keep a straight face when you're told not to laugh."

The clerk was not impressed. "Let's try it again."

Tawny ran a hand across her face as though it would wipe away the urge to smile.

Elaina said, "Take two."

Tawny laughed so hard she snorted. "We'll walk around the store for a while. Maybe I'll get all laughed out. Then we'll give it another try."

"Sounds like a plan." The clerk stowed the camera and returned to the end-cap where she'd been stacking bottles of mouthwash prior to Tawny bothering her to get a passport photo made.

"I should check on Grace." They left her in the car so she wouldn't have to hobble around on crutches. Plus, it was pitch black out. If Grace dozed off then woke up, she might not remember they were at a twenty-four hour drugstore. She might freak out and hurt her foot worse.

"You should probably take her a bottle of water and some of these." Tawny held up a plastic container of sour pumpkin candy.

"It's almost midnight. You think she'd go for something sour?"

Tawny shrugged. "You never know with her."

Elaina spotted a small cooler with bottles of water and soda near the cash register. "Water is always a good idea."

"So are these." Tawny tossed two containers of sour pumpkins, three bags of candy corn, and three bags of fun-size peanut butter cups into a cart. "Do you think Grace is right? That we might have to rescue Steph?"

"I'm not sure about Steph but I might have to rescue you from that candy."

In a rash move, Tawny threw the candy back into the aisle bin.

"Geeze, Tawn', I was joking."

"I didn't get rid of it because of you. I got rid of it because of him." Tawny inclined her head to the right. "It's the ER heartthrob."

"So that's Parker Addison." Elaina inspected him from head to toe while he inspected a display of personal lubrication. She squelched a laugh by putting a hand over her mouth.

"Wait until you see his eyes. Did I mention they're sky blue?"

"I think you did."

Tawny latched onto Elaina's arm and yanked her to Parker. "Dr. Addison."

Elaina keyed on his eyes instead of the giant tube of lube in his hand. They were blue all right; sexy, drop-your-panties-for-me blue.

"Mrs. Westerfield, it's nice to see you." Those amazing eyes darted to the left.

Tawny started to correct him that she was no longer *Mrs.* Westerfield but she stopped abruptly when a brunette came around the corner. "Candace."

Elaina swung her gaze from Parker to Candace and landed it on Tawny. *Uh oh.* From the way Tawny had said Candace's name and the fake smile on her face, she guessed the hot doctor just got caught with a co-worker.

Candace didn't appear nervous that she and Parker had been discovered. She put a possessive arm around his waist. "You're out late."

"I know, right?" Elaina lifted her wrist to display the time. "We should be going. Our friend is probably in a lot of pain." Without any forethought she added, "Not Tawny. Grace. She sprained her ankle earlier. We're here to fill her prescription. You're here," she paused to look at the lube still in Parker's hand, "because you need to fix something that squeaks." She didn't dare look at Tawny.

Chapter Eleven

~ The four hussy homestead! ~

Elaina slid into the only available seat in the Chamber of Commerce assembly room. She opened her day planner and searched for a pen. She wasn't up to discussing business strategies when everything but her business was in chaos. As soon as they'd gotten home from the drugstore this morning – at 12:30AM – Tawny marched upstairs, retrieved the pack of cigarettes she'd hidden in her sock drawer, and headed outside to puff away her angst at seeing Parker with Candace. The swelling in Grace's foot increased instead of going down. And she had an uneasy feeling about Steph being in Maine. Since the Chamber's secretary had sent an email reminding Elaina she hadn't been to the last few meetings, she thought she'd better show her face. The email had been typed in all capital letters. The secretary had virtually shouted for her to attend.

"Well hello there."

Elaina hadn't paid much attention to who she'd sat next to. She was fully aware now. "Hey, Mac, how's it going?"

"Good. Good," he repeated.

Elaina muted a groan. Not only was Jess "Mac" Macintosh one of Cherry Ridge's most successful realtors, he was also Arden's golf buddy. He was the guy she'd called a while back to sell her house and gym when her relationship with the girls had fallen apart for a short time. Devastated and desperate to start over in Texas or anywhere for that matter, she'd contacted Macintosh Realty. In the phone call to Mac he'd revealed that Arden had gotten engaged. The emotional flip of the coin as to whether she'd stay in Ohio or move elsewhere had still been up in the air. Mac's loose-lipped disclosure stirred anger, curiosity, determination, and so much more. It made the coin land heads-up. You couldn't have pried her out of Cherry Ridge after that news bulletin. Basically Mac had shot himself in the foot. Elaina no longer needed his services but that phone call had made things awkward between them.

Mac swiveled in his chair to stare at her. "What do you think about Arden selling his house?"

Elaina almost never said the f-bomb. It was one of those words that made her hair stand on end. Yet Mac's question made that word fire across her brain. "I'm happy for him."

Mac's face scrunched into lines of suspicion. "You're happy for him?"

"I am." She couldn't very well say she didn't give a rat's ass one way or the other. It would make her sound like a bitter shrew.

Mac sifted air through his teeth. "Roberta still can't

believe Arden let you go."

Roberta Macintosh was an awesome lady. She volunteered at the thrift store, spearheaded charitable events, and stuck up for those who got the short end of the stick. She'd had Elaina's back more than once over the years. One Friday night when Elaina and Arden, Mac and Roberta had golfed together, Arden had been in nitpicking mode. The moment they stepped on the green he rode Elaina's butt about her swing, the black smudge on her golf shoes, that her hair was getting too long which he thought made it look hideous, on and on. At the eighteenth hole, Roberta must've had enough of Arden putting Elaina down. She'd said, 'Quit your complaining, Mr. Perfect. My ears are about to fall off from all the bitching.' She'd poked him in the chest with her club. 'You're damned lucky to have Elaina.' The strangest thing happened – Arden apologized, not to her but to Roberta. And he sucked up to her the rest of the night. "Tell Roberta hello for me."

"Will do." Mac moved to face forward again, but tapped his pen on the notebook he had laid open on the table. "I was tickled when Arden called me to list his house. That place is worth a fortune."

"It's incredible, for sure."

Mac turned in his seat again.

Elaina was tempted to take a hold of him and rotate him to face the front.

He lowered his voice. "There's a rumor that Arden is in financial difficulty."

There it was. The hook with the bait had been dropped

in the water. Annoyed that Mac again divulged sensitive information, Elaina swam away from the hook with a stern look. "I wouldn't put a lot of stock in hearsay." She searched the room to locate her ex and found him working his mojo with Mason Glask, owner of Mason's Pizzeria. Arden wasn't easy to like and even harder to love, but she was in awe of him. The man she'd once been married to was the master of millions. In that moment, she knew there wasn't an ounce of truth in the gossip. Arden was a lot of things but careless with his wealth wasn't one of them. Whoever started the vicious buzz had to have a personal agenda.

Elaina baited a hook of her own with a casual laugh. "Arden has more money than he knows what to do with. He could buy Cherry Ridge and kick all of us out. Wouldn't that be something?"

Mac frowned for no more than a millisecond but Elaina had seen it. "Arden wouldn't kick his buddies out."

"Or would he?" Elaina fought a grin.

* * *

A van belonging Henri Flowers and Gifts was parked out front when Elaina arrived home. Obviously word had gotten around about Grace's injury and Dalton James had sent flowers. She'd bet money on it.

Elaina was almost to the door when Chet Daniels, the delivery man walked out.

A huge smile worked to Chet's face when she spotted her. "Elaina, how the heck are you?" Chet was a retired machinist who delivered flowers to stay busy.

"Just peachy." That was a stretch. She was dog tired and starving. "How about you?"

"Couldn't be better. After I'm done with my deliveries, it's beer and cards."

Elaina smiled. "Enjoy."

"I was about to say the same to you, little lady. Woo-wee! You got a lot of flowers."

"I'm sure you're mistaken. Grace is the one with a bum foot. "

"The cards were clearly marked for you."

Chet was in great shape for a man who recently turned seventy, but his eyesight had to failing him. "Okay, well, I'll go inside and check things out." She dug in the side pocket of her purse and produced a ten dollar bill to give as a tip. "Card money."

"Thank you kindly."

The smell of roses met Elaina's nose the second she entered the house.

Grace sneezed, pinpointing her location.

Elaina peeked into the living room. "How's the foot?"

Grace pushed aside the afghan covering her foot. "Better." She sneezed again. "Those flowers, however, are messing with me. My eyes keep watering and I've sneezed a hundred times in the last five minutes." She pointed to the coffee table where vases of red roses with spider mums, yellow roses with gladiolas, purple roses with white wax flowers, and an assortment of carnations in various colors sat in clear glass vases. "It's beginning to look like a funeral parlor in here." A single rose bud accented with baby's breath and a silk bow in a milk glass vase was on the lamp table next to Grace. She jerked her thumb to the solitary rose, "Mine," and then gestured to the coffee table again, "yours." Mischief lit her expression. "Did you sleep with a mortician?"

Elaina surveyed the multitude of arrangements. "Not that I know of, but I must have." She giggled. "That's a freakish display of something. I'd like to say affection but I'm with you, they resemble something you'd send to extend sympathy." She let out a sigh. "Life is getting weirder by the minute." Her phone rang from the kitchen counter where she'd stowed her purse.

"It's probably your secret mortician. I mean… admirer."

Elaina teased Grace by narrowing her eyes. She grabbed her phone and identified the caller as belonging to the gym. "Hello, Val. What's up?" *Please don't say another piece of equipment broke or someone got hurt.* When you owned a gym both things could occur in the blink of an eye. The machines were relatively new but they got used a lot in a day's time. Lately the tension adjusters were giving her fits and she'd had to replace ripped cushions. Neither thing was a big deal but Elaina didn't want anything to crimp the workout experience for her members. Happy members equaled a healthy business. She tried to resolve any issues as soon as possible. Of a more serious nature, a member had fallen off a machine a while back and hurt her arm. Even though the woman claimed to be fine, Elaina had sent her to the doctor to be checked out. Things turned out well in that particular case. The only thing hurt was the woman's pride. She repeatedly apologized to Elaina for being clumsy. Elaina tried to smooth things over by saying it could happen to anyone. She'd also given the woman three free months on her membership.

Val whispered into the phone making it difficult for Elaina to hear.

"You'll have to speak up. I can't make out a thing you're saying."

Val cleared her throat and began again. "Millicent Markward wanted me to pass something on to you."

Elaina noiselessly grumbled. Millicent had been the one who exposed Arden as a handsy guy a few months ago. "What does she think I ought to know this time?"

"You're not going to like it."

Every muscle in Elaina's body tightened. "Go into the weigh and measure room and close the door."

"I'm in," Val whispered as if she was part of a covert operation.

Elaina couldn't fathom why Millicent thought it was okay to draw Val into her private matters. "Hit me with it."

"I'm not sure how to say this."

"Don't sugar-coat it, Val. What did Arden do this time?"

"This isn't about Arden. It's about you."

Elaina tried to swallow past the sudden knot in her throat. "Did I take out a classified ad in the newspaper to meet the man of my dreams?"

"If only," Val stated without an ounce of humor.

"Millicent said someone is burning up the gossip pipeline with the lie that you're into..." She exhaled loudly. "I can't get my mouth to say the words."

Single people were sometimes the target of vicious rumors. No one seemed to know where the gossip originated but the carelessly repeated words inflicted a lot of *nerve* damage before they were put to rest. "Spell them then."

"M-u-l-t... Aww, hell, multiple bed partners."

Stunned didn't begin to describe the effect on Elaina. She went numb all over, including her vocal chords.

Val rushed to clarify her loyalty. "I know it isn't true."

Elaina tried to refute the vile fabrication. Still, no sound would come out.

"Are you there? I'm really sorry." Val's voice cracked with panic. "You're hurt. I would be too."

"I...uh..." Elaina rasped. "Even though I don't need to set the record straight, I'm going to. I've NEVER had multiple partners, nor would I want to. Most days I can't handle one, let alone many. For those into that sort of thing, more power to them." Queasiness charged to the pit of her stomach and inched up her throat. She looked at the flowers and then at Grace whose eyes were round with interest.

"People who know you won't believe it."

Elaina rubbed her forehead. "It was difficult to hear but I'm grateful you called. I'd rather know what people are saying behind my back than to wonder what the snickers are about."

"You're rich, beautiful, built, and available. All of

those things make you a prime target."

Elaina sifted through Val's assessment. Yes, she had money but in no way was she rich. She silently scoffed at the bit about being built and beautiful. Both lay in the eyes of the beholder. In place of generous curves, she had muscle. Arden had called her eyes spectacular; once early in their relationship when he was trying to gain ground romantically and again last night when he was trying to gain a different kind of ground – the dirt her house and gym sat on. As far as being available, it was a state of mind more than anything. She was currently unavailable. "Thanks for the support."

"The wackos who are talking smack about ya must be ugly as sin, bored as hell, and have the disposition of a two-year old that isn't getting attention. They obviously envy your freedom to play and your looks to lure. In other words, the grass looks greener in your yard."

Elaina was frustrated. Contrary to some people's perception, being a divorcee wasn't an exciting choice or lifestyle. It meant the earth crumbled beneath your feet at some point. It meant you'd gone through a crap ton of mental anguish. Some divorcees endured physical pain as well before they were able to cut the bindings holding them in a bad marriage. "I'm going to have to stop using fertilizer."

"Don't stop using fertilizer. Sprinkle that stuff everywhere."

Elaina forced a chuckle. "You're awesome, Val."

"Thanks, boss. You're pretty awesome yourself. Oh crap. I have to go. One of the members just knocked over the display of protein shakes. Sorry for ruining your day, Elaina, but I thought you should know what had been said."

"You didn't ruin my day. I appreciate the heads-up."

After Val disconnected the call, Elaina drooped into the recliner. "I have to move."

Grace frowned. "I pieced together bits and pieces. I take it someone's engaged in a smear campaign."

Elaina propped her elbows on the arms of the chair and cupped her face with her hands. A heavier burst of frustration gushed from her chest. "I allegedly entertain more than one man at a time."

Grace's light blue eyes darkened with anger, but Grace was Grace so her automatic response was humor. "That explains the noise I hear coming from your room every night. I thought you were a heavy snorer."

Elaina closed her eyes. "It's not heavy snoring. It's heavy coitus. Apparently." She relayed the conversation she'd had with Mac earlier.

"Wow. Arden's headed to the poorhouse and you have a sexual appetite that causes quite a stir. Who knew?"

Elaina made a face.

Grace moved in her chair to get comfortable. "Don't let the halfwits rattle you. You know the truth."

"I don't get it, Grace. I don't mess with folks. They shouldn't mess with me."

"You're good to people. You're even nice to your ex." Grace looked thoughtful for a moment. "The past couple of weeks have been strange. We've had a possible stalker. Arden asked you to dinner. His lawyer shows up at the restaurant. Together they tried to strong arm you. Then you received a bossy email from the Chamber secretary. Mac proceeded to inform you that Arden's going to one day be penniless. You came home to funeral flowers from God knows who. Now it's come to light that you're a two bit hussy."

"Thanks for the recap." Elaina felt deflated. "Someone is getting their jollies by messing with me."

Grace cocked her eyebrow a fraction of an inch. "Or are they?"

"Meaning?"

"Things aren't always as they seem. There's definitely something going on but I doubt it's directly aimed at you." Grace moved her neck from side to side to work out a kink. "My head says Arden isn't behind this but my gut wants to implicate him."

Elaina sat up straight. "Why would Arden stalk us? He's not blond, by the way. And why would he use Mac to take a pot shot at himself? He's a financial investor whose business relies on gaining the client's trust. Why would he put it out there that he might go belly-up?"

"To throw you off." Grace shrugged. "My gut is seldom wrong. My advice to you is to stay in Cherry Ridge with your head held high. Laugh off the rumors. Remain the sweet, loving person that you are. The bad people or persons will eventually trip themselves up." She sneezed. "Now about those flowers…"

Elaina pulled up out of the chair, grabbed one of the floral cards and read it out loud. "Thanks for last night." She took another card. "We had a special rhythm last night. Let's keep it at three from now on." The anger that started to subside came back. "Whoever's behind the rumors..."

Grace said, "Arden."

Elaina finished her thought, "...also sent the flowers."

"Sloppy work on their part. You can find out who it is by nagging or bribing the florist."

"I wouldn't put that kind of pressure on the florist."

Grace mocked with the lift of her eyebrows. "You're too stinking nice. You know what they say – nice guys finish last."

"Do I really want to know who's up to no good?" Elaina answered her own question. "I don't think I do. I just want it to stop."

"You can't roll over and play dead on this one. To save your self-respect and reputation you have to call him out."

"I hate confrontation."

"You'll confront people on our behalf but you shy away when it affects you. The more you shy away the bigger the bulls-eye. Stand up for yourself or I will." Grace raised her foot. "I'll kick him in the peaches."

"With your bum ankle?"

"Whatever it takes."

"You're right. I can't ignore this, but I have to do some detective work so I don't rip into the wrong person."

"While you super-sleuth, I'll order a pizza for dinner." Grace pulled her phone from beneath the afghan.

Elaina studied the floral arrangements, shaking her head and concluding that someone had gone to a lot of expense to give the appearance she was having too much fun as a single woman. It couldn't be Arden. He was the one who'd forced single status upon her. Unless... No way. He didn't want her back. He wanted the house. If by some small chance, he did want her back, it wouldn't be wise to taint her name in the community. It would be as good as tainting his name. Plus, there was already a big X through his standing in the business community regarding his finances. Someone was trying to discredit them both. It was time to have a serious meeting with Arden, that didn't include a low-cut neckline or dinner.

Grace dialed the pizzeria located two blocks down the street. "We'd like a fifteen-inch thin-crust pizza with extra pepperoni. Extra onion. Extra banana peppers. And extra cheese."

Elaina slid in her two-cents. "We're going to need an extra crust to hold all that."

Grace wrinkled her nose in amusement. "For delivery, please." The pizzeria employee must've asked for the address. "The four hussy homestead." She winked at Elaina and whispered, "Let's see how long it takes that name to get around."

* * *

Tawny dragged herself into the living room, looking like she'd done a forty-eight hour shift instead of a twelve. "There has to be a full moon tonight. Nothing else explains the day I've had."

Stony came down the stairs and pushed against

Tawny. "In a minute, Stone-man, let me get my bearings first."

Grace contributed that there wouldn't be a full moon until the end of the month.

Tawny dropped her purse beside the sofa and started to sit down. She stopped when she spied the flowers. "What have we here?"

"Thank-you-for-the-coitus flowers." Grace stretched her mouth wide with an ornery grin.

"They're kind of somber for thank-you flowers. Wait. What?"

"I take part in orgies." Emotion welled inside Elaina. She wished she could laugh it off as Grace suggested. Perhaps in time she'd be able to but not now. The cut was too fresh.

Tawny jiggled with a laugh. "It's always the shy ones."

"Someone is messing with Elaina." To save Elaina from telling her story a second time, Grace filled in the blanks.

Tawny was instantly ticked. "When I find out who's up to no good, I'll beat the snot out of them."

"Grace's gut says it's Arden." Elaina uttered a gritty sound of discontent. "Let's talk about your day so I can forget about mine for a while."

Grace sneezed three times in succession. "Can we get rid of those blasted things first?"

"I'll ditch the flowers. Tawn', you take Stony out to do his business. Grace, you wait for the pizza." Elaina placed a twenty in Grace's lap. "My treat."

Stony barked at the front door. A knock followed.

"I take it the pizza has arrived." Tawny snatched the money from Grace. "Stay sitting. By the time you hobble to the door the darn thing will be cold."

The freckle-faced teenage delivery boy read the slip taped to the box. "The four hussy homestead?"

"Excuse me?"

Elaina came to the kid's rescue before Tawny bit into him. "You have the right place."

"Since when are we the four hussy homestead?"

"That's Grace's doing."

"It sounds like a brothel."

The delivery boy smirked.

Tawny gave him a narrow-eyed look. "You're too young to know what that is."

"He'll be old enough by the time you finally pay him," Elaina wisecracked and motioned for Tawny to hand over the loot. "Keep the change."

Tawny looked for a place to set the pizza box.

Elaina began moving the vases. "These flowers are history." She gathered as many vases as she could hold. Stony moved with her.

"Uh, Tawn', you'd better get him outside soon or his bladder is going to burst."

Elaina sat the vases on the umbrella table on the patio. She didn't have the heart to dump them in the trash. The evening air was as good as a walk-in cooler so they'd be fine until she figured out what to do with them.

Stony finished his ritual of sprinkling every tree and bush on the east side of house and barreled toward her. He bumped the table, knocking over one of the vases.

Roses went flying.

Elaina flinched. Stony reacted with a type of whimper. Tweaking the velvet of his ears with her fingers, she let him know he wasn't in trouble.

With no warning, Stony's head shot up. He stared at the steel building at the back of the property and bared his teeth.

Elaina squatted beside him. "What is it, boy?"

"Are you a hussy slash dog-whisperer?"

"Duh," Elaina teased but the humor faded in a hurry. "He senses something or someone at the back of the property."

Tawny cussed and stomped toward the building. "I've had my fill of nut jobs today." Shaking her fists in the air, she shouted. "If there's a nut job on this property he'll be putting ice on his privates."

Stony sprinted to Tawny's side.

Elaina caught up with them as they reached the back of the building. It was well past dusk but the security light mounted on the pole at the corner of the yard shed light on the area.

Like the first time they'd suspected an intruder, there was none to be found. Stony sniffed the ground. He was no longer baring his teeth, but Tawny was baring hers. Elaina put a finger up to encourage Tawny to play along. "There's no one here. Geeze. Do we get spooked easily or what?" She laughed for effect. "Must be our guilty consciences making us jumpy."

Tawny adlibbed, "The weed we smoked had to have been laced with something kooky. It's making us hear and see things that aren't there. Boy that was some good stuff."

Elaina rolled her eyes. She was probably one of the few people on the planet who hadn't smoked marijuana. "Let's get back to the pizza."

"I'm so hungry I could eat a horse." Tawny mimicked Elaina by rolling her own eyes at the lame comment. "Wait. Horses are awesome. I'd never eat a horse. Whoever thought up that saying was an idiot. You should ride horses, not eat them." She mumbled under her breath, "Do I sound high? Or like a moron?"

Elaina started back to the house. "It's not our imagination. Someone was there. Tomorrow morning I'm going to check every inch of the fence. Whoever is spying on us has to have an escape hatch."

"Check it from the other side. If there's a hatch, that's where you'll find it."

* * *

When they returned to the living room, Grace was in tears.

"Grace?" Elaina said.

Grace brushed the moisture from her eyes with the back of her hand. "Cody just called. He's getting married in two weeks." She grimaced. "I've not met Isabella. Shouldn't a mother meet her son's intended before he walks down the aisle?" Her voice trembled with emotion.

Tawny held out a tissue. "Does he sound happy?"

Grace dabbed at her eyes. "He sounds ecstatic."

"Then it's your job to also be ecstatic. For him. For them," Tawny gently said.

Elaina had a hunch Cody getting married to an unknown Italian girl wasn't the sole cause of Grace's anxiety, but rather that he was entering into Holy Matrimony without the presence of his father. Brince, Grace, and Cody had been a trio of love and joy. In an instant on a sunny autumn morning, Brince was gone. Elaina couldn't imagine the strength it had taken to get through the tragedy but she knew Grace would always love Brince and there would always be tears and times of weakness where she'd feel as if she couldn't go on without him. Hopefully looking into the eyes of the son they'd made together and hugging him a thousand times would be enough to get Grace through until the next bout of sadness tried to take over. "You won't face this alone. We'll fly to Italy with you or trot all over the globe if you need us to." She rubbed Grace's arm. "From what you've told us about Cody, he has a good head on his shoulders. He'll choose carefully." She felt compelled to add, "I'm not saying this gal is right for him but he has to follow his heart."

Grace buried her face in her hands and muffled through her fingers, "He's my only child and he sees nothing wrong with getting married five thousand miles from home." She dropped her hands and looked from Elaina to Tawny.

Tawny raised her palms. "Kids nowadays. Whatcha gonna do?" A weird look hit her eyes. "Oh. My. Gosh. I opened my mouth and my mother came out."

Grace's angst split into a small smile. "It was bound to happen. You're forty-seven."

"And you'll soon be forty-two, ya geezer."

Elaina realized just how much they relied on humor to get them through their personal crises. "You have to call Steph and update her about Cody. After all, she's the fourth hussy."

Grace punched stored number five and put the phone on speaker.

Steph answered right away and spoke in hushed exasperation. "Oh thank god! Friends!"

Elaina, Grace, and Tawny exchanged looks. "Is everything okay, Steph?"

"Jack and I are fine; me and his mother, not so much. She's just not taking to me. No matter what I say or do, she frowns. It's as though she made her mind up about me before I arrived. And Jack could possibly be a mama's boy."

"Possibly?" Tawny asked sarcastically. "That woman is a black bear protecting her forty year old cub."

"Tawwwwn'," Elaina warned.

"What? She needs to hear the truth."

Grace asked, "Have you had a few moments alone with Jack to discuss the bear issue?"

"I'm afraid to approach the subject because I know I'll be on the losing end of things. I'm sure in his eyes she can do no wrong." Steph's frustration came through loud and clear.

"Tread lightly, Steph. Most guys have a special relationship with their mom. Don't put Jack in a position where he has to choose you or his mother. The best plan of action is to try to win her over a little at a time. Your cinnamon rolls would be a good starting point." Elaina shrugged. "Or not."

"It'll be a standoff made easier with cinnamon and sugar." Grace also shrugged.

"Pfft. Don't listen to those yahoos. Black bears aren't into cinnamon rolls. They eat grass, roots, berries, insects, fish, and the occasional mammal. Humans are mammals." Tawny snickered. "Whatever you do, don't climb a tree. Black bears are excellent climbers. And don't play dead. Fight for your life."

"Really, Tawn'?" Steph said blandly. "That's all you've got? Don't give them cinnamon rolls or climb a tree?"

"I also said don't play dead."

Steph sighed. "I miss you guys."

Elaina's heart went out to Steph. The battle plan *win the mom-win the son* seemed easy enough. It was seldom that simple though. In most cases it boiled down to strength. Steph had to keep her chin up, while sucking up. "We miss you too, Steph." Elaina cued Grace to share her news.

"Cody's getting married in TWO WEEKS! TWO WEEKS, STEPH! I almost had a meltdown but Elaina and Tawny helped me through it. They're way better than anxiety meds."

"But are they better than a pitcher of sangria?"

Chapter Twelve

~ Jezzy and Belle! ~

Elaina turned on the electric fireplace to take the chill out of the air. "We should write a book about all the crazy things that happen." She curled up on the sofa with a plate of pizza in her lap and a glass of sparkling blueberry wine at her fingertips.

Grace nibbled the end of a slice of pizza and spoke through the chew. "We'd have enough material for a three-book series but we'd have to tout it as fiction. No one would believe any of it to be true, even though you couldn't make up this much chaos. I mean it doesn't get any more real...or bizarre...than coming home to a house filled with funeral flowers, a peeping Tom in the backyard, and a son who's trying to make his mom insane. And I'm not talking about Jack Kirby. Then there's our dear, good friend Steph who's digging potholes as we speak; this time in Maine. In the mix of the madness is the most lovable nymphomaniac you'll ever meet." She put her teeth together in a toothy grin and showed them to Elaina. "Last but not least, nurse Tawny Westerfield battles the butt; cigarette butt, that is. She also works with hospital staff that some days qualify as nut jobs."

"It would make the bestseller's list." Elaina wet her lips with a taste of wine, savoring the sweetness. "It just dawned on me that we haven't given Tawn' a chance to vent about said nut jobs. We've been too absorbed in our own muck. Tawn', the floor is yours."

A loud gush of air whooshed from Tawny. "Do you really want to extend an already hectic day with me whining?"

Elaina sat her plate of pizza aside and wrapped both hands around her wine goblet. "It's not whining. It's releasing the garbage of your day so all that festering, moldy, oozing refuse doesn't explode all over the ER tomorrow."

Tawny puckered her face and shuddered with revulsion. "Gross."

"Exactly."

"It probably would do me a world of good to get a few things off my chest." Tawny's exhale was long and labored. "The head nurse took a bite out of my rump this morning. I didn't even have my car keys put away and she lit into me."

"What's her beef with you now?" Grace asked.

For reasons unknown, the head nurse had taken a dislike to Tawny on day one when she'd moved from the maternity floor to the ER. It was almost five years since then and Tawny still couldn't get in her good graces. Elaina had met the woman a month ago when she dropped lunch off to Tawny. Her first impression had been that the woman had the personality of a grill scraper.

"A fountain cup of soda was left at the nurse's station yesterday. During the shift change, one of the RN's coming on didn't notice the cup, bumped it with her elbow, and cola splashed onto a stack of patient charts. No one claimed responsibility for the cup so naturally she blamed me. I came this close," Tawny showed an inch in width with her fingers, "to telling her to shove the cup where the sun doesn't shine. Instead, I swallowed my temper and calmly informed her I don't drink fountain soda. She gave me the stink eye and walked away. My day tumbled downhill from there. We ran out of non-latex gloves, which apparently was my fault too. I guess she considers me the unofficial stock person. An hour later it took four sticks to get an IV in a patient. I felt bad for the guy but I couldn't find a good vein. And yes, he made sure my boss knew I was incapable of doing my job. The maraschino cherry on top of the crap-parfait? Doctor Hot Body was an extreme grouch. He grumbled under his breath all day and threw – not placed – instruments onto the stainless steel tray when he was finished with them. After lunch, he read the riot act to another nurse for something that wasn't done. In her defense she was on the verge of getting a debilitating migraine. He told her to either go home or take a pill. Essentially, he was cranky, clanging, and contrary."

"He and Candace must've gotten caught in the lube aisle again," Grace joked.

"Or," Tawny finally gave into a laugh, "he had an

allergic reaction to lube. That would make anyone cranky."

"Your boss is probably allergic to it too. That would explain a lot." Elaina smirked over the edge of her wine glass.

That was too much of a visual for Tawny. She laughed so hard she snorted. When she composed herself, she smiled so big it looked as if the edges of her mouth touched her ears. "When my train derails I can count on you guys to put it back on the track." She tugged at her scrubs. The top was decorated with goofy-face pumpkins. "I'm going to change into some real clothes."

Elaina grinned. "Sweat pants?"

* * *

"We're trespassing." Dark clouds set the mood for the murky investigative work. Elaina was so nervous she picked up on noises that normally went unnoticed unless she was in direct contact with them; the rattle of someone's garage door going up, the clank of a metal trash can lid being put back on, a car backfiring in the distance, and the warning bell of gates being lowered at the railroad crossing a few blocks away.

"You're allowed to inspect a piece of land when you're interested in buying it."

"I'm not interested in buying it."

"You know that and I know that, but the public thinks you're a potential buyer."

"No they don't. They think I'm a loose woman,"

Elaina said with a sneer.

"A loose potential buyer."

A red pickup truck putted by and the driver craned his neck for a look.

"Act natural." Grace pulled the tape measure from her pocket; a prop she thought would make them appear legit.

Elaina took the end of the tape measure and walked to the edge of the property. "What are we measuring?"

"How long it takes the nosy guy's laser to bore a hole through us."

Elaina projected her voice. "I think the lot's big enough for a winery." She pulled that idea out of thin air.

"And a dog boarding business." Grace snickered with her head down. "Is he still gawking?"

Elaina said, "Mmm. Hmm," without moving her lips."

The driver pulled his truck to the curb and got out. He was a spry old gent with snappy blue eyes. His t-shirt read: *Retired plumbers sit around and talk sh*t all day!* The asterisk made it funny but the gist of the message was that he had all the time in the world to bug them. "Mornin', ladies." He tipped the frayed bill of his plumber's union cap.

"Good morning to you too, sir," Grace said with more enthusiasm than she was known to have at seven-thirty in the morning.

"You gals are going to build a winery?"

"Possibly." Elaina shot Grace an amused look.

"And a dog boarding business?"

"We love dogs," Grace spouted. "We have a Siberian Husky that thinks he's human."

Elaina conveyed "nice dodge" by raising her eyebrows. Grace accepted the compliment by blinking rapidly; a kind of eyelash Morse code. Elaina looked away to hide her smile.

"I hate to dash your dreams, but this land isn't zoned commercial."

Elaina was well aware of zoning and permits and all that went with constructing and owning a business but she played along. "I suppose that could be an obstacle."

Grace struck a go-away pose with her hands on her hips. "We appreciate the input." Her tone said the opposite.

The busybody ignored the unspoken request to leave. His attention toggled back and forth between them. "I'm sure the city will give the thumbs down to another winery. A dog boarding business would be a good enterprise though. There's only one in town and it's always full. My wife and I have to drive ten miles to board our spaniel when we go out of town."

Elaina looked at her watch, another hint for the interruption to end so they could inspect the fence. "That's our problem too. There's no place for Stoneman to go when we globe trot." Technically it wasn't an untruth. They were headed to Italy soon and would have to make arrangements for Stony and Lula.

The corners of the man's eyes crinkled. "You get around, huh?"

Grace winked. "In more ways than one."

Elaina teasingly glared. If word hadn't sufficiently made its way to every ear in Cherry Ridge about her being an insatiable hussy, it would now. "Time's ticking away. If we don't hurry we'll be late for work."

Interest flickered in the man's eyes. "What do you gals do for a living?"

"Fitness trainer," Elaina replied, but she also rattled off the realtor's phone number from the For Sale sign and repeated it as if trying to memorize it. The number was already in her phone since it belonged to none other than Jess Macintosh – Mac.

"I work at the bank," Grace chirped.

"I do all my banking online," the man said proudly. "My retirement check and social security allotment go right into my account every month so the wife insisted I learn how to pay our bills with the computer."

"Easy peasy. With the click of a mouse your payments are taken care of. Quite efficient," Grace patronized.

"That's what the wife says. I'm old school but she's forcing me to be modern. For my birthday she bought me an iPad. What am I going to do with an iPad?"

"The list is endless. You could tweet or pop into Facebook to catch up with your friends."

"I'm going to catch up with them at the coffee shop. If I don't get moving they'll send out a search party to look for me. It was nice meeting you ladies." He started to walk away but turned to ask, "What did you say your names were?"

Elaina made a split-second decision not to engineer a fake identity. "Elaina Samuels." She nodded to Grace.

"Grace Cordray."

A strange expression flitted across his face. He looked directly at Elaina. "I've heard of you."

I'm sure you have. Elaina walked the tape measure to the fence. "And you are?"

"Rudolph but I go by Rudy."

"It's been nice meeting you, Rudy. Enjoy your coffee."

"Have a cup for me," Grace quipped.

Elaina felt Rudy's blue-eyed radar stay with her even though she was now concentrating on the fence. The tiny voice inside that normally kept her on an even keel was smothered by a big dose of frustration. "Minolta makes a fine camera."

Gawking-Rudy had no clue she was being sarcastic. "I believe ours is a Nikon."

Elaina couldn't look at Grace or he might catch on that she was just being mouthy. "We need to photograph the lot so when we decorate the walls of our winery we can hang before-and-after photos." Even though there was no real plan for a winery she wanted Rudy to know she wasn't a wimp who feared city disapproval.

It was Grace's turn to check her watch. "Your buddies are forming a search party at this very minute."

"Oh right." Rudy walked to his truck, but glanced over his shoulder every couple of steps.

Grace gave him an exaggerated wave each time he looked back. She waited until his truck was out of sight before she made big eyes at Elaina. "I can't believe you gave him our real names."

"You'd prefer I came up with something different?"

"Duh. Jezzy and Belle." A grin quirked the corners of her mouth.

Elaina chuckled when she put the two names together. "Fitting."

A loud clap of thunder overhead warned of impending rain.

"We'd better hurry." Elaina took the left side of the fence and Grace started on the right. After only a few slats had been inspected, the sky gave way to a zillion drops of cold rain.

Just like that, Elaina and Grace were soaked to the skin.

Elaina was determined to find the opening. "I'll finish, Grace. Get in the Escalade so you don't get sick."

"Nope. We're in this together."

"You got rid of your crutches this morning. If you slip on the wet surface and reinjure your foot because of me, I'll never forgive myself."

"Worry wart."

"You can't go to Cody's wedding in a swanky dress and a cast on your foot."

Blinking raindrops from her lashes, Grace got all sappy. "You're always there for me. All I have to do is ask and you make it happen. Sometimes I don't even have to ask. You know what I need. The least I can do is put up with a little bit of ran to help you find where the two-legged rodent is getting through the fence."

Elaina formed an open heart with her hands.

* * *

Elaina experienced a moment of raw indecision at the sight of Arden standing in front of the Garden Café. She clenched and unclenched her hands, contemplating doing an about-face and skirting away before he noticed she was there. "No guts, no..." She was going to say glory but it didn't factor into this in any way. Whether she liked it or not, this meeting had to happen.

Arden checked his watch and folded his arms across his chest; his impatience evident.

Elaina glanced at her watch too, thankful to be on time. Had she been one minute late he'd have no problem articulating his displeasure. She took a breath and sidled next to him. "Thanks for meeting me."

Featherlike wrinkles creased the corners of his eyes and the corners of his mouth tipped into a sexy smile. "I wasn't sure you'd want to see me again after Cornell and I tried to bargain with you."

Elaina tried to ignore the potent smile. It was a distraction she didn't need or want. Steph had once said Arden was model material. Her assessment was spot-on. He was a handsome devil who wasn't afraid to use his looks to his advantage. "Your definition of bargain doesn't match the one in the dictionary." She gave him a good-natured push with her hip. "I should warn you, this rendezvous isn't just about lunch."

Arden's blue eyes glittered with interest.

The hostess, who was also the owner, approached with a larger-than-life smile.

Elaina knew her as one of the newest members of the Chamber of Commerce. "Hello, Madelyn. It's a beautiful day outside."

"Elaina, good to see you." Madelyn took in Arden's presence. A fleeting look of confusion dashed across her expression but the smile returned just as quick. "Good to see you too, Arden."

The business community and most of the people in Cherry Ridge were aware of their divorce and how things hadn't ended on a friendly note. Many also knew there had been another woman involved. For she and Arden to be seen together twice now had to have the rumor mill in a state of bewilderment. Elaina was happy Madelyn's jaw hadn't dropped open.

"The weather hasn't been the best lately so today's sunshine is a gift."

Arden didn't roll his eyes per se but he looked up as though he was already bored with the small talk.

Another couple came in behind them, bringing the chit chat to an end.

"It's open seating right now. The tables near the tall windows provide a breathtaking view of the pond and walk bridge. Enjoy your lunch."

Arden offered tepid thanks.

Elaina chose the farthest table for privacy.

In a gentlemanly move, Arden pulled out her chair. The moment they were seated he leaned close enough for her to catch his cologne. Elaina tried to pay no attention to the pleasured assault on her senses.

He smoothed the front of his navy striped two-button Armani suit jacket. "You've decided to sell me the property."

Unfolding her napkin to spread across her lap, Elaina chuckled lightly. "Are we there yet?"

"What?"

"Why dither when you can be a little kid in the backseat, asking if we're there yet. You cut right to the chase. So I'll cut to the left. Yeah, no, I haven't decided to change the name on the deeds for the house and gym to yours."

Arden's agreeable expression tightened. "I hate when people say yeah no. It's either yes or no. Yeah, no," he mocked.

Elaina shrugged. "It's a catchy saying."

"It shows a lack of class."

"The mayor says it."

Arden curled his upper lip.

Elaina scooted her chair away from the table to give the impression she might leave. "If you're going to find fault in every little thing there's no point in spending a half hour together."

Arden put up his palms. "Sorry." He laid the burgundy cloth napkin in his lap. "Believe it or not I'm trying to be a better person. Every now and then I backslide."

Elaina went still, wondering if this was one of those crazed tests or mind games some exes were known to play. "You're trying to be better?"

"I was a lousy husband, Elaina." His voice softened. "My behavior was atrocious at times. I knew it but I couldn't seem to stop."

On the ride to the café, Elaina imagined a hundred ways their lunch would go. In no way did she anticipate

Arden taking responsibility for the collapse of their marriage. His admission jerked her to the core. It made her even more nervous and a tad suspicious. She fumbled for an appropriate response to such a strong statement. "We had some happy times."

Arden reached across the table to give her shoulder a gentle squeeze. "Do you remember when we went skinny dipping in Lake Michigan?"

The warmth of his hand permeated the polyester golf-type shirt bearing the gym's logo. Elaina wanted to edge away from his touch. It was disturbing. At the same time, it felt good. "I remember. I was super reserved back then. You dared me to do a strip tease in the boat and to dive into the water. You practically ripped off your clothes and dove in after me. We scared the fish with our...umm, swimming. When we got back in the boat you couldn't find your underwear. You went commando until we got to our hotel room in Ludington."

"We should do that again sometime."

YEAH, NO! Elaina shouted vociferously in her head.

Their waitress brought glasses of ice water, a basket of crackers, and menus. "I'm Janine. I'll be taking care of you today. Our specials include a tuna melt and cup of vegetable soup for $3.99 or grilled chicken salad with a side of cottage cheese for $4.99."

"We'll both have black coffee and grilled chicken salad, raspberry vinaigrette dressing on the side. Forget the cottage cheese." Arden handed back the menus.

Janine didn't bother to write down the order. "That was easy."

Elaina smiled sweetly but she wanted to kick Arden under the table.

Arden's phone buzzed with an incoming text message. He glanced at the message and put the phone back in his pocket. The former version of her ex would've eaten up their time sending messages back and forth to whomever had initiated the communication. Maybe he really was trying to be a better person. "I can't get away from the office for five minutes without someone bugging me. Apparently I have a client who inherited a ton of money and he's eager to invest. Celeste put him off until 12:45, which means I have to eat fast and you have to get to the heart of whatever prompted this rendezvous."

Elaina was glad the trip down memory lane was over but she wasn't excited to begin a dialogue that would inevitably raise both of their blood pressures. She sipped from her water glass and shifted in her chair. "There are some weird things happening I thought you should be aware of."

He ripped the cellophane from a package of crackers. "Such as?"

"For starters, I think someone is stalking me."

Arden's somewhat-relaxed posture stiffened and his brows drew together to form a strict V. "Stalking you?"

The abundance of disbelief in his tone ticked her off right away. "I'm not making it up. Tawny thought she saw someone while we were in the hot tub the other day. We think he returned last night. This morning Grace and I checked the wooden fence and found screws missing at the bottom of two slats. The screws at the top were loose so the slats could move. It appears someone is slipping onto the property using the fence and making his escape the same way."

Arden's brows were still tightly knit together. "Elaina, it's normal to feel insecure when there isn't a man around, but a stalker?" The disbelief in his tone had changed to 'get real'.

"You think this is about me being insecure?" Elaina's anger increased. She fisted her hands and laid them on the table. "I had a feeling you wouldn't believe me. In your eyes I'm a drama queen."

What was left of Arden's easy-going demeanor fled the scene and his blue eyes turned a shade darker. "I called you that *one* time." His phone buzzed with another message. This time he let it go without checking it. "You said Tawny *thought* she saw someone. You *think* he returned last night." He scoffed. "Have you notified the authorities?"

"No." It was a half-truth. She'd secretly notified a high school friend, Tim Smith, who was a Special Deputy affiliated with the Sheriff's Department. While his position was voluntary, non-compensated, and usually only needed for special functions, he was trained in all areas of law enforcement. Elaina had called him after the first incident. They had a lengthy discussion and Tim urged her to file a report. Elaina wanted to stay low-key on this for the sake of her business and Arden's. She'd put Tim in a precarious position by sharing the information but tying his hands on the matter. When he asked why she contacted him if she wasn't going to let him proceed with protection, she'd simply shrugged. "We don't have any hard evidence, Arden. And I wanted to get your opinion first."

Arden tugged at the collar of his starched white shirt. "You should call the cops. Have them take a look at the fence. You're still using the home security system, aren't you?"

"When I remember to turn it on, I use it. There are four of us going in and out so much it's easy to forget." Elaina prepared herself for a lecture. "Before you tell me to stop being a ditz, I want you to know I don't feel as though we're in danger. Neither do the other girls. We think it's a case of snooping rather than stalking-stalking." She sighed. "It's just that with the gossip..."

"What gossip?"

"About you and me."

Arden bit into a cracker and made an annoyed face at the crumbs that fell onto the table. He took the time to brush them into the cracker basket. "People are always going to talk, Elaina. When they get bored with their pathetic existence, they dissect someone else's."

"I'm not talking about our divorce."

Janine came to the table with a pot of coffee.

Elaina flipped her cup upright so it could be filled. Arden made Janine flip his cup.

"Your food will be ready in a few minutes."

Elaina smiled. "Great. I'm starving."

Arden tapped the table until Janine walked away. "Are they ragging on me because I put my house up for sale?" His snicker was filled with disdain.

"Your house is the least of the gossip."

"What are they saying?"

Things were going smoothly between them but it was still emotionally draining to be in this man's company. Elaina only had herself to blame for the discomfort. She was the one who arranged the meeting. "Let me lay it out for you. I'm sleeping with more than one guy at a time and you're close to being penniless because of bad financial decisions."

Expecting Arden's jaw to drop open and his eyes to bulge, she was baffled when he just sat there with little to no change in his expression. "Say what?"

Elaina wouldn't repeat the rubbish.

"I knew you were involved with a truck driver but I..."

"Don't go there or so help me I'll give you a bloody nose."

Arden expelled an arduous sigh. "I know you don't frolic between the sheets with more than one guy. Anyone worth their salt knows it too. Regarding my monetary well-being, let me just say I'm better off now than before we split."

Elaina couldn't believe his calm and nonchalance. That was so unlike him. He did say he was trying to change, but real change took time and effort, and it was never this drastic. "You're not angry or concerned that someone is out to give us black eyes?"

"I'm offended but not surprised." Arden propped his elbows on the table and steepled his fingers. "When you're successful not everyone is happy for you. In fact, some of my so-called friends would throw a party if the rumors were true. They'd drink to my demise. I'm not happy though that someone's trying to wreck your good name." He sifted air through his teeth, the only real indication he might be upset. "As cockeyed as this might sound, I'm wondering if the attempt to tarnish you is just another way to mess with me."

"And the stalker?"

"He's probably part of the package deal to make me sweat...through you." Arden wrapped his hand around Elaina's and stroked her skin with his thumb. "You really should talk to the police." He released her hand to dig for his phone. "I'll make the call for you."

Elaina felt a warm fluttering in her chest from his concern, but her brain urged caution. Arden had gone from thinking she was insecure to worrying about her safety in a matter of minutes. "Don't. If you call 9-1-1 they'll send a squad with lights flashing and sirens blaring. The media will have a field day. I don't think either of us wants that kind of negative publicity."

"You shouldn't have to put up with a mangy creep lurking about, 'Laney."

Holy Mother of Pearl, Arden hadn't called her 'Laney in forever.

"Like I said, we don't fear for our safety. Besides, the three women I live with have vowed to kick the guy in the peaches when we catch him."

"As tough as you think you are, you don't want to take on a lunatic." He snickered. "The peaches?" Arden chuckled but stifled the mirth when two older ladies sat at the table behind Elaina. "You have such a casual approach to, well, just about everything. Therein lay the difference between us." He tightened the knot in his tie. "Money makes my world turn. I enjoy the perks that come with wealth. Armani suits and Christian Dior sunglasses are in my wheelhouse. My vacation destinations include Paris, Santorini, and St. Bart's. You, on the other hand, don't lust after wealth or its benefits. You're content to commune with three strangers and drink wine while wearing sweat pants. We're so far apart in who we are, and what we want out of life."

All this soul-baring from Arden was incredible. It's as though he woke up this morning and had a giant epiphany. He kept diverting the discussion with his striking realizations. "Designer clothes and fancy vacations are great but I just want to be happy."

Arden took her hand again. "Marriage didn't work for us but that doesn't mean we can't spend time together." He lifted an eyebrow without the usual cockiness. "An occasional dinner or tropical getaway wouldn't hurt either of us." He put a finger across her lips as though he anticipated a rejection.

Elaina's brain was in a quandary, trying to make sense of this somewhat-gentler adaptation of the man she'd once loved and grew to loathe. She wouldn't fool herself into thinking his callous edge was completely gone, but the fact remained, it was no longer brutally sharp and pointy.

Janine brought their food and refilled their coffee cups.

Arden grimaced at the plates of grilled chicken salad and looked at Elaina. "Old habits die hard, 'Laney." In front of Janine he apologized. "I should've given you the opportunity to choose what you'd like to eat."

Elaina's heart did a ridiculous somersault in her chest. Dammit.

Chapter Thirteen

~ Start the freaking blender! ~

"I'm a free woman for three whole days. To celebrate, we're going to Bernard's Nightclub to drink, dance, and raise a little hell." Tawny stood at the sink and guzzled a glass of water. "We'll call Steph when we get there."

"We should stay home and book our flights to Italy." Grace sat at the kitchen table with her laptop. "We have to make a list of things to take along." She put a hand on her forehead. "I need a dress. I've been searching for something subtle yet elegant but nothing has called my name. What's the weather like this time of year in Italy? Do I need a wrap? Dang. I forgot to ask Cody if it'll be an outdoor wedding or held in a chapel."

"He's a guy. They assume we know what to do. The good news is we have time to pump him for details." Elaina massaged Grace's shoulders. "Take a deep breath. This doesn't have to overwhelm you. We'll help you find something to wear regardless where it will be held. Won't we, Tawn'?"

"You know it. After you get off of work tomorrow,

we'll head to the mall."

Grace blinked up at them. "The last time we went to the mall together we were shopping for swimsuits. Wasn't that a hoot? You went gaga over the guy at the cash register in Macy's."

"He was cute."

"He had big ears."

The humor had a calming effect, not only on Grace who relaxed under Elaina's fingertips, but also on Elaina. She was relieved to be in their company versus Arden's. Before they parted earlier, he'd kissed her. In the café. In front of God and at least a dozen people. He'd pulled her up and out of her chair and into his arms. He'd laid a lip-lock on her that spiked her pulse and turned her legs to jelly. The kiss shouldn't have been a huge shock, but frankly, it might've been the biggest one since he'd proposed all those years ago.

"What was Big Ears name?" Grace asked, drawing Elaina from her thoughts.

"Dirk," Elaina said without having to wrack her brain. That particular day had been outrageous and laugh-out-loud funny. It had been a day of warmth and bonding. The memories would forever be etched in her mind. "Dirk blushed when we teased him and you blushed when he called you Tawny P. Westerfield. Steph asked what the P stood for and you said precious."

"That's because I am."

"Yes you are. What does the P really stand for?" Elaina asked.

"Pia."

"Doubtful," Grace stated.

"Would I lie to you?"

"Uh huh."

"You wound me."

"No I don't. Your middle name isn't Pia. Not that it's a bad name but it doesn't flow well with Tawny."

"I'm telling you it's Pia."

"We'll know for sure when your new passport comes."

Tawny groaned. "I paid extra for it to get here on time. What if it doesn't?"

"It'll be here. In the meantime, let's get to Bernard's. I'm in dire need of a mega-size glass of wine."

"Because?"

"I had lunch with Arden."

* * *

"What's that noise?" Steph asked.

"You mean the thing that sounds like rocks being chopped up in a blender? Oh that's some guy trying to sing *Eye of the Tiger*." Tawny and Elaina fist-bumped.

Steph laughed. "Where are you?"

"At Bernard's, for some dancing and wine therapy. Had we known ahead of time it was karaoke night I would've had a hard time talking Elaina and Grace into coming along. I was aided by the fact that Grace is *still* a wreck about Italy and Arden is *still* toying with Elaina. FYI, my boss *still* despises me. So we're primed and ready to consume an exorbitant amount of wine."

"How's Arden messing with you, Elaina?" Steph asked.

"By being nice. I can't handle it. I can from anybody else, not him. He kissed me and I'm not sure if I should throw up or let it happen again."

Tawny gasped. "No wonder you're in a funk. You left out a big part of the story, missy."

Elaina ran a finger around the rim of her glass. "I left out more than one part."

"I can't hear you. Those rocks being blended is making it hard for me to latch onto the juicy details."

"You haven't missed much. It seems Elaina's been holding out on us."

Steph was eager for information. "Walk us through what happened."

"I'd rather not, especially here."

"Don't make me nag."

"Stephhh."

"Elainaaa."

With monumental reluctance Elaina spilled her guts. "Arden was so freaking nice today I should be in a sugar-coma. He kept touching me." She handed Tawny her drink so she could close her eyes and lace her fingers behind her neck so her elbows jutted out. In those few seconds with the world shut out her heart took her through a gamut of emotions. She wanted to call Arden and tell him to stay away. She also wanted to ask if she could come over. She wanted to sleep with him. She wanted to delete his number from her phone. She wanted... Elaina opened her eyes. She preferred the madness of the nightclub over the things going on in her head. "He wants us to have an occasional dinner and to vacation together."

Tawny offered her opinion. "He might want those things but that's not what he's truly after."

"I know. He wants me to be his bootie call."

"Probably. But that's still not the ultimate prize. No offense."

Elaina pushed Tawny with her forearm. "None taken." The rocks in the blender combined with rocky thoughts tumbling around in her brain made it difficult to think. "What *is* the ultimate prize?"

"Man he's proficient at distracting you. The thing he's been badgering you about is the ultimate prize."

"The house."

"Booyah."

"I'd tell you to run, but I'm a good one to talk," Steph said. "I ran to Maine to please my man. Speaking of which, Mr. and Mrs. Kirby have flipped a switch or something. They went out of their way to be kind today. Jack, on the other hand, was in a foul mood. He was as stiff as a board and wouldn't look at anyone, including me. A few times he started to say something but Georgia kept interrupting. When he took me back to the hotel, I asked him about it and he clammed up. Ugh. It's been two-steps-forward, three-steps-back. But hey, I made headway with his parents. I'm chalking the day up as a win."

Grace interjected her two-cents. "Maybe Jack hasn't fully adjusted to the move."

"He seems like a wussy boy to me."

Elaina gave Tawny a pointed look.

Tawny simulated innocence. "What?"

"I hate to admit it, Tawn', but I'm starting to think the same thing." Steph didn't seem saddened by the conclusion.

Tawny lightened the discussion. "Oh. My. Gosh. You should hear the gal butchering *Love Shack* by the B-52's."

"I wish I was there with you. Since I'm not, enjoy the music and have a drink for me."

"Keep us posted about wussy boy and his strange family," Tawny quipped.

Again Elaina gave Tawny *the look* which she ignored.

"Yikes. The woman must've swallowed a parrot with a husky squawker." Tawny held the phone up for Steph to hear.

"I doubt we could do better," Elaina said in support of the blonde who was shamelessly belting out the lyrics even though she was out of time with the music.

Tawny's eyes twinkled. "Challenge accepted."

Elaina wagged her finger. "That wasn't a challenge." She changed the subject. "We booked the flights, Steph. We couldn't wait for you to come home. We had to book them now. If we held off any longer, the price would've been outrageous."

"Did you book one for me?"

"We did."

"I haven't cashed in my ring so I don't have the money to pay you back. And my boss called this morning threatening to fire me if I don't show my face in the office soon. As much as I want to go to Italy, it may not happen. Sorry, Grace."

Grace's face fell but she turned so Steph wouldn't see.

She'd been an emotional wreck since Cody made the marriage announcement. Elaina feared Grace was on the verge of some serious tears now that Steph might not be able to attend. Grace coughed and twisted back around with a half-smile. "We'll see how things play out, Steph. Get your butt home. I miss you."

Elaina was glad for the commotion of a new song. The woman with the microphone was doing a great job singing *You're So Vain* by Carly Simon. "She's impressive."

Tawny scoffed. "Don't flatter the competition."

* * *

Tawny cupped her mouth and shouted, "Look who's here." To heighten the embarrassment she pointed. The nightclub was dimly lit for atmosphere but there was enough lighting for safety and to illuminate a memorable face.

Grace knocked Tawny's hand down. "Could you be any more obvious?"

Elaina's gaze zipped to where Officer T. Marley sat drinking a draft beer. Dressed in a green golf shirt, he was off duty and staring in their direction; more specifically, his eyes were all over Grace. "Wave to let him know it's okay to approach."

"Dalton and I aren't officially over."

Tawny raised and lowered her eyebrows impishly. "Officer Marley has access to handcuffs. Just saying."

Grace poked Tawny in the ribs with her elbow. "I do love a man in uniform but I'm not into handcuffs."

"How do you know? Weren't you the one who was all gung-ho to try something different? You put purple streaks in your hair and suggested we get nipple rings and tattoos."

Grace tried to hide a laugh but her body shook, giving her away. "How exactly does one use handcuffs?"

"Let your imagination guide you."

Elaina slapped a hand over her eyes. "I'm trying not to get a visual."

Tawny gave Grace a playful push forward. "Go hit on Officer T. Marley or we're going to sing karaoke. Your choice. One or the other will happen."

"It must be hook-up night." In a more tactful manner than Tawny, Elaina quietly said, "Grady's here."

"Get out of town."

"I'm not joking. He's sitting alone, four tables over from Officer Marley."

Tawny followed Elaina's line of vision and dropped an expletive. "The world is coming to an end. I should fall to my knees and ask forgiveness for my sins, because life as we know it is over."

"Because Grady's seldom in a nightclub?"

"He isn't into nightclubs or nightlife of any kind unless it involves watching TV until the wee hours of the morning."

"The world isn't coming to an end just yet. The zombie apocalypse hasn't begun either. And your ex is gracing the nightclub with his presence." Elaina put an arm around Tawny. "Do you think he's trolling? Or is he here for you?"

"Trolling. Definitely. He's probably just as surprised to see me as I am to see him."

"He doesn't look surprised. He looks like he wants to devour you."

"Ick. Double ick. Triple ick."

Tawny could say ick a hundred times but she wouldn't convince Elaina she meant it. The second Tawn' had seen Grady she struck a sexy pose – shoulders pulled back, torpedo boobs thrust high. The corners of her mouth had dimpled into a come-and-get-me smile. Tawny might not be aware, but she was ready to engage her ex. Grace was in similar form with regards to Officer Marley. Elaina didn't want to be a third wheel. "I have to pee. If by chance things work out the way I think they're going to and you gals decide to leave, text me so I don't worry about you."

"Yes, Mom." Tawny winked and headed toward Grady.

Grace tucked a wayward wisp of hair behind her ear and wet her lips with her tongue. Her gaze was locked with Officer Marley's. "I don't want to ditch you, Elaina."

"I'm a big girl. Just be safe." Elaina giggled. "And don't lose the key to the handcuffs."

Grace covered her mouth to deaden a squeal of delight and adventure. She slinked away with a soft sway of her hips.

Elaina shook her head, conscious that being part of a four hussy homestead filled most of the void in their lives but there would be times when they'd be overtaken by hormones and a need for intimacy. Earlier, lust for Arden had surged in her to the point she would've gone skinny dipping with him again. Good thing it was autumn and they'd get hypothermia if they jumped in the water.

A whisper beside her ear made Elaina do a slow turn. "Tim Smith," she said, feeling the need to use his last name.

"In the flesh."

The DJ who'd been manning the music table announced he'd be taking a small break to burn one outside. "Freshen your drinks or dance cheek to cheek with someone special. I'll be back in twenty." He slipped in a CD with music to last until he returned. The timeless classic, *Lady in Red* by Chris De Burgh, filled the club.

"Hey, I'm special. Let's dance cheek to cheek." Tim grinned.

"You're special all right. A special-Special who'd have to sleep on the couch if his wife found out he danced with a former classmate. Besides, I'm not wearing red." Elaina referred to her black silky blouse by pulling at the material.

"I should've asked you out when we were in high school."

"But ya didn't." Elaina gave him a friendly shoulder-bump. "Where is the lovely Mrs. Smith?"

"With her friends, at a women's retreat in California. I'm here with the husbands they left behind. Since you're thwarting my pretend advances, let's talk about the skulking snoop. Anything new to report?"

"Honestly, Tim, I don't stay home long enough to know. Arden insisted I set the security alarm when I leave so that happened tonight."

Tim nodded. "Good idea. If you have a security system, you should use it. I've been thinking about why you didn't go to the police."

"I told you, I don't want the negative attention."

"That may be true, but it's not the only reason. Here's my take on things – you already know who's doing it and what their end game is. That's why you're not quaking in your boots like most women would be if they had a stalker. You involved me because I'm an additional pair of eyes and I'll be discreet."

Elaina ran a finger over her eyebrow and dropped her gaze to the floor.

"Am I right?"

"Special Deputy Timothy Smith, you're brill'. I'm 99.9% certain I know who's toying with me and their motive. And yes, I trust you. We never had chemistry but we've been friends for a lot of years and I know if I need you, you'll have my back."

"That's what friends are for, Elaina."

She nodded. He nodded. And the music changed from slow and romantic to fast and crazy.

"Care to do the chicken dance? I won't get in trouble with the wife if I'm flapping my arms and acting like a bird-brain."

"You're on."

One chicken dance and a glass of sangria later, the disc jockey was back.

"Let's get this party started again." A few whistles and one "woohoo" indicated the audience was geared up for more off-key madness. The DJ thumbed through the stack of cards filled out by those willing to engage in a little blender action for the sake of entertainment. He thudded the microphone a few more times to get and keep everyone's attention. "Next up, we have Tawny, Grace, and Elaina. They'll be singing *We Are Family* by Sister Sledge."

"No they won't," rolled off Elaina's tongue. Her head zipped around the establishment that was possibly twenty people shy of being in violation of the fire code for capacity. The red letters of the Exit sign beckoned. Two steps toward the door, she was body-blocked. "I'm not singing." She tried to maneuver past Grace, only to be blocked a second time by Tawny.

"Grace, shouldn't you be making googley eyes at Officer Ted? And Tawny, your ex foamed at the mouth the second he saw you. Why are you two bugging me when you can be over there smooching on your men?"

"Officer Ted isn't my man. He's yummy but I'm not feeling it."

"Try harder, Grace."

"Piss poor advice, if you ask me."

"Grady isn't my man either. He used to be. He isn't now. Don't tell me to try harder or I'll put you in a headlock," Tawny threatened. "As it turns out, he met someone online and they're supposed to meet in person for the first time tonight. He told me to go away. I'm such a meanie. I stayed there until he begged me to leave."

Grace took one of Elaina's arms, Tawny took the other. They pulled her toward the table with the karaoke machine. She resisted with a tug that sent her reeling into none other than Officer T. Marley, who guided her back to Grace.

They fast became a spectacle. The more Elaina resisted, the more the audience got involved. "Make her sing. Make her sing," bounced off the ceiling and walls. One rogue heckler improvised. "Make her sing by herself."

Elaina wasn't the *Lady in Red* earlier but she was bright red now. Her cheeks flamed so hot she anticipated blisters. She squinted with reproach at her friends. "I hate you guys."

Grace contradicted the claim. "You love us."

Elaina gave one last yank and got nowhere. "Start the freaking blender."

Chapter Fourteen

~ *Saturated with sangria!* ~

Tawny climbed into the backseat of Ted Marley's GMC Acadia. "That was epic! Wasn't that epic, Officer Ted?" She hiccupped then laughed. "I may have had too much sangria."

Ted didn't give his opinion. Smart man.

"I didn't have *enough* sangria." Elaina was still sweating and her heart-rate hadn't settled down. The three of them managed to destroy what had once been a great song.

"We could get a recording contract." Grace pushed against Elaina in an effort to get her to move over so she could get in.

"People applauded but it wasn't because we were good. They clapped because we finally stopped making their ears hurt." Elaina used her elbow to keep Grace from getting in the backseat. "Up front, Grace. You're riding shotgun."

Grace narrowed her eyes. "The big get-even?"

Elaina mumbled, "Oh yeah."

Tawny took over. "Officer Ted doesn't bite hard. Do

you, Ted?" Not leaving room for him to answer she also purred and said he smelled nice. "Thank you for taking our sorry butts home. We intended to drink just enough to take the edge off a crappy day. As you can see we overdid it a little." And then she delivered a zinger. "Grace thinks you're hot."

Grace tried to shush Tawny. "Stop. Just stop."

In their slightly inebriated state, everything seemed magnified and funny. Elaina pealed with laughter.

Grace joined Ted in the front and peered through the opening in the headrest. "I'll make you pay."

Tawny leaned forward so she could speak over Ted' shoulder. "Do you keep a set of handcuffs handy? I'm asking for a friend."

Ted ignored the question. Again, wise man.

"You wouldn't also happen to have a roll of duct tape, would you?" Grace asked.

"There might be one in the trunk. Why?"

"Because she's going to yap all the way home and we can put a stop to it."

"Ladies, don't make me tase you." Ted guffawed. He cleared his throat when Grace crossed her arms. "There's no need for duct tape or a taser. Trust me, I've heard a lot worse coming from the backseat of my cruiser." He drove from the nightclub parking lot onto North Street.

"You've never ridden with Tawny Precious Westerfield."

Tawny snorted. "I told you, it's Pia."

"It doesn't roll off the tongue, which means it's an alias." Grace tapped Ted's arm. "Could you run a background check on one Tawny Pia Westerfield? If you come up empty we could have a notorious criminal on our hands."

Ted's mouth curved into a grin. "I might have to put that duct tape to good use after all."

"Ert!"

Ted's amusement was replaced by a look of confusion. "Ert?"

"It's condensed sarcasm, Teddy. Grace made it up. She didn't start saying it until we moved in together. Between you and me, she's very odd."

"See what I have to put up with? Day in and day out. Talk. Talk. Talk." Grace used her hands to mimic Tawny speaking.

Elaina raised her eyebrows at Tawny. "Grace hasn't shut her pie hole since we got in the car."

Tawny reached around the headrest to smooth her hands over Officer Ted's shoulders. "You didn't answer my question. On a scale of one to ten, how was our singing?"

"A definite ten."

"I didn't ask you how I look, I asked how we sang?"

"You didn't give me the address, Grace."

"Good dodge, Officer T. Marley."

He chuckled again.

Grace rattled off the street name and house number using a bedroom voice, which Elaina and Tawny camped onto right away and teased her about it until Ted pulled into their driveway.

"I was going to take these yahoos to my son's wedding

in Italy but they'll misbehave so badly we'll get thrown out of the country." Grace batted her eyelashes. "Would you like to go with me, Officer Ted?"

"It's just Ted." He put the car in park. "I should probably stay in Cherry Ridge and track down people who use aliases."

"See, Tawn? He thinks you're hiding something too."

When they were out of the car and standing on the sidewalk Grace blew him a kiss. "Thanks for being our taxi, just-Ted."

"Anytime, ladies."

Tawny mentioned the bank where Grace worked. "Stop in and see her anytime."

Ted didn't respond with a "maybe" or an "okay" or anything. He merely waved as he put the car in reverse.

"That's the last I'll see of just-Ted, unless he nabs me for speeding."

* * *

Elaina sat at the kitchen table with a strong cup of coffee, waiting for the other two Sledge-sister wannabes to make an appearance. She replayed the video Arden had sent at the crack of dawn with the message, 'What's gotten into you?' She groaned and asked herself the same question. Someone had recorded their musical atrocity and uploaded it to YouTube. Whoever produced the video shared it with Arden.

Stony padded into the kitchen and dropped at her feet. Lula had yet to make an appearance.

Taking her first sip of piping hot coffee, Elaina seared a few hundred taste buds off her tongue. She flinched and spilled coffee on the table when another text message pinged on arrival.

I keep watching that ridiculous video. I'm not impressed, Elaina. Those women you're living with are a bad influence. You no longer dress for success. At the restaurant yesterday you showed up in yoga pants with an extra-long shirt. I didn't say anything because I didn't want to fight. You said people are talking about you, about us. Well, you quite possibly are sending out a subliminal invitation to rip us apart with your sloppy attire and careless behavior.

"I'm not in the mood, Arden." She wouldn't waste time explaining that last night just sort of happened, because he'd go into a lengthy rant about business people being held to a higher standard. Tapping her phone, she winced and typed a reply. *I had the morning shift yesterday; hence the attire was appropriate as your suit was for your job. Stop ragging on me about my behavior. I had fun last night.* Embarrassment aside, she'd had a blast. *I don't have to justify why I do what I do, especially to the guy I'm no longer married to. In order to have a relationship with me, you'll have to take me as I am. Or not.*

Grace stumbled into the kitchen looking like she'd pulled an all-nighter. "Remind me how old I am."

"You'll be forty-two on Valentine's Day."

Grace stretched her neck from side to side and read her own pedigree. "You'll be forty-two, Grace Vivian Cordray. Forty-two." She carefully lowered herself onto a chair. "At the nightclub, I saw some gals I work with.

I'm sure they were more than amused by our theatrics and I can say with absolute certainty I'll be the talk of the bank."

"Let me reiterate – it wasn't my idea. You and Tawn' went bonkers and decided we'd be good at karaoke. We weren't." Elaina hit play on her phone. "Enjoy."

Stony raised his head at the grating noise.

Grace's light complexion paled even more. "If that isn't a reality check, I don't know what is. We sound like three cats that got their tales caught in a rat trap." She pulled up off the chair. "I don't know about you, but I'm going upstairs to pack."

"For the trip."

"No. Because we have to move."

"It's tough to see the humor in that video, but look closely." Elaina played it again. "As horrible as it is, we're smiling. Pure gold, don't ya think? We're not moving. We're going to go to work and face the music."

"Nice play on words."

"What's a nice play on words?"

"Why are you up? It's your day off, Tawn'."

"I don't have a snooze button on my internal clock." Tawny poured a cup of coffee and shuffled to the back door where her Crocs sat on a rug. Above the rug was a white shelf with a row of hooks. She took the first jacket, which happened to be Grace's. "It's still dark, Stoneman, but I need a breath of fresh air and so do you." Her shoulders rose with an inhale and fell with an exhale. "After a top night on the town, I need a cigarette." She fumbled in the pocket. "Ugh." She took off Grace's jacket and found hers.

"Could you use some harmonious pleasure before you proceed outside?"

Tawny's brows bumped together. "I don't want an overload of stimulation or I won't be able to go back to sleep. Today I'm all about laundry, cleaning the bathrooms, and hugging my pillow."

"Hug this." Elaina played the video and turned the volume up to the highest setting.

* * *

One of the gym members leaned over the desk. "Could I interest you in one of my handmade wreaths?"

Elaina had been preparing the days' receipts to be deposited in the bank. "Sure, Rita. Show me what you've got."

"Awesome. I'll be right back. They're in my car."

While Elaina waited, she recounted the money and put it a zippered pouch. New membership had been sluggish the last few months. She'd either have to lower the price for people to join or think of something else to make folks take notice. Businesses had to be creative to stay competitive. Maybe a two-for-one special would do the trick. Or a free week would be enough enticement to rack up new members.

Rita returned with a suitcase on wheels. "Don't you just love autumn," she said cheerily.

"I do. There's nothing better than the orange hues at sunset or a pot of hearty soup smelling up the house."

"Or rag-wreaths on your front door." Rita held one up that looked like a giant sunflower. She waited for Elaina's nod of approval.

"It's nice."

"How about this one?" It was made of brown burlap with an orange satin ribbon interspersed between the puffs of material. A subtle chocolate bow was wired at the bottom.

"That's the one. Actually, I'll take two; one for the house and one for the gym."

"Are you sure you want two? They're thirty-five dollars each."

Elaina examined the wreath close-up. "They're well made. I don't have a lot of decorations for autumn, or really for any of the seasons."

"Why not?"

"It's a long story involving an ogre who thought they were a waste of time and money."

Rita looked perplexed.

"My ex hated the stuff. Now I can decorate to my heart's content." Elaina ran her fingertips over the silk ribbon. "You're not asking enough for these."

Rita came around the desk and gave Elaina a hug. "Thank you so much."

"You're welcome." Elaina wasn't sure the purchase was worthy of a hug but she'd never turn one down.

Rita returned to the suitcase. "Our church is making and selling them to raise money for a needy family of eight who's part of our congregation. They moved here from the southern part of the state after the dad lost his job making television screens. The plant he worked in moved overseas and now they're having a rough go of things, especially the kids."

Elaina's heart clenched. "I love kids. I wish I would've been able to have a few of my own." She opened a drawer to retrieve her purse. "I'm going to buy all the wreaths."

Rita's eyes grew in size. "You don't have to do that."

"I want to. Life has thrown me a few curves, but I've never had to struggle for the necessities."

Elaina counted twelve wreaths in all and tallied the cost. She bumped the total up to seven hundred dollars and wrote the check.

Rita's eyes watered. "This is beyond kind, Elaina."

"We have to help one another."

Rita's voice cracked with emotion. "We do." She turned the check over a couple of times with a thoughtful look in her eyes. "I'll say a prayer for you."

"That would be nice."

"Is there anything you'd like for me to pray for?"

"World peace. An end to hunger. No one losing their job. The list is long."

"I pray for those things anyway. What do you need specifically in your life?"

Elaina clicked the pen a couple of times. "You could send up a prayer for me to make good choices."

"Consider it done." Rita rushed around the desk again and gave Elaina another hug. "Be blessed, my friend."

* * *

Grace spun the rack of elegant dresses. "I can't see myself in any of these."

Tawny held up a black, stretchy form-fitting dress with a dangerously low neckline. "This one is totally you."

"That's totally me?" Grace scoffed. "I'm the mother of the groom. I shouldn't look hot at my son's wedding."

"Afraid you'll upstage the bride?"

Grace made mean eyes at Tawny. "I can't wait until you're in my shoes. You'll be tearing your hair out trying to fit those puppies," she pointed to Tawny's abundant chest, "into something motherly." She moaned. "If my cells weren't still saturated with sangria I'd suggest we pop over to the bar across the street."

Elaina placed a hand on Grace's shoulder. "No adult beverages until we find a dress that will wow the Italians." She traipsed to a clearance rack and sorted through the thick wall of clothing. A champagne-colored, below-the-knee dress with a flowing jacket all but jumped out at her. It was stylish and elegant, and the material glittered without being gaudy. "Maybe this one?" She wiggled the price tag. "It's fifty-percent off."

Grace's mouth dropped open for a second. "Do they have one in size ten?"

Elaina circled the rack. "You're in luck."

Grace laid the fabric against her arm. "Does the color make me look washed out?"

"Not at all." Tawny inspected the dress more closely. "It complements your skin tone."

Elaina suggested she try it on to know for sure.

"After you see how great it looks let's head to the jewelry counter. We passed it earlier and I happened to see a strand of champagne pearls."

Grace hugged the dress. "This may sound corny but it's a special moment. I have one child which means I'm only going to buy a mother-of-the-groom dress once. I'm glad you're here to share it with me. I wish Steph was here too."

"She can be." Tawny pressed the FaceTime app on her phone. The sound of the awesome technology connecting Cherry Ridge with Portland, Maine brought a smile.

Steph's face came into view. "My friends!"

"Stephanie Irene Mathews, Grace would like your opinion."

Steph leaned close to the screen making her eyes and nose look huge. "On getting a tongue ring or vulture tattoo? My opinion is noooooo. Don't do it."

"Ha. Ha. Keep your day job. Wait. Your day job is to assist a hundred-miles-an-hour executive. Nix the day job and write that cook book." Grace bunched her face into an elfin grin. "Sorry. I'm supposed to be seeking an opinion, not giving one."

Steph whispered, "Since Jack drops me off at the hotel every night around eight, I have time to kill before I go to sleep. I've been watching cooking shows and getting ideas. I've started a file folder with recipes that may someday become...wait for it...a cookbook."

Elaina, Grace, and Tawny cheered.

Tawny moved the phone away from Grace. "That's awesome, Steph. Why are you whispering?"

"I don't want Jack to know about the cookbook."

"I see. Actually, I don't. I guess it's a conversation we can have when you get home. Grace wants to show you something."

While Tawny and Grace fussed over the dress, Elaina keyed on that tidbit of information about Jack, and determined Maine wouldn't become Steph's permanent address after all. She was torn for being happy that Steph would reside in Ohio and sad that her friend hadn't found love.

Steph gave Grace a nod of approval regarding the dress. "The flights are a done deal. Our passports are up to snuff. Mostly up to snuff. Tawny's still waiting for hers, but it's on the way. You have your dress. What about lodging?"

"Isabella's parents have a guest bungalow behind their home. They've offered it to us. It's small but we can make it work. A week from tomorrow we'll be flying across the Atlantic to the Mediterranean." Grace steadied herself by holding onto the nearest clothes rack. "I hadn't thought of a gift for Cody and Isabella. Ugh. I feel lightheaded."

"Hold her upright, Elaina and Tawn'. We'll figure it out tomorrow night. Who's available to pick me up at the airport? Four-ish?"

Another round of squeals bounced around the Ladies department. They were mature women – although some might argue otherwise – who easily expressed their emotions no matter where they were.

Chapter Fifteen

~ A few tears with lobsters dangling from their ears! ~

"Bad news." Grace made a series of disgruntled noises in Ferdinand's backseat. "It looks like we won't be going to that Halloween party after all. Dalton has a horrendous sore throat. Truthfully, we've been so busy I forgot about the party."

"You should make Dalton some chicken soup." There was nothing better than chicken noodle soup when you were sick. Elaina's mom would add a few cloves of garlic to her soup. She'd said it might not kill the virus but the germs would have stinky breath. Elaina smiled fondly at the memory. Her mother had a quirky personality, just like Steph, Tawny, and Grace.

"Good idea, although I'll have to get Steph involved. If I'm left to my own devices it'll be soup from a can."

Tawny drummed the steering wheel with her thumbs. "We are so not culinary-inclined. I suppose it's the reason we've not had much luck with men."

Elaina flicked Tawny on the arm. "I disagree. The way

to a man's heart is NOT through his stomach. That's a theory women have passed down through the ages. Real men love their women for who they are, not what they can cook for him."

Tawny chortled. "I disagree with your disagreement. Men are wired different. They want a woman who's on the same level intellectually, but to keep them happy you have to be skilled in more than conversation. There are two areas where they insist on expertise. One is the kitchen. The other goes without saying."

"I respectfully disagree with your disagreement of Elaina's disagreement. Ha. Say that three times fast. Anyway, not all men are cut from the same cloth. Brince didn't mind my lack of kitchen talent. Some nights we had hot dogs with a side of macaroni and cheese that came from a box. And to be honest, I was no vamp in the bedroom. On the flip side, he didn't get an A every night either." Grace sighed. "I can only speak for myself. The reason I don't have a solid relationship with a man right now has nothing to do with my inability to be a gourmet chef. It's because deep down I don't want one. I thought I was ready to move on, but I'm not. I may go on the occasional date but I prefer the company and comfort of my besties."

Tawny parked Ferdinand in a space on the second floor of the parking garage at the Dayton International Airport and shut off the engine. "You were lucky to have a man like Brince. I knocked myself out trying to..." She paused. The faraway look in her brown orbs indicated some internal analysis was taking place. "My apron-wearing, apple-pie-making grandmas, great-grandmas, and great-great grandmas lived for their husbands. They didn't work outside the home. When they put in a twelve-hour shift it was to can green beans and apricots, make homemade bread, pressure cook meat, and iron everything they washed because nothing was made of polyester." A wicked smile curved the corners of her mouth. "I'm sure when they kicked off those orthopedic shoes and removed their hairnets they were hellions in bed too." She looked toward the sky. "Forgive me, Grandmas. Nothing personal. I'm just trying to make a point." She glanced at Elaina and then back at Grace. "I wasn't Julia Child in the kitchen but I made some tasty dishes from scratch. When it came to being amorous, let's just say I didn't win any blue ribbons. Don't get me wrong, I enjoy a good romp but not after I've been on my feet all day. My perfectionist husband wanted a perfect wife." Her giggle was laced with sarcasm. "I've developed a pattern of navigating to men who want specific things from me. When I don't deliver, they get pissy." She patted the dash. "I'm sticking with Ferdinand. He gives me unconditional love and I give him regular tune-ups. Rant over."

Elaina listened intently to what had been said and sifted through the wisdom as it applied to her relationship with Arden. He was the ultimate outdated version of the American male. His idea of a wife mirrored Grady's. He also wanted a faultless woman who could cook scrumptious meals, keep his castle spotless, fulfill his every fantasy in the bedroom, and be successful running her own business while making him look good in his business. She tried to be that person, but in his eyes she didn't measure up. He figuratively ripped the S from her chest and searched for a new superwoman. Elaina wasn't sure the woman existed who could live up to his requirements. But that was Arden. He was who he was and she was who she was. Their alliance didn't pan out and they were now free to forge a new one with whomever they wanted. Michael came close to being the type of man she could settle down with again, but he came with strings. At her age, most men did. Michael's strings had pulled him back home. "I'm going to explore and enjoy life before I give all my affection to one guy, no matter how good-looking or smooth-talking he might be. If you catch me swerving in that direction, take me by the shoulders and turn me around. In the meantime, let's embrace who we are or aren't and have a Halloween party with just the four of us."

Tawny seconded the proposal. "Tomorrow night, trick-or-treat begins at six o'clock and ends at seven. After the kiddies stop ringing the doorbell, let's put on our sweat pants, sip a little vino, and watch a movie. A bowl of candy corn is a must."

Grace placed her chin on the front seat. "Let's find a roadside stand on the way home and buy a pumpkin. Cody and I used to carve some gnarly-looking jack-o-lanterns in our day. They'd have fangs and we'd make one eye droop lower than the others. By the time Halloween came around he'd have drawn on an eye patch and blackened the fangs."

"We're going to have to find you an eye patch, Grace, for old times' sake. You could wear it when Cody escorts you to your seat in church."

Grace shook her head. "I'm a dork most of the time but for the wedding I have to be on my best behavior."

Tawny mocked with an eye roll. "Who's she kidding, Elaina?"

"This is important to Grace. Not only is she going to be on her best behavior, so are we. Capish?"

Tawny grumbled under her breath that they were a couple of stick-in-the-muds.

Elaina checked her watch. "Steph should be landing any minute. The three hussy homestead will be back to four." *As it should be.*

* * *

Tawny wasn't one to beat around the bush. "Did Jack sweeten up before you departed Maine?"

A smile engulfed Steph's face. "He did. On the way to the airport he apologized at least a hundred times. Okay, maybe not a hundred, but a lot. He walked me to the TSA security checkpoint and held me so tight I could barely breathe. He kissed me until we had to come up for air." She fanned herself. "That was probably the best kiss I've ever had. He said, 'Come back to me, Steph.'" She made a dreamy sound of contentment. "It took him a while to show his romantic side, but when he did it was awesome."

"So you *are* going to be a Mainiac maniac," Tawny probed.

"It sure looks that way." Steph talked a mile a minute. "I can't wait for you guys to come to Portland. It's awesome. In the short time I was there it spoke to my soul. I know that sounds a bit out there, but it's true. I felt at peace even when the Kirbys were being less-than-sweet." Excitement continued to pump out of her. "I brought gifts."

"Like what?" Tawny maneuvered off of Interstate 75 and onto an exit ramp.

"You can't wait?"

"I have to get gas, silly."

The moment Ferdinand came to rest at the gas station Steph hopped out of the car and rummaged through her suitcase. She came out with three plastic bags stuffed to the hilt. After they were all seated again, she passed out bottles of maple syrup, jars of cranberry relish, moose key chains, can coolers with pictures of Portland's Head Light House, and lobster earrings.

Elaina held the card holding the earrings up to her ear. "Steph, you're a treasure."

"I know, right."

Tawny took off her gold hoop earrings and replaced them with the lobsters. "These will go perfect with an eye patch." She looked in the rearview mirror at Grace. "Just saying."

"What about eye patches?"

Everybody seemed to talk at once. Grace explained about the pumpkins. Tawny mentioned the video of them singing. Elaina said they'd be leaving on Wednesday for Italy. And Steph asked for suggestions on how to tell her boss she was breaking up with him.

"Tawn', you should be on hand when I give him the news. He's going to need CPR."

"I've seen your boss. These lips aren't going anywhere near his."

"I think the method for giving CPR has been modified to just chest compressions so you don't have to put him in a lip-lock."

"Untrained bystanders should only provide Hands-Only CPR. I'm trained, which means..." Tawny shuddered with a goofy grin.

"You're such a drama queen, Westerfield."

"Yes I am, Mathews."

Grace mentioned that Tawny blew right by a farm that had a trailer heaping with pumpkins for sale.

"Want me to double-back?"

"Nah. We'll see another one."

"What are we doing?" Steph inquired.

"Buying things for our Halloween party."

"It's more of a girl's night than a party," Elaina clarified.

"You're in charge of the appetizers, Steph." Tawny told her she could make spooky eyeballs using deviled eggs, and mummies from hot dogs and crescent rolls."

"What are we? Nine?" Grace teased. "But we," she corrected, "I could use a pot of your famous chicken soup."

Elaina peeked over the top of the headrest. "Welcome home."

* * *

"Come with me. All of you," Grace pleaded.

"Scared to be alone with Dalton?" Tawny asked.

"No. It's just that it'll be easier to leave if you're with me."

Steph chimed in with, "What she means is that she doesn't want to mother him. When we get a cold, we buck up and go about our day. Guys tend to lay around in misery, worrying that they're one step away from pneumonia. Or maybe that was just Corbett. He was such a baby."

Grace rapped her knuckles on the door.

They expected Dalton to be dressed in pajama pants, with tufts of hair sticking out everywhere from having slept on the couch.

A thirty-something curly-haired brunette greeted them instead. "Hello. Can I help you?"

It was easy to see that she was as curious about them as they were about her.

Grace spared a questioning glance at Elaina before asking the girl if Dalton was there.

"He's, uh... Yes, he's here." She turned. "You have company."

"Tell whoever it is to come in." Dalton's usual warm voice creaked with rasp. When he laid eyes on Grace something akin to guilt washed across his expression. "I wasn't expecting you."

Grace smiled sweetly but the sugar didn't reach her

eyes. "I suppose not." She held up the stainless steel pot of soup. "Steph made you chicken soup to help your throat."

To their shock the brunette spouted that chicken soup doesn't cure a cold. "It's a myth."

Grace started to say something but Tawny crowded in front of her. "Nothing cures a cold, but chicken soup can help relieve the symptoms. Chicken has an amino acid that thins out mucus, which limits the amount of time the virus is in contact with your throat or nose."

"Are you a nurse?"

"Yessss. And you are?"

"Wondering why four women brought my boyfriend soup."

Tawny pressed her lips together and took a step back. "That'll teach me to butt ahead. You're up, Grace."

"No she isn't. I am." Steph moved around Grace. "You have a lot of nerve."

Grace tugged the back of Steph's fleece jacket. "I've got this." She handed Steph the pot of soup. "Dalton."

He sat up.

Elaina whispered, "Would you like some privacy?"

Grace squared her shoulders. "No. This won't take long." She walked to the couch and put a hand on Dalton's shoulder. "Things wouldn't have worked out for us anyway. I'm a terrible cook." At referencing yesterday's conversation, she slanted a smile at her friends.

Even though Grace said she didn't care for privacy, the three of them and Dalton's new squeeze relocated to the porch.

Elaina shoved her hands in her coat pockets and hummed.

Tawny moved a leaf back and forth with the tip of her ankle boots.

Steph repeatedly flicked the stainless steel pot with her fingernail.

The squeeze crossed her arms at her chest and glared past them.

Grace finally emerged. There were no tear stains streaking her makeup and she appeared remarkably chipper for someone who'd just kicked a guy to the curb.

The squeeze slipped back inside the house without a word.

"Well that was awkward," Elaina said for lack of something better to say.

Grace put an arm around Elaina's waist as they walked to Steph's Ford Escape. "Not for me. It was cathartic. I like Dalton but... Blah. Blah. Blah. Time for a new chapter in my life. I could really go for some Vitamin C and a bottle of hand sanitizer. Dalton hugged me goodbye and now I feel like I have germs crawling all over me. If he gets me sick I'll come back and clobber him. Head to the nearest dollar store, Steph."

"I know what we're having for supper." Steph stowed the pot of soup on the backseat between Grace and Tawny.

Elaina breathed a sigh of relief. Breaking things off with Dalton didn't appear to be a huge upheaval for Grace. She'd be fine. Until she got to Italy.

* * *

Steph backed out of Dalton's driveway and almost got sideswiped by a van. She slammed on the brakes, lurching the SUV and everyone in it, forward.

Tawny shrieked.

Elaina put the door handle in a death grip.

A four-letter word slipped from between Grace's lips.

"Where did he come from?" Steph's head moved rapidly from right to left a few times and eased carefully onto the roadway. "He wasn't there a minute ago."

"Apparently he was." Elaina tilted to catch Tawny's eye. "See? I told you her driving sucks. She's either on the gas or the brake, nothing in between. Remember when I texted you about her driving on our way home from the grocery a while back? You thought I was joking."

"It's not my strong point."

"If it makes you feel any better my night blindness is getting worse."

"Why would that make me feel better? It just tells me not to ride with you at night."

Elaina covered her face with her hand and spoke through her fingers. "Not my circus, not my monkeys."

"You tried that motto when we first met, then you asked us to move in." Tawny slapped her thigh and laughed.

With Steph at the wheel they made it to the dollar store in record time.

Grace took a basket. "I'm headed to Health and

Beauty Aids."

"We need a cart." Steph removed the basket from Grace's hand. "That thing won't hold Halloween decorations."

"We don't need any decorations. I have wreaths we can use; twelve to be exact. Make that eleven. I'm going to hang one up at the gym."

"You have eleven Halloween wreaths?" Grace pointed out they didn't have that many doors.

"They're autumn wreaths. We'll use a few and donate the rest to the nursing homes."

"Grace could wear the catwoman mask when we drop them off."

"We want to do something nice, not give the residents heart failure."

* * *

"It's October thirty-first. In four days we head to Rome. I'm not terrified of flying and the language barrier apparently is no biggie, but I'm scared shitless of my son getting married. I know he said not to worry but all kids say that."

Cody had sent an iMessage earlier on Grace's iPad with the following information and heartwarming/heart-wrenching note:

Mamma,

Ti amo e mi manchi. (I love and miss you)

Thank you for sending my birth certificate, baptismal and confirmation certificates. Everything is properly filed with Rome and the church. I had to go to the U.S. Embassy to obtain the Dichiarazione Giurata (affidavit) stating there's no legal impediment to me getting married. (i.e. I'm not divorced from someone else) From there I had to get an Atto Notorio, which is another declaration in addition to the Dichi-Guirata. Isabella, Karina, and I went to the town hall a couple of weeks ago and had to make a Declaration of Intention to Marry. Whew! Who knew getting hitched would be so complicated. I love her, Mom. I love Karina too. It's going to be weird being a husband and father but I know I'll do just fine because you and Dad showed me how marriage is supposed to go. While Dad won't be there in body to hear me declare my love for Isabella and Karina, I know he'll be there in spirit, holding your hand and urging you to be brave. It's hard to type this without crying. Guys aren't supposed to cry but when I think of how crushed I'd be without Isabella and Karina, it makes me understand how difficult it was (and still is) for you without Dad.

I've said it before but I'll say it again, I'm happy that you're with Elaina, Stephanie, and Tawny. They sound like amazing women and I can't wait to meet them in person.

Are you packed yet?

It might be helpful to learn a few Italian words on the long trip across the pond. I'm just a phone call away if you have any difficulty.

I'm counting the days, hours, and minutes until I can hug you and soak up some of that Mamma-warmth.

Your loving son,
Cody

Grace had shared the e-letter and all four of them hugged and cried like babies. Once they got the tears out of the way, Elaina smoothed Grace's bangs across her forehead. "It's going to be okay. He loves this girl and her child. He has everything ready. If he were my son, I'd be a wreck too. I'm sure it comes with the territory." She handed Grace a cup of chamomile tea. "This will help."

Grace put the tea to her lips for a taste. "I won't relax until I see the actual joy in his face."

Elaina decided on caffeine-free orange tea. She steeped the tea bag and added a few drops of honey to give it just a hint of sweetness. Her peripheral caught movement outside the kitchen window. "Son of a…" She bit back the last part of the exclamation for Grace's sake. Her friend was already a mess. If she made it known that someone was outside it might be the trigger for a full-blown meltdown.

Grace stretched to look around Elaina. "What's wrong?"

Elaina hated to lie but it was necessary. "Scalded my finger with hot water."

"Be careful. We can't risk any more injuries or it will make our jaunt across the ocean a bit tricky." Grace lifted her foot. "I'm glad it was a mild sprain and not a break. I feel a twinge of pain when I move it a certain way."

"You should prop it up and put a cold pack on it. Just to make sure you're good to go for the trip." Elaina took an ice pack from the freezer. "I'm going to take Stony on his last trip outside for the night. Tawn'," she hollered, "come with."

"Come with?" Tawny smirked when she came into the kitchen. "Scared of the dark?"

Grace said, "Ert," and carried her cup of tea into the living room. Elaina followed with the ice pack.

Steph was curled up on the couch, texting back and forth with Jack.

"We'll be back in a few minutes so don't start the movie." Elaina wanted to sound as normal as possible.

Back in the kitchen, at the patio doors, with Stony leashed and chomping at the bit to enjoy the cool outside air, Elaina typed "stalker" on her phone, showed it to Tawny and sent it out to Tim Smith.

Tawny frowned hard and dug into the pocket of her jacket. She produced a tube of lipstick. Pulling off the cap, she mouthed, "Pepper spray."

Elaina nodded and quietly informed Tawny she had a pocket-size flashlight.

Tawny held up a finger and stepped into the half-bath off the kitchen. When she returned she had an empty loose-knit, drawstring-style laundry bag.

Elaina put her hand palm-side up and quietly asked, "What?"

Tawny demonstrated pulling the bag over someone's head.

Okay then. Elaina tried not to convey with a smirk that there was a small chance they'd get the bag over the guy's head. Very small chance. "I'm about to lie through my teeth. Follow my lead," she whispered.

Armed with a lovable dog that would possibly lick the guy to death, a tube of pepper spray, a laundry bag, a flashlight, and a flimsy plan at best, they proceeded outdoors. Elaina still didn't feel as though she and Tawny were in danger because like Tim had suggested, she was more than certain she knew who the trespasser was and why he skulked in the shadows. She hoped Tim noticed the text though and understood he was needed at the four hussy homestead. If she was right about the intruder, it would be to their benefit to have an unbiased fifth party – Tim – to shore up their finding. Nothing said they'd be able to detain the trespasser long enough for Tim to get there but Elaina would try her damndest.

Elaina stepped into the darkness with Tawny on her heels. "Brr," she said, starting the dialogue of fibs. "It's freezing out here, but hey, it would be a great night to get in the hot tub...naked." She said an "ahhh" of pleasure. "I love the privacy of our backyard. We can misbehave all we want and no one's the wiser." Dang, she was laying it on thick but she wanted the guy to hear every word and to build the thrill for him.

Tawny didn't miss a beat. "In the light of day we're just four ordinary women. A gym owner. Nurse. Bank teller. And secretary. After dark, the ordinary goes away. I'm so glad I moved in with you, Elaina. I'm free to be me – the wild child my parents and ex-husband tried to tame."

"The three of you have given me courage to be me." Not a fib. It was the complete and utter truth. "Behind the lilac bush," she said under her breath, and continued to chat. "Arden held me down, not in a fun way. I couldn't laugh in public unless it was proper and lady-like. I had to be good all the freaking time. He'd go into cardiac arrest if he knew the things I did now. Whew! All his arteries would blow at once."

"He wanted a beautiful, submissive, stuffy spouse?"

"You got it."

Tawny forgot herself and started to mention Arden's mischief with being handsy with some of the women in the community. Elaina said a quiet yet staunch, "No." She wanted this fake discourse to be more about them and less about Arden.

Elaina guided Stony to the far side of the yard to keep him from discovering the prowler just yet. "This afternoon I ordered a few things online from Victoria's Secret."

"Ooooh," Tawny said in a sex-kitten voice, "do tell."

"I bought a black, see-through halter bralette. It's from their new high-neck collection. I'll be able to tease with it by wearing it under a V-neck sweater or button-up blouse." Elaina clicked her tongue. "It's sheer in the right places, if you know what I mean." She kept an eye pealed for movement. The guy was staying put. She tried to think of something to lure the snoop out in the open but she came up empty, so she went back to sexing things up. "I keep having this dream where I'm making love with this guy on the deck of a boat with a news helicopter flying overhead."

"Holy mackerel, woman, you have exhibitionist tendencies." Tawny laughed. "Who's the guy?"

"I don't know. I can't see his face but I know he's blond and a real hunk. What do you think it means?"

Stony had hiked his leg on six trees so far. Pretty soon he was going to run out of water.

Elaina took a lengthy and noisy inhale. "I love autumn air. It's so clean and crisp."

"I actually like the smell of burning leaves this time of year. When I was a kid we'd pile up leaves and make forts out of them. At night we'd set them on fire and roast hotdogs and marshmallows. Let's do that tomorrow, for old time sake."

There had been a city ordinance implemented a few years ago where residents were no longer allowed to burn leaves. You had to rake them to the curb and one of those city vacuum trucks would suck them up. The only burning allowed was in backyard fire pits. "You want to defy the law?"

"Sure. Why not? After all, we're baaaad girls."

"The cops do have handcuffs." *Get your keister here,*

Tim. She wasn't sure how long they could keep up this farce. They were running out of things to say and if they stayed outside much longer Steph and Grace would come looking for them. The chance of exposing the rat would dwindle to zero.

"Grace would like a little of that action. She's the biggest surprise of all of us. I would've never imagined the things she's into. What a woman!"

A bright light lit up the backyard.

Elaina shielded her eyes against the extreme beam coming from the spotlight.

Stony barked.

Tawny said, "The Calvary has arrived."

It wasn't the Calvary. It was Tim, all by himself, dressed in plain clothes.

Expecting the living, breathing body still hidden behind the lilac bush to bolt, Elaina was surprised when he remained secreted away.

"You ladies okay?"

Tawny said they were fine but that they'd exhausted their arsenal of slutty stories.

Tim settled his gaze on Elaina. "I wouldn't mind hearing a few of those." He clicked his tongue.

She cocked an eyebrow to let him know he was kidding himself.

"Killjoy."

"Yep." She discreetly inclined her head toward the lilac bush.

With all the swiftness and stealth of a tiger, Tim pounced on his prey. In less than a minute the guy was shoved into the bush and held immobile with the peril of a taser close to his neck. Elaina was glad Tim hadn't pulled his gun. She was sure he had it with him.

Elaina gasped when she recognized the spiky-haired blond son of none other than...Jess Macintosh - Mac. Her lips curled in disgust. Her intuition had been right. Why did she have to be right? Her stomach convulsed with instant bile. Thinking it might be him had been one thing; confirming it by seeing his frightened face made her sick. "Landyn, what are you doing? Why are you stalking us?"

His eyes darted wildly. He trembled but remained tight-lipped.

Tim moved the taser closer. "Answer Elaina or you'll be writhing on the ground from being tased. She has every right to call the cops. You think you're scared and embarrassed now. Wait until they slap on the 'cuffs and shove you in the back of their cruiser. I'm giving you one last chance to speak up. If you don't tell Elaina what she wants to know, she'll make the call and press charges."

Landyn's voice squeaked like he couldn't get the words to come out. "I'm... I'm sorry, Elaina. My..." He cleared his throat. "My dad..." He hung his head. "My dad and your husband wanted to frighten you out of the house and off the property." His breaths came in choppy gulps like his lungs couldn't function properly. Elaina feared he might pass out. "I was supposed to sneak around every now and then. I was afraid I'd get caught but your husband told me not to worry. He said you wouldn't call the law. He promised me a new car."

"The rat bastard! I played right into his hands by saying I didn't want the negative publicity."

"That rat bastard knows how you'll react. Prove him wrong. Call the cops. Call the newspapers. Call the radio station." Tawny turned sideways so Landyn wouldn't see her wink.

"Oh god!"

Elaina thought he was going to cry. He needed to cry. He needed to know the huge error in judgment he'd made. "Aren't you studying to become a lawyer?"

Landyn closed his eyes. "Yes," he replied sullenly. "I got a scholarship, my dad pays some of my tuition, and I'm expected to come up with the rest, which I've been able to do. I don't have any extra money to fix my car. It's on its last leg. It's the reason I agreed to this disgrace. I need a reliable vehicle to take me back and forth to school."

Elaina was madder than she'd probably ever been in her life. Arden and Mac took advantage of Landyn's situation and put him in the direct path of having his scholarship ripped out from under him. Landyn might be twenty-one and keen on the law, but he was also naïve and easily coerced; not good traits when it came to juris prudence. "Open your eyes this minute." After she had his full attention she continued. "Shame on Arden. Shame on your father. Shame on you, Landyn. Remind me not to hire you as my lawyer should I need one further on down the road." Elaina handed Tawny the leash so she could strike a hostile pose. She crossed her arms, stood feet shoulder-width apart, and frowned until she couldn't wrinkle her forehead any more. "Your mom is going to be so hurt."

The tears Elaina hoped for came in an instant. "No! Please! Don't tell my mom. I'll do anything. She's a good woman who doesn't deserve this stress. It'll crush her."

"You should've thought of that before you turned to a life of crime, bucko." Again, Tawny twisted out of his view to raise and lower her eyebrows at Elaina.

"What do you want to do, Elaina?" Tim asked.

"Arden needs to be taught a lesson, so does Mac." She looked hard at Landyn without blinking. "You do too."

"I'm ruined." Landyn cried harder.

"Stop the tears right now, mister," Elaina ordered. "I won't be swayed by them." Sheesh, she sounded brutal. She sounded like Arden.

Landyn flicked off the tears and sniffed a few times because his nose was running.

Elaina softened. "Here's how things are going to play out. Roberta Macintosh is a good woman who *deserves* a better son and husband. She *doesn't deserve* the fallout of your shady dealings. Landyn Macintosh, you just caught a break. I'm not going to call the law. I am, however, going to call your dad and Arden and read them the riot act. Your dad may climb all over you for getting caught, but I can guarantee your mother will never find out what you did. Arden is going to pay big time, in more ways than one. You *will* get a new car from him. It's the least he can do for talking you into being his pawn." She glared again. "If you breathe a word about any of this the dean of your law school will be notified. Have I made myself clear?"

"Yes, ma'am." Landyn wiped his nose with the back of his hand.

"You're one lucky S.O.B.," Tim stated firmly. He backed away and stowed the taser.

"Tomorrow when it's daylight I want you to fix those slats in my fence."

"I really am sorry," he said miserably.

"I know you are. Oh, one last thing. All that garbage talk me and Tawny did was to keep you here until Tim arrived. None of it is true."

"I think I knew that. My mom speaks highly of you. She wouldn't if you were a..." He stopped. "She thinks the world of you."

"Be good, Landyn. Make your mother proud. Now go."

"I will." He dashed off.

Tim waited until he was out of earshot. "Bravo, Elaina. You handled that like a pro."

Elaina burst into tears. "I'm going to string Mac and Arden up by their peaches. If they think they can scare me out of this house, they're dead wrong. It would take something big to pry me out of this place. Since that's never going to happen they can kiss my ass." She criticized them using even stronger language.

"Atta girl." Tim put an arm around her. "Get the shock and harmful anger out now so when you approach them you'll also handle that situation like a pro. Go at them with a clear head and without your fists."

The patio porch light came on.

Grace opened the door. "What's taking so long? Why do we have a spotlight on the yard?" She came outside without a coat and in furry slippers. "Tim Smith? What are you doing here?"

"You fired four questions in less than thirty seconds," Tawny teased.

"We're supposed to be watching a movie."

Tim explained that he promised Elaina he'd keep an eye on the place. He happened to be driving by and spied someone in the backyard. "It turned out to be Elaina and Tawny." He petted Stony on the head. "And this amazing dog. He's so well-behaved."

"He's no guard dog. When you flicked on that seven thousand lumen high-intensity spotlight, which almost blinded me by the way, Stony barked but didn't go after you."

"He doesn't have to go after anyone. His presence is ominous enough. As soon as I saw him my whole body clenched."

"Wuss," Tawny teased.

"Damned straight I am. I'm not wearing a cup and didn't want my *peaches* torn to bits."

"That's more information than I needed. I'm going inside." Tawny pulled on the leash to get Stony moving. "Thank you for coming to our rescue."

"Your rescue?" Grace asked.

"Funny story. Let's go inside. You're not going to believe it."

"Yes, thank you, Tim. This wouldn't have gone the way it did without you. I owe you."

"I was happy to help. And you don't owe me a thing. I'm a Special because I want to make a difference. You made a difference tonight too, whether you know it or not. I have a feeling Landyn will turn out just fine because you thought things through and cut him some slack." He bumped her with his shoulder. "Have a good night, classmate."

"You too, Tim."

Tim gathered his spotlight and headed to the front of the house where his car was parked.

Tawny was waiting for Elaina at the back door. "So this dream you've been having..."

Chapter Sixteen

- The flea bag motel! -

"I don't care if he's in a meeting. Get him out here pronto." Elaina bore down on Arden's secretary, Celeste, with an unyielding look of determination. Celeste had worked for Arden since he'd started the business. She had a sharp mind and a no-nonsense personality. Her world revolved around her boss. Whatever he did, she considered brilliant. Whatever he said, she thought should be etched in stone. That level of loyalty was awesome, and a bit unnatural. "Celeste, I'm serious."

"He doesn't wish to be disturbed."

"I'm not concerned with his wishes." Elaina handed the phone receiver to Celeste. "Make the call." She felt a smidgen of guilt for raising her voice and trying to push her way in.

Celeste held firm. "You need to go away."

"Fine." Elaina would give the appearance of compliance. She turned to walk away. A few steps later, she swiveled around and darted to the heavy double-doors of Arden's posh office. She pounded hard on the

220

wood and then backed up, expecting the firestorm she'd ignited to burn through the door any second.

Celeste gasped.

"It isn't your fault. He won't yell at you." Elaina studied a ginormous portrait of Arden that hung on the wall. "Narcissistic bast..." The comment was left unfinished thanks to the abrupt opening and closing of Arden's door.

"What in pray tell are you doing here?" His face contorted with anger.

"Talking to your picture. Calling you a narcissistic bastard." She turned to Celeste. "Your bladder has to be full given that you have a coffee mug the size of a gallon pitcher. Go to the Ladies room. Please?"

Celeste's gaze flew to her boss.

Arden gave his approval with a nod. He waited for Celeste to scurry away. "Have you lost your mind?"

"One would think so, but no, I haven't. You on the other hand, have lost yours."

Arden sneered vilely to terrorize her. It didn't work. She wasn't the least bit intimidated. Adrenaline pumped hard through her veins. She closed the gap between them and came inches from his face.

"Don't keep me in suspense. Tell me what has you so riled up."

"You," she poked him hard in the chest. The padding of his suit, shirt, and undershirt protected his chest from her fingernail. "You're a despicable creature who had me fooled into thinking you'd changed. Ha! You've gotten worse."

"Keep your voice down. I have clients."

"Whoopty freaking doo! I don't care if you're having a conference with the Pope. How could you stoop so low? You are the lowest of the low, Arden Blackheart Samuels."

Arden took her by the arm and tried to lead her into the hallway.

Elaina pulled loose. "Don't try to shush me or I swear I'll shout so loud every window in the building will break."

Arden put his hands on his hips. "State your business or I'll have Security haul you to your car."

"You'd enjoy watching me get dragged away, wouldn't you?" Elaina had made her point that she was thoroughly pissed. Now she intended to yank out his dark heart and toss it in the trash. "How dare you use Mac's son to stalk me, to frighten me into leaving my home." Elaina had been palming her cell phone the entire time. She raised it to his face and snapped a picture. "This is what guilt looks like."

Arden made a swipe for the phone.

Anticipating such a move, Elaina dropped her arm and slid the phone into the end pocket of her purse. "We caught Landyn in the act last night."

"What in the hell are you talking about?"

"Don't play stupid because you're not. You're wily as a fox. But even a fox gets caught now and then. You, mister, have been nabbed in an illegal deal of harassment."

Arden scoffed. "What have you been smoking?"

"I have witnesses and Landyn's statement on tape."

Small fib. She hadn't thought to tape it.

"Witnesses? You call those hellcats you live with witnesses? A court of law would discredit them in a heartbeat."

"No it wouldn't. My friends will swear under oath how things went down last night."

"I didn't hire anyone to harass you into moving. Who'd want that flea bag motel you live in anyway? There's a mountain of dog hair in it." He looked at his watch. "I have things to attend to."

"You're right. The place is heaping with dog hair and the fleas are huge. They can barely jump." She made a sound of derision. "Just so you know, I have a witness other than the sweet women I live with."

Arden hooded his eyes. "Who?"

"That'll stay in the vault until I need his expert testimony."

"For the love of..."

Elaina clamped a hand over his mouth. "Do not say love. There's no love here. You don't love me. You never have. You love the house. The house you'll never get. You might as well take down the For Sale sign in your yard because you won't be moving into my flea-infested hairy-palace." Elaina's pulse throbbed at her temples and the hollow of her throat. "We are done, mister! For now and for always. Don't call me. Don't text me. Don't look at me if we happen to bump into each other at the grocery." She cut him with the dagger of her eyes. "Or I'll get a restraining order." She turned to take her leave. "You owe Landyn a car and you'd better buy it this afternoon.

If you don't, things will get…interesting." Elaina was on her way to the elevator when she swiveled around and stomped back to him. "It had better be a Cadillac SUV. I mean it, Arden. Don't chintz out on Landyn. There will be serious repercussions if you do. One more thing," she poked his chest again. "Call Mac and tell him he's a rotten father who'd better go easy on his son or he too will feel my wrath." Elaina felt empowered but a 4.5 tremble on the quiver-scale quaked through her body. It had to be her backbone adjusting to its new role.

* * *

"It's over. The love-hate relationship with my boss has come to an end. I walked into his office and he lit into me for taking vacation. He said the temp couldn't keep up. Really? He races around the office at the speed of light, tosses napkins or scraps of paper on the desk and wants a letter drafted from them. When he doles out a project that should take a week to complete, he wants it done in a day. At quitting time, he thinks of something else that needs sent out. He's exhausting to watch let alone work for. And he was mystified as to why the temp didn't get everything accomplished. I listened like a good little secretary then asked if I could take more vacation to go to Italy. He went ballistic. This parting of the ways has been coming long before I had the nerve to want more time off." Steph shrugged. "I'm jobless, heading to Italy and then to Maine, and I'm scared out of my mind." She took a carton of ice cream from the freezer and a spoon from the silverware drawer.

"Don't be scared. You closed one door and opened another. You cleared the way for things to work out between you and Jack. I'm sure you'll find a job in Portland and you can write your cookbook at the same time."

"My boss won't give me a good reference, Elaina. He called me a few choice names and demanded I vacate the premises immediately."

"I told him he can't fire me because I quit. Then I cried all the way to my car."

"Things will work out, Steph. They always do."

Steph removed the lid from the Moose Tracks ice cream and spooned a bite into her mouth. "It's hard to step out of the safety zone."

"Your job wasn't the safety zone. If you kept working for him there was a good chance you'd be hauled off to jail for locking him in the supply closet with duct tape binding his hands and piece across his mouth."

Steph took another bite of ice cream and licked the spoon. "I wasn't just referring to my job as the safety zone. I'm talking about leaving everything I know and cherish in Cherry Ridge. I'll be leaving you guys."

"This isn't a safety zone either. We had a stalker."

Steph didn't smile.

"You can come home anytime you want and your room will be here if you need it."

"Thanks, Elaina."

"Stop hogging the ice cream."

Grace came down the stairs with an overnight bag.

"I'm headed to Kentucky."

"We leave for Italy in three days. Why the sudden trip to the Bluegrass State?"

"My in-laws insisted. They haven't seen me in a while and they want me to pick up Cody's wedding present. He called and invited them to the wedding but they already have a trip booked to Hawaii with friends and can't back out. They feel horrible about missing their grandson's wedding. I told them when Cody, Isabella, and Karina come to the states we'll have another small ceremony and reception." She sighed. "I hope I can deliver on that promise."

"Do you want me to go along?"

Grace shook her head. "Thanks for the offer, but I'd rather go alone. I need time to think." She smiled and left by the back door.

Tawny came in the back door.

"Like two ships that passed in the night." Elaina rinsed some dishes and stuck them in the dishwasher.

Tawny sat some plastic bags on the counter. "What's that supposed to mean?"

"That life in this house is a blur. Someone is always coming and going."

"Life isn't just a blur it's freaking nuts. I was at the stop sign at Washington and Main. Carter went buzzing by in a small teal-blue car. I waved and honked. He looked but kept going."

Steph offered a reasonable explanation. "Maybe he had to pee."

"I gave him the bird."

"He probably didn't see you. Call him and find out." Elaina searched through the cupboard for paper plates and a sleeve of Styrofoam cups. "Let's use these for the next few days. The less mess we make the less we'll have to do before our trip. If you haven't started packing it might be a good idea to at least figure out what you're going to take."

"He looked right at me."

"I had a heated exchange with my boss. You might as well have one with Carter." Steph stuffed the ice cream carton back into the freezer. She peeked in one of the plastic bags. "What have we here?" Steph pulled out a cardboard package containing at least a dozen eye patches."

Tawny snatched it away. "Those were supposed to be a surprise."

"It worked. I'm surprised."

"Ha. Ha." Tawny stormed out of the kitchen and up the stairs.

"She's wound tight."

"We all are."

* * *

"Care to talk about it?" Elaina stuck her head around Tawny's half-opened door.

Tawny sat propped up against her headboard with her feet crossed. "There's not much to say, other than it's getting increasingly difficult to be a nice person. My passport didn't come today. I'm tired of my boss's head games. Carter's being a jerk. I want a cigarette so bad and Quentin and Bo don't know I exist."

Elaina climbed onto the bed and scooted in position next to Tawny. "I have faith your passport will get here on time. Your boss will always be a crank, it's her nature. Carter hasn't come around lately. I'm not saying his only interest in you relates to a car sale, but you might want to find out. Regarding those adorable guys you call sons there's no excuse for them not calling their mama. From what I hear at the gym when the members talk about their kids, it's always the daughters who communicate with them; the sons not so much. I don't have much to offer on your desire for a cigarette, except you've come this far without one. Don't give in to the craving or you'll beat yourself up afterward."

"You're the most positive person I know, Elaina. How do you do it? I mean when life strikes you down, you bounce right back. That's a gift not many people get."

"It takes me longer to bounce back than you think. I grieved a long time when my parents got killed. I'm still grieving for them. I don't think anyone really gets over the loss of loved ones. The pain is always there but you go into a type of pain-management. I learned that without the help of Arden. Then my marriage fell apart and I wallowed in a different kind of anguish. But I came out stronger. I still have nights when I weep into my pillow. By morning I'm good to go again. I attribute the strength to God, you, Grace, and Steph. You came into my life at the right time. I love you guys to infinity and back." An idea popped into her head but she'd save it for later.

"We love you too." Tawny nudged Elaina with her foot. "I always feel better after talking to you. I'm sorry you had to deal with the deaths of your parents without Arden's help. For that reason alone I despise the man. You're better off not being married to that, that... There are no words bad enough to describe him."

"How about Japanese beetle?"

"What?"

"The Japanese beetle skeletonizes certain foliage. That fits Arden to a tee. He ate all the leaves of our marriage. He's a serious, destructive pest. I really shouldn't throw him into the same category as Japanese beetles because they have some redeeming qualities. They eat other harmful insects."

"You're a weirdo."

"Uh huh. I am. Want to learn some quick Italian?" Elaina's cell phone rang. She didn't recognize the number and considered letting the call go to voice mail. Instead, she answered. "Hello."

"It's Landyn."

Elaina made big eyes and pointed to her phone. "Hey, Landyn, what's up?"

"You're what's up. I'm in your driveway with a brand new Cadillac SRX Crossover. Elaina you came through for me. Come take a look."

Elaina couldn't stop smiling. "We'll be right out." She disconnected the call. "Come on, Tawn', let's forget our problems and help Landyn celebrate his good fortune."

"See. You're doing it again. You're this happy, forgiving woman. Landyn did you dirty yet he now has an expensive vehicle because of you."

"I'm a weirdo, like you said."

* * *

Steph had a stack of folded clothes on her bed and was cleaning out another drawer.

"Come with us." Elaina motioned for her to follow.

"Where are we going?"

"To an Italian restaurant. With Landyn Macintosh. In his new SUV."

"We are?"

Elaina chuckled. "He doesn't know it yet, but yes, we are. We could use some pre-Italy atmosphere to set the mood for our trip."

They converged on Landyn who had the radio cranked up and was singing the country song, *Take Your Time* by Sam Hunt. He flinched even though he'd known they were on the way.

"You have an amazing voice." Elaina slid into the front passenger seat while Tawny and Steph took seats in the back.

He avoided the compliment. "Look at this thing, Elaina. It's incredible. The navigation system blows my mind. It also has a host of sensors and cameras to keep an eye on things around me. The surround-sound is more than a guy could hope for." He forgot himself and touched her thigh. "Oops. My bad. This is my space." He made a circle around him. Then he leaned across the console and made a circle around her. "This is your space.

I'll try to remember that." Landyn did take her hand though and placed a kiss across her knuckles. "You saved me and I'll always be grateful. If there's ever anything I can do for you, don't hesitate to ask."

"Landyn, take us to Angelo's." Elaina smiled. "Don't panic, I'll pick up the tab. Tonight is all about Italy. We're going to eat their food, drink their wine, and learn to speak their language. You get to be our designated driver."

"You're on."

Chapter Seventeen

~ A bit of magic in the air! ~

"Ciao!" Elaina said to the dark-haired, dark-eyed man who greeted them when they walked in.

He smiled so big all his teeth showed. "Salve signora!" The man counted heads. "Four for dinner?"

"Si."

Again he smiled like she'd made his day. "This way, signora."

They were taken to a table in the back of the tiny, hole-in-the-wall restaurant, Elaina embraced the ambiance. It was decorated with plastic grapes and assorted bottles of wine. And it smelled of garlic and marina sauce. Her mouth watered and it made her even more eager to fly to the country shaped like a boot.

The waitress introduced herself as Sofia and commenced taking orders. When she got to Elaina, she called her "Signora." The man out front must've passed along that she knew a few words.

Elaina ordered Tuscan Chicken served over fettuccine. "Could we see a wine menu as well?"

"Si signora." Sofia left to get the wine list.

Tawny dipped a piece of bread into a bowl of olive oil and herbs. She took a bite. Her eyes rolled back in her head with the blissful taste. "Oh yeah, I'm going to love Italy."

"Speaking of which," Elaina smiled at Landyn, "I have a huge favor to ask."

Landyn followed Tawny's lead and dipped bread into the olive oil and herb mixture. "Anything. Name it."

"Remember the adorable dog you assumed was vicious?"

He grimaced. "How can I forget?"

"We're headed to Italy for a few days and need someone to care for Stony and our cat Lula while we're gone. I know you're busy with school. Is there any possible way you could help out?"

"I'm your man. Tell me what I need to do and consider it done."

"Don't be so quick to offer your services. You have no idea what you're in for." Elaina giggled. "Stony thinks he's human. He loves to be around people. When he's left alone too long he gets into trouble. Lula's much the same way, although unlike Stony she's independent. She likes to watch everything from a distance until she's ready to cause mayhem."

"I would take care of them if they were the worst two pets on the planet."

"Just to be clear, you don't owe me a thing. If you do this, it's because you want to."

"You're wrong. I do owe you. Anything you want, I'll

do." He cocked a blondish-brown eyebrow. "Anything."

Tawny broke into a hearty laugh at the same time Sofia arrived with a plate of antipasto. Sofia flinched. The plate wobbled dangerously in her hand. Thin slices of salami and prosciutto, mozzarella and provolone cheeses, black and green olives, and pepperoncini peppers were in danger of decorating the floor. Landyn sprang into action and steadied the plate, graced Sofia with his killer smile, and helped set the antipasto in the center of the table.

Elaina watched his subtle flirtation and surmised that Landyn Macintosh would be one heck of a lawyer, contrary to her earlier opinion. He had charisma, good looks, and despite his flub with his dad and Arden he was a smart guy. He was also genuine. The tears he'd cried had been real. The love and respect for his mother was heartwarming. And his effort to make things right won her over.

"Grazie, signora," he said to Sofia in the kind of voice a man uses to snag and keep a woman's attention.

Elaina met Tawny's eyes. They grinned at the bit of magic in the air.

"Prego." Sofia blinked coyly and hurried away.

"Landyn Macintosh, you smooth operator," Steph teased. "If I were your age I'd be stalking *you*."

Landyn smiled but the implication made it fade rather quickly.

"I do know how to kill a moment. Sorry, Landyn."

Elaina sipped from her water glass. "You know how to speak Italian?"

"It was one of my college electives sophomore year. I loved learning about the Italian people and their culture so much that I wanted to take a semester off to check out their country. The funds weren't available so I did the next best thing. I made friends with some Italian-Americans on campus. They're warm people who made me feel like family."

"Is that why you're attracted to our waitress?" Tawny asked.

The tips of Landyn's ears reddened in a blush. "Possibly, but she's also beautiful."

"Landyn." Elaina put a hand over her mouth in awe. "Most guys your age wouldn't use the word beautiful to describe a girl. They'd say she's hot, cute, smoking, a babe. You get big points for calling her beautiful."

The blush reached his cheeks and he shifted in his chair. "Awkward in Italian is imbarazzante."

"Noted."

* * *

When Grace drove her Chevy Equinox into the driveway, some of the knots in Elaina's muscles relaxed; knots she hadn't realized had been there. Without her knowledge she'd turned into Mother Hen – weird because she wasn't the oldest of the flock.

Another twinge of awareness made her bite down on her bottom lip. When one of her three best friends wasn't there everything felt out of synch. Soon Steph would fly the coop for good. The cackle of four hens would be reduced to three. Realistically, some day there'd be one chick left in the nest – her. While Tawny and Grace wanted a 'breather' from the roosters, eventually they'd wander off to another pen to hear the cock crow in the morning.

"How'd it go with the in-laws?"

"The way it always goes when we visit. Happiness, tears, more happiness, more tears. All the emotion takes its toll. It gets harder and harder to be with them. They're such a gentle yet brutal reminder of Brince. If that makes sense."

"It makes perfect sense, Grace. They're tender and loving, but it hurts your heart to look in their eyes and see their son reflecting back at you."

Tears gathered in Grace's eyes. She put a hand over her face and shook her head as though she was telling herself 'not again'.

"It's okay, Grace," Elaina said gently.

After a few minutes, Grace swiped at the salty droplets dripping from her cheeks. "I'm such a baby."

"No you're not. You're a brave woman who still loves her husband very much. Brince Cordray was a lucky man to have found you. And you were a very lucky woman to have found him."

Tawny joined them with a steaming hot cup of coffee for Grace. "I thought you might need a caffeine buzz after that five hour drive."

Grace sniffed, took the coffee, blew away the steam, and took a sip. "Ahhhh. The only thing better than coffee is my amazing friends." A small smile slipped into place.

"Well, there's wine. It's right up there too."

Elaina was relieved to see Grace's mood improve.

Tawny reached around to her back pocket and produced a small blue booklet. She danced in a circle and waved her passport. "It came this morning."

"Sweet. Trying to sneak you into a foreign country without it would've been difficult. We would've done it though. Right, Grace?"

"Uh, yeah. We would've. Not."

They laughed.

Grace looked around. "Where's Steph?"

"Packing."

"Good Lord, how much stuff is she taking? We're only going to be there for four days."

"She's packing her things to move."

Grace frowned. "She needs to cut that shit out."

Again, they laughed.

In that moment, everything was right with the world.

* * *

"Stone-man, behave while we're gone. Do not give Landyn an ounce of grief." Tawny pulled tenderly at his ears.

Stony whimpered like he knew what was about to take place.

Elaina handed Landyn a checklist. "Any questions?"

"Nope. I think I've got it."

"Thanks again for agreeing to dog-sit and house-sit."

"It's an arrangement that works for all of us. I have

two major tests coming up and I have to study someplace quiet. At home the silence comes in small increments. Dad has the TV on whether he's watching it or not. Mom's always cooking something which means a lot of clanging of pots and pans. Here I'll get lost in the quiet. My brain will soak up all the information I need to pass those tests. It's a win-win. Stony won't be a problem. Will ya, boy?"

Stony leaned into Landyn.

"He likes you," Tawny said.

Landyn smiled. "What's not to like?"

"I know, right?"

"Did my dad get a hold of you to apologize, Elaina? He said he was going to."

"He did." Elaina wouldn't add that Mac texted his regret instead of calling her. His message had been short and to the point – *I was an ass. Please forgive.* Her response was also short and direct – *You're right. You were a manipulative ass. I'll give your request for forgiveness some thought.*

"Good. I hope you and him will remain friends."

"No worries." The vague answer kept her from having to fib or promise. There was a good chance she and Mac would mend their rift, but she'd make him sweat for a while.

Grace crouched to peek at Lula under the table. "Watch out for this one. She's been known to drop from my headboard onto my face while I'm sleeping. Good thing she's declawed. It jerks you awake like a bad dream."

"I'll keep that in mind."

Elaina opened the fridge. "Fully stocked for your dining pleasure. There's beer in the extra fridge in the garage." She pointed to the wine rack. "Vino if the mood strikes you." She raised her eyebrows authoritatively although she knew she didn't need to. "No parties."

"Yes, Mom." He winked. "I mean Elaina."

"I guess we're good to go."

"Safe travels, ladies."

The suitcases were already packed in Elaina's Escalade so the only thing left to do was pile into the vehicle.

On the way out the back door, Steph grumbled, "Did I mention I get antsy on an airplane?"

"A thousand times."

Chapter Eighteen

~ To infinity and beyond! ~

"I think I'm going to pass out." Steph fanned herself with the airplane safety instruction card.

Elaina leaned forward to look at Tawny. "You're a nurse. What should she do?"

"For starters, quit reading that dang card. It's stuff every passenger should know. Yes, your seat can be used as a flotation device. Yes, you should identify the exits. All good information but you shouldn't be reading it every fifteen minutes because you're scaring yourself." Tawny snatched the card from Steph. "For the love of Pete, take a nap."

"I can't sleep on a plane."

Tawny was clearly annoyed. "Your inability to shut your eyes shouldn't interfere with the ability to shut ours."

Elaina undid Steph's seatbelt. "You're free to roam the cabin. That should help you get your equilibrium back. If it doesn't, hold onto the seats as you walk but don't fall into anyone's lap. They might not appreciate an unexpected guest."

"Side-splitting funny," Steph retorted sarcastically.

"Actually, I was trying to be helpful. You really should walk around. Ask the flight attendant for a glass of water."

Tawny fumbled for the barf bag tucked in the pocket of her seat and handed it to Steph. She unlatched her seatbelt and stood in the aisle while Steph vacated her seat in the middle. "Don't bother Grace. She's sleeping."

Grace was wedged between two rather meaty men in the center section of the plane. She had her eyes closed.

"I don't think she's sleeping. I don't hear her snoring."

Tawny narrowed her eyes to slits. "Leave her alone. She has a rough few days ahead of her so every bit of sleep she gets will be beneficial."

"You're not the boss of me."

Tawny clutched a handful of Steph's shirt. "Wanna bet?"

Elaina laughed until she snorted.

Steph had taken maybe five steps maximum when the plane hit a pocket of turbulence. She flew backward and landed spread eagle.

Elaina shook her head. "That's our Steph."

* * *

"Two hours to Dayton. Two hours to New York City. Seven and a half hours to Frankfurt. An hour and forty-two minutes to Rome. That's over thirteen hours and it doesn't include the layovers at each airport. I'm completely wiped out." Grace staggered up the Jetway that would take her to the terminal of the Leonardo da

Vinci International Airport.

"You've got this, Grace," Elaina encouraged with what little oomph she had left. Traveling by air was faster than by boat but it siphoned just about every bit of your energy. The time difference played a big part too. They'd arrived on a red-eye flight which put the time at two in the morning. Back home it was eight in the evening. They'd eaten up a full day and was into the second one, which basically meant they'd love on Cody, Isabella, and Karina for a short time, watch Cody and Isabella get married, make their rounds at the reception, and board a plane for the long flight home.

"Keep moving," Tawny said. "One foot in front of the other. We'll make it."

"Where's Cody going to meet us?" Steph inquired.

"He isn't. We're going to take a taxi to Isabella's parents' villa. We're dog-tired but there's no reason for them to be."

Steph's eyes widened with panic. "We're in a foreign country with just a handful of words to communicate. Gah! I know you love your son and don't want to put him out, but geeze, Grace."

Grace reared up to say something but her shoulders drooped. "I'm too tired to argue."

At the luggage carousel, they retrieved their bags and the present from Cody's grandparents. Grace's eyes flew to Elaina's in alarm. "Dear God in Heaven, I didn't get Cody and Isabella anything." The exhaustion and emotion pooled together to make Grace sway. "What kind of mother am I?"

Despite her own exhaustion, Elaina kept Grace from hitting the floor. "Take a deep breath, Grace Vivian Cordray." She used Grace's full name as a subconscious command for Grace to pull herself together. "I have a plan."

A gentleman waiting for his luggage to circle saw Grace wither. "E lei sente poco bene?"

Elaina's mind was too fuzzy to try to comprehend what he'd asked. "I'm sorry. I don't understand."

"Americano?"

"Si."

"I always use my home language first." Even though the man had a thick accent he was fluent in English. "Is she feeling unwell?"

"Her son is getting married."

"Ahhh. She'll be okay then?"

Elaina nodded. "Eventually."

"My wife was much the same when our daughter wed."

Elaina smiled appreciatively and asked for instructions to a taxi stand.

The gentleman provided the location and tipped his hat. "Welcome to Italy. Enjoy some gelato before you leave the airport."

"Do you hear that, Grace? Let it sink in. We're in Italy! They have gelato."

* * *

"Mom!"

The three-letter word sent a rush of warmth through

Elaina. She could only imagine the powerful effect it had on Grace.

Cody was the spitting image of his father but when he smiled he was Grace through and through. "My mom!" His happiness spilled out and onto everyone else. "I thought this day would never get here." He was tall and thin and shadowed tiny Grace. Gathering her in his arms, he kissed her head at least a dozen times. "I love you, Mom." He lifted her off her feet and swung her around.

Elaina, Steph, and Tawny stayed a good distance back to allow for a much needed private reunion. A lovely dark-haired girl, along with an older man and woman, remained on the steps of the villa, Elaina assumed for the same reason.

Grace and Cody laughed and hugged, cried and hugged, and laughed some more.

"They'd better knock that off or I'm going to bawl like a baby," Tawny said. "Seeing their happiness makes me miss Quentin and Bo more than I already do."

Steph patted Tawny's back. "When we get back to the states you'll have to arrange for them to come to Ohio or you can fly off to meet them somewhere between California and Oregon."

"Sounds simple enough but putting it into play would be like stepping my bare foot in scalding hot water. I won't whine that the other nurses can take all the time off they want but when I ask... Forget it. I'm in Italy. I don't want to taint the pleasure of being here by going off on a tangent about my boss."

Cody motioned for Elaina, Tawny, and Steph and did the same to Isabella, Francesca and Niccolo. Still holding his mom as though he thought she might leave if he let loose of her, he introduced his in-laws-to-be.

In true Italian style, Francesca and Niccolo kissed Grace on each cheek and took her hands for a gentle squeeze. They allowed Cody to introduce Isabella.

"Mom, this is my heart of hearts – Isabella."

Isabella nodded politely at first, but the pulse of the introduction turned heartwarming. She embraced Grace with so much energy there wasn't a dry eye. "Mia suocera. My mother-in-law. So happy to finally meet you."

Grace's blue eyes glistened with joyful tears. "It's good to meet you too, Isabella, and I can't wait to see sweet Karina."

"She wanted to stay up but she didn't make it much past nine o'clock. You'll need vitamins when you meet her in the morning. She's vivacious after a good night's sleep."

Steph yawned.

"Let's see," Cody tapped his chin and studied Elaina, Tawny, and Steph. "You must be Steph."

"Why must I be Steph?"

"Because you're the adorable redhead my mother goes on and on about." At Steph's wide eyes, he clarified, "All good, I assure you." He kissed her hand.

He moved on to Tawny. "You're Tawny. My mom says you keep everyone on their toes." He kissed her hand too.

Finally, he smiled at Elaina. "Elaina Samuels. You're

the glue that keeps this fearsome foursome together. Thank you for everything you've done for my mama." He also kissed her hand.

Cody's gaze raked humorously over them. "I hear you sing a mean karaoke."

Steph piped up that he could watch them on YouTube. "Zip it, Steph."

"It's freaking hilarious, Cody," Steph said in defiance of the order to keep quiet.

Grace frowned at Steph. "Oh what the heck. I'm too tired to care. Watch it all you want." She yawned and started a domino effect.

* * *

Elaina hadn't been asleep long – at least it felt as if she'd just closed her eyes – when she felt a poke in her ribs. She tried to roll over and ignore whatever was trying to roust her awake.

"Elaina."

"Go away," she said groggily.

"It's important."

The haze lifted enough for her to recognize Grace's voice.

She propped up on an elbow and rubbed her eyes. "What's wrong?"

"I'm fatigued to the point of collapse but I can't sleep until I know the plan."

Elaina gave her head a shake to get the blood flowing to her brain. "What plan?"

"I was worried I didn't have a gift for Cody and Isabella. You said you had a plan."

"You couldn't wait until morning?"

"Technically it is morning."

Elaina puffed out a breath of stale air and sat up. "Give Cody and Isabella a card. Inside write that you're giving them and Karina an all-expense paid trip to America; more specifically, to Maine. Steph will be there. We'll all be dying to see her too so it makes sense that's where it should happen. Your in-laws can drive or fly to Maine. And it will all be good. Now let me go back to sleep."

"There's just one fly in the ointment of that plan."

"There's no fly. I have plenty of money. I'll loan it to you to give to them. Seriously I need sleep."

Grace squeezed Elaina's hand and gently guided her down to the pillow. "I'll pay you back plus interest."

"How about interest in catching a few Zzz's?"

* * *

The sun peeked through the part in the curtains, hitting Elaina square in the face. She popped open an eye, then the other. It took her a second to remember where she was. A knock on the bedroom door made her pull the covers over her head.

"Time to get up, buttercup." Tawny entered holding two cups. "Coffee with milk. Or as Francesca said, 'caffe latte'. You need to get a quick shower. Francesca and Niccolo are giving us a tour of Rome."

"What time is it?"

"Seven-thirty."

Elaina put the pillow over her face and muffled that they hadn't gone to bed until almost four.

"I'm up. Steph's up. So you're getting up. Drink your caffe latte."

The four of them made their way to the main villa from the guest house.

As soon as Grace saw a small version of Isabella she put a hand across her heart. "Karina!"

Elaina didn't believe in love at first sight. Until now. Grace's expression was gooey. Her blue eyes sparkled and she had an endless smile.

"Karina," she said again.

"Go to her, Grace."

Grace practically ran to the little girl but she held off picking her up until Karina gave the go-ahead.

"She's one happy grandma." Elaina winked at Tawny. "It's your turn next."

After breakfast, the nine of them were off for a day of exploring Rome. It took three Renault cars to haul them around.

They visited the historic tombs of Pantheon, the eighteenth century sculpted Trevi Fountain, the Colosseum, and Vatican City where they took in St. Peter's Basilica and Michelangelo's Sistine Chapel. It was a brilliant autumn day filled with history and getting to know Grace's son and new family.

At midday they stopped for panini and sweet red wine, accompanied of course, by gelato.

Grace insisted on paying for dinner. They dined at a

traditional Italian restaurant and enjoyed lasagna, steak, prawns, risotto, salad, and tiramisu for dessert.

Cody encouraged them to try limoncello; an Italian lemon liqueur.

It was well past dusk by the time they pulled onto the brick-driveway of the villa.

"Tomorrow a wedding will take place," Niccolo said with a smile. "Our lovely daughter and your amazing son will become man and wife."

The prospect of Cody getting married no longer appeared to jar Grace. "I can't begin to describe how happy I am."

Cody shifted Karina in his arms to bend down and kiss his mom's cheek. "Just triple what you're feeling and that's where I am."

"I have a special surprise for you and Isabella." Grace corrected the comment. "Cody, your father and I have a special surprise for you and Isabella." She slowly slipped off her wedding rings, brought them to her lips, and then held them out to him. "This feels right." At his look of surprise, she said, "There's no pressure for you to use them as your weddings rings. I…we…just wanted you to have them." She tucked a wisp of hair behind Karina's little ear. "My present to the three of you is a trip to America."

Joy hit Cody and Isabella's face.

"The rings…" Cody could barely speak. "They're…" He cleared his throat. "They're perfect. Are you sure you can part with them, Mom?"

"It would do my heart good to know they're with you

and Isabella." Grace's eyes watered.

Niccolo and Elaina were on the same wave length. He proposed they give the happy couple and Grace some private time. He hoisted Karina into his arms. "Come, nipotina. Granddaughter. Early bedtime for you."

Elaina was grateful for so many things, but at this particular moment she was thankful fate had stepped in the day she, Tawny, Steph, and Grace had met at that cash-for-gold event. A great friendship began, distracting the reason they were at the jewelry store. Instead of Grace's rings being melted down by the jeweler for their cash value, they were now in the hands of two people who would cherish them for their sentimental value. Fate had definitely stepped in that day, but because of her faith, Elaina knew fate was another word for a well-orchestrated move by the power above. "Thank you," she whispered.

* * *

Grace was beautiful...and surprisingly composed.

After Cody and Isabella said their vows, they repeated a second set of vows that included their devotion to Karina. It was the most touching display of affection Elaina ever had the pleasure of witnessing.

Of course, the day wouldn't have been complete without a tribute to Brince. Cody took Grace's hand and honored her and his father with an accounting of sweet memories. Boxes of tissues made their way around the reception hall.

A scrumptious meal was served and the dance began.

Elaina, Tawny, Steph, and Grace laughed when they tried to do the Italian folk dance.

The thing that made the reception distinctive was when Cody's sense of humor mirrored his mom's. He took the DJ's microphone. "Mom, Elaina, Steph, and Tawny, your presence is requested up here."

Elaina said under her breath, "This better not be what I think it is."

Just like in the nightclub, Tawny and Grace – aided by Steph this time – had to drag Elaina to the front of the room.

Cody's grin was just as impish as Grace's. "It's only fitting that you sing *We Are Family* by Sister Sledge." He sobered. "Because that's what we are. Everyone in this room is family."

Touching words but the fact remained they had to sing. Elaina moaned.

"We'll be an international sensation," Tawny joked.

"Remember when I said we had to behave or we'll be kicked out of the country? When we make their ears bleed they'll load on us the first plane headed to the states."

Tawny knuckle-bumped Cody.

Cody retrieved a padded pouch from under the table where the karaoke machine sat. He borrowed the microphone from the DJ. "My new friend, Tawny, brought something special from America. It took me a second to remember what the things in this package meant. Thank you for making me laugh."

Tawny nodded.

Cody continued. "Now it's time for me to make all of *you* laugh."

Elaina clutched Tawny's arm. "What did you do?"

"Nuttin'." Guilty amusement etched Tawny's face.

"Turn around so your backs are facing the crowd," Cody instructed. He handed them each an eye patch and signaled for them to put them on. He put one on too.

Grace could hardly get hers on she was laughing so hard.

"You've got to be kidding." Elaina put on her patch, even though she didn't want to.

Cody gave permission for them turn around.

It was a hilarious scene. Not only did they have eye patches on but so did everyone else.

Laughter rocked the dance hall.

"Crazy Americans," Grace said.

"You know it," Elaina agreed.

When the members of the four hussy homestead sang *We Are Family* any and all mice in the building and for miles, squeaked and ran to find ear plugs.

* * *

"I don't know when I've had more fun at a wedding," Steph admitted. "We ate, drank, danced until our feet almost fell off, and laughed so much our stomachs hurt. Epic wedding, Grace. Epic."

Grace had been abnormally quiet on the airplane and she was still keeping to herself on the drive home. "It *was* pretty great, wasn't it?"

"You're a mother-in-law and grandma. How does it feel?" Elaina looked in the rearview mirror at the woman whose life had drastically changed the moment her son took Isabella's hand and repeated after the priest, 'Lo viglio. Ti prendo come mia sposa. I do. I take you as my wife.'

"It's unlike anything I've ever felt. I'm still trying to sort through it all."

"It's going to be great. The newlyweds and their daughter are excited to be coming to America. To Maine. At Christmastime. How cool is that?"

A genuine smile perked Grace's face.

"I could use some gelato," Steph said.

"When we get home you can make some." Tawny laid her head against the window. "If I didn't have to work tomorrow I'd sleep the whole day."

Steph's cell phone chimed with a text message. "I wonder if he missed me." She collected her phone from her purse and read the message out loud. "*Call me ASAP.*"

"I'd say he did." Elaina veered onto Route 40 from Airport Road.

"I hate to make the call while we're in the car but he said ASAP."

"Go ahead, Steph. We don't mind." Grace asked for confirmation. "Do we, girls?"

"Fine by me but I draw the line at phone sex," Tawny said humorously and tried to spread out in the bucket seat to get comfortable.

Elaina said, "Go for it."

Jack must've been waiting by the phone.

"We're baaaack. Uh huh, our plane landed thirty minutes ago. The wedding was so great."

Elaina tried to tune out the conversation with thoughts of Landyn, Stony, and Lula, to give Steph some privacy but her subconscious directed her ears to listen.

Route 40, which would take them to the interstate, quickly became a congested mess. Elaina could only imagine how insane traffic would be on I-75. She didn't mind a little automotive commotion but when people weaved in and out of their lanes, and jockeyed for position, it made her nervous.

The ASAP call didn't last long. "I'm flattered Jack wanted to hear from me so soon but he sounded weird; like he wanted to say something important but he didn't. You know that feeling you get when someone's holding back? He said to call him back when we get home."

"I heard you tell him we landed a half-hour ago which means you're in the car with an audience. Whatever he had to say could be so personal he doesn't want back-feed from three other women." Elaina put on her blinker. "Maybe he's going to pop the big question."

Steph put up a hand. "Whoa! Don't go down that road."

"Why not? It's inevitable one day he'll ask. You are moving to be with him."

"No, really. You're going down the wrong road. I mean the wrong exit. This is for I-75 south."

Tawny raised her head from where she'd anchored it on the window. "Steph's right. We're headed into Dayton not away from it."

Elaina raised her shoulders in a shrug. "Oops."

Grace ended the game she was playing on her phone. "You never say oops when you mess up. You cuss. What are you up to?"

Elaina clicked her tongue. "You'll see."

Grace took a guess. "You're taking us to that new steakhouse on Route 35, aren't you?"

"It's too early for dinner but my stomach is rumbling so I could eat. That teeny bag of pretzels they gave us on the plane wasn't enough to tide me over until we get home," Steph said. "You know what I've been hungry for? Grilled pineapple."

Traffic on the interstate wasn't bogged down at all.

Elaina drove a mile and took the first exit.

Tawny reiterated Grace's question when Elaina bounced the Escalade over a speed bump in the parking lot of a strip mall. "What *are* you up to? There aren't any restaurants here."

"You'll see." She took a parking space in front of a tattoo parlor and shut off the ignition.

"You're joking, right?" Steph's voice sparked with panic.

"Grace wanted to shake things up by doing something different. Why not a tattoo?"

"You were dead-set against it, if I remember correctly," Tawny pointed out.

Grace said, "Hmm. When I made the suggestion I might have been having a midlife crisis. I thought I wanted a tat but deep down I don't see it happening. Fire up the Escalade and get back on the interstate."

"Hear me out." Elaina swiveled so she could see their reactions when she presented her case. "You're right, Tawn'. I was dead-set against getting one. I've been thinking about how things are changing every day for us. The thing that doesn't change is our friendship. In my heart I know that no matter where we go or who we end up with, we'll stay best friends forever. With Steph leaving soon, I thought... I wanted.... Aww, hell. Let's get the infinity symbol tattooed on the inside of our ankles."

Grace's mouth dropped open, as did Tawny and Steph's.

* * *

"I thought I was going to faint when the tattoo artist said, 'Your skin will be pierced repeatedly, creating a wound that will need to heal.'"

"He had to put it out there, Grace, so you knew what to expect. Plus he wanted us to know the importance of aftercare."

Tawny scrolled to the pictures of their ankles. They'd grouped together to take a photo of the artwork. "How cool is this, ladies?"

"I did not see this coming, but I'm glad you talked us into it." Grace moved her head back and forth in amazement. "You're a sentimental sap, Elaina."

"I didn't know I was until you guys came into my life."

Steph walked to the car like she had a corncob up her behind.

"What are you doing?" Tawny asked.

"Babying it."

"Most people would guess you just had a colonoscopy." Tawny gave Elaina a high-five. "Booyah."

Chapter Nineteen

- *Sisters of the heart!* -

"Home sweet home!" Tawny smiled in the direction of the house. "I love going away but there's nothing more humbling and incredible than coming home.

"I agree." Grace opened the hatch and grabbed her suitcase.

Steph waddled to the back of the Escalade, still favoring her ankle. "I'm going to make a pitcher of sangria to celebrate returning from our journey and getting tattoos."

"As hectic as the drive home was, I'd drink straight tequila if we had a bottle." It had been easy getting to the tattoo parlor. Coming home was a different story. Elaina breathed in a lungful of cool air and exhaled. "Some drivers shouldn't be on the road until they take a remedial driving class. They were out of control. The speed limit is 70 miles per hour. I swear some of them were doing 95."

"They have a need for speed," Tawny said.

"Or they're just psychotic." Elaina snickered and

dragged her suitcase into the house.

"Landyn?"

"In here."

Elaina found him sitting on the sofa with Lula in his lap and Stony at his feet. "Would you look at that?" she marveled. "Miracles do happen."

Stony practically leaped in the air when he saw Elaina. He yowled that distinctive happy noise that made her heart swell with affection. She didn't have kids but she had Stony and Lula. She chuckled when Lula raised her head but remained on Landyn's lap. She knelt down to pet Stony and to bend his ears with baby-talk. "I missed you so much, boy. Yes I did." She kissed his head and snout. Stony was so excited. He poked her with his nose a few times and leaned hard into her. It was one of the best feelings in the world.

"I can't thank you enough for taking care of our babies."

"My pleasure, Elaina. Stony and Lula are actually pretty cool. It took them a while to warm up to me but once they did it was great."

"You're a good friend, Landyn." She handed him an envelope. "You're deep into getting your degree, but anytime you need a Stony-fix or a Lula-fix or just want to hang out with four slightly older women, stop by. We'd love to hear how things are going with you."

"I'll do that." He waved the envelope. "What's this?"

"A little something to ease the burden of school. It's not a lot but it might buy a few textbooks or fill the tank of your SRX once or twice."

Landyn ripped open the envelope to look at the check. "Wow! That'll buy my books for the next semester and fill my tank for a month. I can't accept this. You've done so much already. I deserve none of it."

Elaina wrenched an arm around him. "You made a mistake. I've forgiven you. Now you need to forgive yourself. Look at it this way – we're supposed to be kind to one another. I'm paying it forward. I hope you'll do the same to someone who needs a little help."

"My mother was right about you, Elaina. You are a special lady."

Tawny brought them both back down to earth. "She's grouchy in the morning."

The room filled with laughter.

"Would you like to stay for drinks? Steph's making sangria."

"As entertaining as you ladies are, I'd be a fool not to stay. But...I have a date with another special lady."

"The one from Angelo's?" Elaina asked.

"Mmm-hmm."

After Landyn left they dumped their dirty clothes in a pile and Elaina commenced the task of laundry. Tawny got reacquainted with the furry love of her life by taking him for a long walk.

Grace snatched Lula and headed upstairs to call Mr. and Mrs. Cody Corday and child, to let them know they'd made it home safe and sound.

Steph put together the pitcher of sangria. "I'm going to miss this place. It's home."

"Remember when you moved out of your parents'

home to get married?"

Steph snickered. "It was difficult for my parents, not for me. I was ready to cut loose and play house. What a disaster that was! Married a month and we realized what a foolhardy thing we'd done." She poured two glasses of sangria. "That was a lesson-learned, for sure."

"Life seems to be non-stop lesson. Some days the lessons are subtle. Some days they whack us upside the head." Elaina sipped the wine and smacked her lips. "Tasty."

"All those lessons build character." Steph smirked. "Or so I've been told."

"You're doing great, Steph. When you stumble you pull yourself back up and keep going."

"It's easier with friends. If Jack is half as supportive as you guys are, I'll be a happy woman."

Elaina was disturbed by Steph's use of the word *if.* She almost mentioned that Steph should already be aware of Jack's level of support. She stopped herself at the last second. There were some things a gal had to figure out for herself. Besides, Steph would know everything there was to know about Jack in short order. Elaina made a solemn vow that if Jack Kirby hurt her friend, the forests of Maine wouldn't be thick enough for him to hide in. "Speaking of Jack, aren't you supposed to call him back?"

"I'll call him after I help you sort the laundry."

"He's probably pacing."

"He did insist I call as soon as I got home."

"Then go."

"I'll tell him you said hello." Steph plodded up the stairs.

Elaina slouched against the counter, happily exhausted. The trip to Italy had been a success. She was sporting a tattoo. And her world was on an even keel despite Arden and Mac's attempts to flip it upside down.

Tawny and Stone-man returned. "Brr. The air is damp. It feels like it could snow."

"It's November now so anything is possible."

"I can't believe it snowed on October fifteenth. Weird, huh?"

A loud racket upstairs made them both frown.

Elaina took the steps two at a time. Tawny was fast on her heels.

At the landing at the top of the stairs, Elaina heard heart-wrenching sobs coming from behind Steph's closed door. "Uh oh."

Grace met them at Steph's door. "Not good."

"Everything was great five minutes ago." Elaina rapped lightly on the door. "Can we come in?"

"No. Yes. No." Steph was hysterical.

Elaina twisted the doorknob to no avail. "Unlock the door."

The pitiful wails intensified.

Grace took a stab at getting Steph to open up. "Whatever's going on, we're here for you."

Stony rushed to the scene.

"You're scaring Stony," Tawny said.

The click of the lock being opened made Elaina sigh.

Steph was a mess. Her eyes and nose were red from crying. Rivulets of tears didn't streak down her cheeks; they fell by the buckets full. She was despair personified.

"Stephhh," Elaina said tenderly, "what happened?"

Hiccupped sobs wracked Steph's body. "He...They... I'm..."

Elaina moved in to put a consoling arm around Steph.

"What did he do," Grace demanded hotly.

"He... They... They're moving..." Steph pushed away and walked to the window. "They're selling the..." Her body trembled. "They don't want the bed and breakfast. It's up for sale."

Elaina let the f-word slip out.

"Ohhh, Steph." Grace walked to Steph but was straight-armed. .

"It feels like I'm being zapped by a thousand volts right now. Like I'm short-circuiting."

Elaina looked to Tawny for medical guidance. "Can that happen?"

Dread coated Tawny's expression. "Calm down, Steph," she said soothingly. "Take a breath."

"I can't take a breath. I quit my job for those..." Steph fisted her hands and shook them. Her face was contorted with pain.

"You quit your job for you, not them," Elaina said, trying to rationalize from a different angle.

Steph went completely still. "That's exactly what I did."

"How does Jack feel about things not going according to plan?" Grace asked.

"He's upset."

"Does it change things between you?"

The question was the catalyst for an even more

powerful burst of emotion.

"Instead of returning to Cherry Ridge they're moving to Florida. Not just Mr. and Mrs. Kirby and Georgia, Jack's going with them." Steph fell face-first onto the bed and screamed into her pillow.

Elaina sat on the bed, wanting to rub Steph's back but afraid to touch her. "Are you following him to Florida?"

"No!" She muffled loudly. "I asked if he wanted me to and he wouldn't answer."

Elaina's anger surfaced at an alarming speed. She wanted to tear Jack apart. He was damn lucky he wasn't within reach. "This isn't the time to tell you there's an upside to this travesty, but there is. We just have to find it."

"You're right. This isn't the time," Steph moaned. "I know you guys care but I want to be alone."

* * *

Elaina couldn't sleep. She turned on her side and then flipped to the other side, going crazy from the anger pumping through her veins. She punched her pillow. "You jackals," she said of the Kirbys. Perhaps she was being unfair since she only knew a fraction of what prompted them to sell but right now the only thing she could focus on was that Steph was hurting. "I wish I could fix this for you, Steph, but I can't."

A tiny voice deep inside countered the proclamation with a kernel of an idea.

Elaina sat straight up and dragged a hand through her

hair. The seed of inspiration grew larger by the second, shoving her anger by the wayside. She grabbed her cell and dialed Arden.

"Elaina?" he asked groggily at first, but then he must've looked at the clock. "What's wrong? What happened?"

"There's no emergency."

He yawned into the phone. "Then why are you calling me at three in the morning?"

"To tell you to be in Mac's office tomorrow... I mean this morning. At ten. Bring your checkbook." She turned her cell phone off so he couldn't call back. The home phone by the bed rang. "Crap. I should've unplugged the darn thing." Although, she would've had to unplug all five phones. Each bedroom had a landline phone and there was one in the kitchen. To keep from waking the others, she grabbed the phone on the nightstand. "What?"

"That's how you answer a phone?"

"I knew it was you and now isn't the time to lecture me about phone etiquette."

"Still, not cool. I can't be in Mac's office at ten I have a meeting I can't get out of."

"Arden, I said ten."

"Be flexible, will ya? I can be there at nine. Will that work for whatever scheme you're planning? I have a feeling it isn't going to be good."

"You won't know until tomorrow. Sweet dreams." Elaina hung up the phone. With a thousand thoughts racing through her head, she padded down to the kitchen and sat at the table. Drumming her fingers, another idea popped into her head. Finding the app on her phone where she bought e-books, she scrolled until she found the one she wanted and downloaded it. She began to read.

"It's twenty after three. What are you doing up?"

"Geeze, Tawn'. Make some noise. You scared me half to death."

"You made enough noise for the both of us." Tawny opened the cabinet for the coffee filters and proceeded to make a pot. "What in Sam hell are you doing up so early?"

"I've got a plan."

"I hate to sound like a complete and utter ass, but you *always* have a plan. Couldn't you have a plan at six o'clock when my alarm was supposed to go off, instead of in the middle of the freaking night? And yeah I heard the phone ring at three. I also heard you slam the receiver."

"Sorry."

"Sorry my butt. You need to relay that plan right now or I'm going to dump coffee on your head."

"I know you didn't get your regular beauty sleep, but why so ouchy?"

"I don't want to go to work. I had such an amazing time the last few days. I laughed, cried, did a folk dance, ate gelato, and laughed some more. It made me realize I work for a toxic boss. She drags me down so much. I'm blaming my cigarette addiction on her. Grady shares some of the blame, but I'm giving the lion's share to her."

"What about a lion?" Grace shuffled into the kitchen, looking haggard too. "Noisemakers, the lot of you."

"Elaina has a plan."

"Great. We could use a plan. Wait. It's about Steph's dilemma, right?"

"Yep."

"Well then, I'm all ears. Poor gal. She fell apart."

"We all did." Elaina poured Grace a cup of coffee. "Would you guys allow me to actually put the plan into play before I share it?" She thrust her hands in the air in case Tawny made good on her threat to dump coffee on her head.

She received an exuberant "yes" from Grace and a whiny "okay" from Tawny.

* * *

"Show no fear. Show no fear." Elaina repeated the mantra as she rode the escalator to the second floor of the building that housed Mac's office. They would try their best to chew her up and spit her out but she was determined to see this through.

She'd texted Mac shortly after Grace and Tawny went back upstairs to shower.

He tried to text-grill her about the nature of the meeting. She told him to wait and see, and didn't read or reply to the dozen text messages that followed.

Mac's secretary jumped from her chair when she saw Elaina arrive. "Mr. Macintosh is expecting you."

A snide "duh" tipped her tongue but she bit it back. There was no need to be nasty to Mac's secretary, especially since the poor gal had to put up with the likes of him all day. "Thank you," she said courteously.

When Elaina walked through the Mac's office door, she took a silent breath. *Ready or not, here I go.*

Mac sat in his high-back leather chair with his legs crossed, staring ominously in her direction. Arden was hunched in an armchair across from Mac, tapping the arms with his thumbs.

"Elaina," Mac said in a tight voice.

Arden stood and greeted her with a half-hug.

Elaina cringed.

"Have a seat."

Elaina shook her head. "No thanks. This won't take long."

"Lawsuit," slid from between Mac's clenched teeth.

Elaina jerked with surprise. "I hadn't thought of that but maybe I'll look into it."

"Mac, you're an idiot," Arden spouted.

"I'd give you the finger if there wasn't a woman present." Mac uncrossed his legs and sat up straight. "What can we do for you?"

Elaina dug in her purse for two sets of keys and ceremoniously dropped them onto the desk. "The house and the gym are for sale."

Arden swore.

Mac's eyes fired with interest. "You don't say."

"I'm going to throw a lot at you and you have to respond without thinking it to death. A simple yes or no will suffice. If I don't get the answer I want within a few seconds the offer will be null and void."

"I'm listening." Arden crossed his arms.

Elaina turned to the right to keep them from seeing her throat bob when she swallowed the plum-size clog of unease. Facing them again, she lifted an eyebrow. "You can have both places for a million and a half."

"Pfft. You're insane."

Elaina made the sound of a buzzer going off. She snatched up the keys and headed for the door.

"Wait!" Arden was out of the chair in a flash. He blocked the doorway.

"There is no wait. You didn't give me the right answer."

"That's because you shocked the hell out of me. You know I want the house and gym. But I should remind you it's going to take a lot of money to clean the house of all that dog hair. And the gym needs some updates. I'll give you a million for both."

"Move," she ordered.

Arden put his elbows out so she couldn't circumvent the blockade. "Play fair."

"Play fair?" Elaina shook her head in disbelief. "You hired Landyn to stalk me and you want me to play fair?" Spittle sprayed Arden in the face. It hadn't been on purpose but she was glad it happened.

He called her a bitch with his eyes but his mouth said, "Okay. A million and a half. When can I take possession?"

"There's one small catch."

"Somehow I knew there would be. You were so pliable when we were married. What happened to you?"

"I became fully aware of my backbone."

Elaina walked to the desk again, dropped the keys on

Mac's desk calendar and took a seat. "There's a place for sale in Maine. Will you look into it for me?"

"In Maine?" At her fierce look, Mac said, "I'd be happy to." He was breathing hard and his eyes were jumping all over the place. She'd either made his day or he was having a heart attack. "Give me the information and I'll see what I can do."

"Do it now, Mac." Elaina shoved a piece of paper across the desk. "I'm not leaving until I know which way this is going to go."

* * *

It had been difficult keeping things under wraps until dinnertime. Elaina sat at the table Steph had decorated with miniature pumpkins and placemats with pictures of a scarecrow and bales of straw.

"I wanted to thank you for shoring me up when I thought the walls were crumbling down." Steph lifted her chin to show she was better now. The dark circles under her eyes told the truth – she wasn't okay. "I made smothered chicken in the Crockpot, mashed potatoes and gravy, succotash, and grilled pineapple." She smiled but it was weak.

"It sounds amazing."

"Oh, and I made two pitchers of sangria to celebrate. It seems like we drink a lot of wine, but we've had a rough few weeks. We deserve it."

Tawny met Elaina's eyes but spoke cautiously to Steph. "What are we celebrating?"

"Life without a plan."

"But Elaina has..."

Elaina subtly shook her head.

"You mean you're meeting the future head on," Grace said.

"I am." Steph's voice wobbled. "I've wanted to write a cookbook, and darn it, I'm going to. Beyond that I haven't a clue what's going to happen."

"Awesome about the cookbook. You can write it anywhere," Elaina said.

"I know. I can take my laptop to the library or the park. Or hole up in my room."

"Or you could write it in Maine."

Three sets of eyes zipped to Elaina.

Tears instantly lined Steph's eyes. "You know that isn't going to happen."

Elaina hopped from her chair to retrieve three sealed envelopes. "Don't discount the idea. It *can* happen." She handed each one an envelope but told them to hold off opening it until she was finished. "If I get a thumbs down there's no point in risking a paper cut by opening it."

"You have something up your sleeve." Tawny's brown orbs danced with curiosity. "Hit us with it."

"Before I do, tell me about your day."

"You're like one of those mean people who have candy but make kids work for it."

"I'm serious. This is relevant. Tell me how things went."

"You know how mine went. It's the same old stuff every time I go to work. Instead of the boss being happy to have me back from vacation, she was extra crabby. There's no pleasing that woman." Tawny sighed and scooped a huge helping of potatoes onto her plate.

Grace stabbed a pineapple spear. "My job doesn't change much either. I was actually bored until my drawer didn't balance. I was a $1.25 off. The way the boss complained you'd think I was off a hundred and twenty-five. He needs to take a chill pill."

"Steph?"

"I cried. Put away my clean clothes. Vacuumed the house. Took Stony for a walk around the block three times. I cried some more. Freshened Lula's cat box. And now I feel another round of tears coming."

Elaina threw a hand up. "Hold them off if you can." She pointed to the envelopes. "Go ahead and open them." She watched their expressions change from puzzlement to astonishment.

"W-what does this mean?" Tawny asked.

Grace said, "I'm not sure I'm seeing what I think I'm seeing."

Steph put a hand on her mouth.

"I have a proposition. Would you gals like to follow me to Maine to run a bed and breakfast? It's a lot to ask, but if you're willing, I'd love to have you."

Steph almost knocked over a pitcher of sangria to get to Elaina. "Oh my gosh!" Tears, hopefully happy ones, flooded her eyes. "I'd follow you to the moon."

Tawny squealed. "Are you freaking serious?"

Elaina nodded.

"I'm in!" Tawny shrieked. "I'm totally in! I know

there's a lot to iron out – health insurance, dental, Ferdinand, and ton of other things, but I am so in!"

Grace's face lit up with a huge smile. "Where do we sign?"

"You're right. There's a lot of details and logistics to iron out. But we have a plan. A solid plan. We're going to own and run a bed and breakfast."

"You're going to own a B & B. We'll be there to help you though."

Elaina quirked an eyebrow. "Take another look at the offer I made on our behalf to the Kirbys."

Grace grabbed the document. "It has all four of our names on it."

"We're all going to own it. Equally. It'll be our bed and breakfast."

"One small problem. I don't have money to put toward it." Tawny looked like she, too, was on the verge of tears.

"Not to worry. You'll contribute. Just differently. In the meantime, we have our work cut out for us." Elaina went on to say that with her business expertise they should do fine. With Grace's accounting background she could keep the books. Steph could dazzle their guests with some amazing breakfasts and snacks, while completing her cookbook. Tawny could be their secret weapon. As an in-house nurse they could attract some older clientele. "We all have a role to play and I know we can make it work." She smiled at Grace. "In December when Cody, Isabella, and Karina come to Maine, they'll be coming to a B & B that bears your name."

"I hate to crimp the excitement even for a millisecond but we don't know anything about running a bed and breakfast."

Elaina addressed Tawny's concern. "I bought a book this morning. I know how cheesy that sounds but we have to start somewhere. We have four incredible brains. We'll figure it out."

"This is too good to be true, Elaina. You've amended your life to fix ours." Steph held the document to her chest.

"No I didn't. This is what sisters of the heart do." She lifted her foot to show the infinity symbol on her ankle.

"That's a sideways eight, not a heart," Tawny spouted, being cocky as usual.

"We have another ankle and we happen to know where there's a great tattoo parlor."

They laughed and hugged.

"I can't wait." Grace clapped.

"We'll be our own boss," Tawny said.

Elaina was filled with an indescribable happiness – another well-orchestrated move from the one up above. "Thank you. I won't let you down," she murmured quietly. To Steph, Tawny and Grace she said, "I'm ready to sip sangria. Maybe a little merlot too. In Maine."

~ The End ~

About the Author

Jan Romes grew up in northwest Ohio in the midst of eight zany siblings. Married to her high school sweetheart for more years than seems possible, she's also a mom, mother-in-law, and grandma. Jan writes contemporary romance and women's fiction with sharp, witty characters who give as good as they get. When she's not writing, you can find Jan with her nose buried in a book or engaged in some sort of activity to stay fit. She loves spending time with family and friends. A hopeless romantic, she enjoys sunsets, sappy movies, and sitting around a campfire. Though she doesn't claim to have a green thumb, she takes pride in growing all kinds of flowers. She loves to hear from her readers.

You can follow Jan here:

www.authorjanromes.com
www.jantheromancewriter.blogspot.com
www.twitter.com/JanRomes
www.facebook.com/jan.romes5
www.goodreads.com/author/show/5240156.Jan_Romes

Other books by Jan Romes

Texas Boys Falling Fast series:
Book #1 – Married to Maggie
Book #2 – Keeping Kylee
Book #3 – Taming Tori
Book #4 – Not Without Nancy

One Small Fib
Lucky Ducks
Kiss Me
The Gift of Gray
Stay Close, Novac!
Stella in Stilettos
Three Wise Men
The Christmas Contract
Mr. August
Three Days with Molly
Big on Christmas
I'd Rather Be Growing Grapes
Wild Goose Chase

Wine and Sweat Pants series:
No Sweat Pants Allowed – Wine Club
Sipping Sangria
Merlot in Maine (coming soon)

Made in the USA
Middletown, DE
18 February 2022

61439355R00166